Are Parents People?

Are Parents People?

Alice Duer Miller

MINT EDITIONS

Are Parents People? was first published in 1924.

This edition published by Mint Editions 2021.

ISBN 9781513212005 | E-ISBN 9781513210803

Published by Mint Editions®

MINT
EDITIONS

minteditionbooks.com

Publishing Director: Jennifer Newens
Design & Production: Rachel Lopez Metzger
Project Manager: Micaela Clark
Typesetting: Westchester Publishing Services

Contents

Are Parents People?

I

THE GIRLS MARCHED INTO CHAPEL singing Jerusalem the Golden. Some of the voices were shrill and piping, and some were clear and sweet; but all had that peculiar young freshness which always makes old hearts ache, and which now drew tears to the eyes of many visiting parents looking down from the gallery, and trying not to crane their necks conspicuously when their own offspring appeared in the aisle below.

On Sundays the whole school came out in blue serge and black velvet tam-o'-shanters. The little girls marched first—some as young as eleven years—and as they came from the main school buildings and marched up the long aisle they were holding the high notes, "Jerusalem the golden," and their voices sounded like young birds', before the older girls came crashing in with the next line, "With milk and honey blest." They marched quickly—it was a tradition of the school—divided to right and left, and filed into their appointed places.

Last of all came the tall senior president, and beside her a little figure that hardly reached her shoulder, and seemed as if one of the younger children were out of place; yet this was an important figure in the life of the school—Lita Hazlitt, the chairman of the self-government committee.

Her face was almost round except for a small point that was her chin; her hair—short curls, not ringlets—curved up on her black velvet tam, and was blond, but a dusky blond. There was something alert, almost naughty in her expression, although at the moment this was mitigated by an air of discretion hardly avoidable by the chairman of the self-government committee in church.

In this, her last year at Elbridge Hall, she had come to love the chapel. Its gray stone and dark narrow windows of blue or amethyst, the organ and the voices, gave her a sense of peace almost mystic—a mood she could never have attained unaided, for hers was a nature essentially practical. Like most practical people, she was kind. It was so easy for Lita to see what was needed—to do a problem in geometry or mend a typewriter or knit a sweater—that she was always doing such things for her friends, not so much from unselfishness as from sheer competence.

The seniors sat in the carved stalls against the wall, and Lita liked to rest her hand on the rounded head of a dragon which made the arm of her chair. It had a polished surface and the knobs of the ears fitted into her fingers.

"Dearly beloved brethren, the Scripture moveth us, in sundry places, to acknowledge and confess—"

Lita loved the words of the service, and she noted that part of their beauty was the needless doubling of words—dissemble and cloak— assemble and meet together—requisite and necessary. Yet Miss Fraser, who taught English at Elbridge, would call that tautology in a theme. . . She sank on her knees, burying her small nose in her hands for the general confession.

As they rose from their knees and the choir broke out into O Come, let us sing unto the Lord, Lita allowed herself one glance at the gallery, where her lovely mother was just rising, slim and erect, with a bearing polite rather than devout. Lita could see one immaculate gray glove holding her prayerbook. She was a beautifully dressed person. The whole school had an orgy of retrimming hats and remaking dresses after Mrs. Hazlitt had spent a Sunday at Elbridge. She was as blond as her daughter, except that somehow in the transmission of the family coloring she had acquired a pair of enormous black eyes from some contradictory ancestor. Even across the chapel Lita could see the dark splotches that were her mother's eyes. It was great fun—the Sundays that Mrs. Hazlitt came to the school, and yet Lita was always a little nervous. Her mother said anything that came into her head—simply anything, commenting on teachers and making fun of rules. The girls loved it, of course, but sometimes— The First Lesson had begun.

The service went on. It was not until the Second Lesson was being read that Lita, glancing idly toward the ante-chapel, saw that a terrible thing had happened: Her father had arrived too—unexpected and unannounced. He was standing there under the gallery, his hat and stick and gloves all held in one hand, and his mouth just not smiling as he at last contrived to meet her eyes. There they were—her mother looking down at her so calmly from the gallery and her father waiting so confidently for her below, each unaware of the other's presence. What in thunder was she going to do?

Their divorce had taken place a great many years before, when Lita was so young that her mother was not much more important to her than her nurse, and her father very much less so. She was accustomed to the idea of their divorce; but she did wish they were divorced as Aurelia's parents were—quite amicably, even meeting now and then to talk over questions of Aurelia's welfare. Or the way Carrie Waldron's were—each remarried happily to someone else, so that Carrie had two amusing sets of half brothers and sisters growing up in different parts of the country. But Lita was aware of a constrained bitterness, a repressed hatred between her parents. When they said, "Perhaps your father does not quite take in, my dear—" or "I would not interfere with any plan of your mother's; but I must say—" Lita was conscious of a poisoned miasma that seemed to rise from old battlegrounds.

And now, in a few minutes, these two people who had not spoken for thirteen years would come face to face in the cheerful group of parents which every Sunday brought to the school. The few minutes after the service when everyone stood about on the grass outside the church and chatted was a time of public friendliness between three inharmonious classes—parents, teachers and pupils; and there these two dear foes of hers would be, each waiting so confidently to claim her undivided attention. She must prevent it.

She had the sermon to think it out, and for the first time in her life she hoped it would be a long sermon. The preacher, a fine-looking old missionary bishop, with a long upper lip like a lawyer, and a deep-set eye like a fanatic, was going up into the pulpit, turning on the reading light, shaking back the fine frills of his episcopal sleeves.

"My text," he was saying, "will be taken from the eleventh chapter of Isaiah, the sixth verse: 'The wolf also shall dwell with the lamb, and the leopard shall lie down with the kid; and the calf and the young lion and the fatling together; and a little child shall lead them.' The eleventh chapter of Isaiah, the sixth verse."

Well, the text was not inappropriate, Lita thought; but she had no intention of listening. The situation, besides its practical difficulties, brought all the emotion of her childhood's worries and confusions. One of her very earliest recollections went back to a time when her parents still loved each other. She and her mother had been sitting on the floor playing with paper dolls, and suddenly her father had appeared unexpectedly in the doorway—returned ahead of time from a journey. What Lita specially remembered was the way her mother sprang up in one single long motion and flung herself into his arms, and how they had clung together and gone out of the room without a word to her, leaving her conscious, even at four, that she was forgotten. Presently her mother had sent her nurse, Margaret, to finish the game; but the game was already over. Margaret was desirable when one was tired or hungry or sleepy, but absolutely useless at games of the imagination.

After that Lita could just remember days when she would see her mother crying—peculiar conduct for a grown-up person, since grown-up people were never naughty or afraid and could do anything they wanted to do, and did. It shocked Lita to see her mother cry; it was contrary to the plan of the universe. And then, soon after this, her father, as far as she was concerned, ceased to be; and it must be owned she did not greatly miss him.

He ceased to be as a visible presence; but at immensely long intervals—that is to say, once a year, at Christmas—magical presents arrived for her, which she knew came from him. The first was the largest doll she had ever seen. It came from Paris and brought a trousseau in a French trunk. It was an incredible delight. She dreamed about it at night, and could hardly believe each morning on waking that it was reality. The only mitigation of her delight was that her mother did not admire the doll. She said it had an ugly, stary face. Lita, beginning the stupendous task of writing a letter of thanks, with a lead pencil on ruled paper, wrote, "Dear Father: Mother thinks the doll has a stary face, but I love her—" Only Margaret said that wouldn't do, and she had to begin all over again, her round, cramped hand pressing on the pencil until her nails were white.

When she was eight a gold bracelet arrived, set with red stones. This time her mother was even more outspoken. She said to Aunt Minnie, "Of course, she bought it! Isn't it just what you'd expect?" Lita guessed that "she" meant her father's new wife, for she knew vaguely that he had married again and was living abroad. She herself thought the bracelet beautiful; but it was put away, and she was never allowed to wear it. And now, only a little while before, she had seen it in an old jewelry case of her mother's and had been surprised to find it was just what her mother had said it was.

Then two years later a set of sables had come. This, too, her mother had utterly condemned.

"Sables for a child of ten!"

Aunt Minnie had suggested that Lita's mother wear them herself and had been well scolded for the suggestion. Lita was content that these should be confiscated. She preferred her own little ermine set.

Until she was sixteen, except for presents, she lived the life of a child with only one parent, and a very satisfactory life it was. Even when her father was in the United States he did not always take the trouble to see her. Perhaps it was not made too easy for him to do so. But within the last two years things had changed. His second wife had died and he had come back to New York to live. He was older, he was lonely, and a pretty daughter almost grown up was very different from a troublesome child who couldn't walk as fast as he did, who required meals at strange hours and could eat only innocuous food. In his own silent way Mr. Hazlitt began to bid for his daughter's affection.

Lita liked the process and she liked him, although she felt immediately that the feeling was a betrayal of her lovely, devoted mother. It wasn't right, she reflected, that her father, who had forgotten her existence for so many years, should come back, and just because he was nice looking and well off and knew the art of life should be able to capture her affection as much or more than if he had stayed at home and been a good parent. It wasn't right, but it was a fact.

For two years the struggle had been going on, steadily rising in intensity. Her father had begun by asking for very little—hardly more than an outlawed parent could ask—but Lita knew that she was becoming dearer and dearer to him, and that her parents were now contending for first place in her heart. Soon it would be for her exclusive love. The pain of the situation to her was that she was to them not only a battlefield but a weapon and the final trophy of the war. As they never met, and wrote only through their lawyers, she was their most vivid channel of communication. She loved her mother the best— much the best—but her mother was a presupposition of her life, part of the background, whereas her father was an excitement, a stranger, a totally new experience.

When she dined with her mother, that was the solid comfort of everyday life; but when she went out to a restaurant to dine with her father—that was a party.

When her mother told her she was looking well the compliment often meant only that Mrs. Hazlitt approved of her own taste in clothes; but if her father said so it was the reaction of an outsider, a critic, a man of the world; it raised the whole level of her self-esteem. She couldn't help valuing it more.

The sermon was nearing its end. Twice already the bishop had begun a sentence, "And now in conclusion—" The next time, Lita thought, it might take. If only Aurelia were about! Aurelia was an authority on the management of divorced parents, though usually with mercenary intent. Aurelia had studied the art of intimating to one parent that the other did you rather better. It brought Aurelia great affluence; but Lita did not quite approve. She thought it too easy to be sportsmanlike; the poor dears were so innocent. But Aurelia was stern. She said children ought to get something out of the situation. Unfortunately, this Sunday, of all Sundays, Aurelia was laid up in the infirmary with a strange and violent form of indigestion which Lita was afraid would turn out to be appendicitis. Miss Barton, the head of the school, believed it to be indigestion merely because she had discovered that Aurelia the night before had eaten peanuts, peanut butter, chocolate cake and tomato mayonnaise. What of course one could not tell Miss Barton was that Aurelia had been eating just such illicit Saturday night suppers ever since she came to Elbridge.

Lita had only said very gently "I'm afraid it's more than indigestion," and Miss Barton had just glanced at her as if she were a silly ass.

If Aurelia had been about she would have been sent bounding up the gallery stairs to detain Mrs. Hazlitt, while Lita herself would have run out and explained the situation to Mr. Hazlitt. Well, as it was, she would have a minute or two. The gallery stairs were narrow and it took people a little while to come down.

The sermon was over. The organ rolled out into Praise God, from whom all blessings flow, an anthem which Lita in her childhood had always supposed was introduced at this point in order to express gratitude that the sermon was over.

The girls sprang up as if on wires. Presently they were all marching down the aisle again. Lita looked up in the gallery and smiled at her mother, looked down and smiled at her father; and then, as soon as she was back again in the main school building, she turned and ran as fast as she could go to the main door of the chapel.

A crowd of parents and teachers had already gathered, all being as civil to one another as if they were not naturally hostile. Lita had once overheard Miss Barton exclaiming, "Of course, anyone could keep a good school if it weren't for these parents!" Her father was standing a little apart, waiting. He had put on his hat at the slight angle at which he wore it—a sort of defiance to his forty-two years. She ran up to him and flung herself into his arms.

"Pat, darling," she said—Mr. Hazlitt's name was James; Pat was a corruption of Lita's early attempts upon the Latin tongue—"it's simply great to see you back; but—"

"I only got back last night," said Mr. Hazlitt, as if he himself were surprised at his own eagerness. "I have Miss Barton's permission for you to lunch with me—"

"Pat dear!"

"—and spend the afternoon."

"Father!"

Out of the narrow doorway that led from the gallery stairs Lita could now see her mother emerging. She was dressed in soft blues and grays like a pigeon's breast, and her eyes, dazzled by the March sunlight, were darting about in search of her daughter among all the other figures in blue serge. Then Lita saw that Miss Barton had stopped her and introduced the bishop. That meant another minute or two; her mother would feel she simply must be civil to the bishop.

"Father."

"Don't interrupt me, Lita. You're just like—it's a very disagreeable habit."

"But you see mother's here, too, father."

Every trace of expression vanished from Mr. Hazlitt's face—his own way of expressing emotion.

Then he said in a hard, even voice, "My first Sunday!"

"I know, dear, but you see it's her regular Sunday."

"Of course. I'm not criticizing your mother," he answered, in that tone in which the phrase is so often used, as if he could do it magnificently if he let himself go. "Only I must say that after three months' absence I did hope—" He stopped; his face, which had been blank before, now became set like steel, and Lita saw that his eyes had fallen on the former partner of his life. It was most alarming. At any instant her mother might grow weary of the bishop and turn from him. Lita laid her hand on her father's arm.

"So, you see, dear," she said rather glibly, "I can't possibly lunch with you."

"I don't see it at all," replied her father. "Your mother has had you to herself all this winter. I'm afraid I shall have to insist. There is something I want to talk over with you."

Lita had not anticipated the least difficulty with her father. He usually yielded his rights in silence, and afterward her mother explained to her how mistaken he had been in supposing he had any rights. She sighed, and he caught the sigh.

"Unless," he added, "you don't want to lunch with me."

His feelings were hurt. She couldn't bear that.

"Of course, I always want to lunch with you," she said, and she was glad this hearty assurance did not carry so far as her mother's ears. "I'll run and explain, and I'll meet you at the main gate in half an hour."

She turned away. Miss Barton, to whom Sunday was a terrible day, devoted to placating visiting parents, who always had one disagreeable thing to say before they left, had rather mistakenly abandoned the bishop entirely to Mrs. Hazlitt. As Lita approached them she heard her mother saying: "But I think it's so much nicer for wolves to be wolfish and leopards leopardy. I'm sure the heathen are ever so much happier the way they are, sharpening their teeth and eating one another up, poor dears."

"But they are not happy, my dear madam," said the bishop, driven by a sense of duty into correcting her mistake, and yet discouraged by a sense that whatever he said she would interrupt him before he had said it. "They are not happy. They are full of terror. Darkness and night are to them just a recurring fear."

"To me too," said Mrs. Hazlitt. "The heathen have nothing on me, as these girls would say. I look under my bed every night for a giant spider I read about when I was a child. You ought to be so careful what children read. So interesting—your sermon, bishop. I'm sure you could convert me if I were a heathen. Oh, I see you think I practically am. Oh, bishop, your face! Lita, the bishop thinks I'm a heathen. This is my child. May we go to your room before luncheon? Well, I never know. I'm so afraid of breaking some of their silly rules in this place. Oh, I hope Miss Barton did not hear me say that. I've asked that nice fat girl with the red hair to lunch with us at the inn. I'd rather like to ask the bishop too—he's rather sweet," she added regretfully as Lita began to lead her away in the direction of her dormitory. "But I suppose you girls wouldn't be amused by a bishop."

"Mother dear," said Lita, "prepare yourself for a shock."

"You've been expelled," said Mrs. Hazlitt as if it had come at last, as she always knew it would.

"No, it's almost worse. Father is here too."

Mrs. Hazlitt stopped short and looked at her child.

"What?" she exclaimed, and the final t of the word was like a bullet. "But this is my Sunday."

"But he didn't know that."

"Didn't he, indeed? It's been my experience that your father usually contrives to know anything that it's to his advantage to know—and the other way round. He just thought he could get away with it. Well, he can't!"

"He's been away on business for three months, mother."

"Has he so? Fortunately I am no longer obliged to keep track of your father's comings and goings—especially the latter. When I did attempt to—"

She paused, bitterly brooding on her past anxieties; and Lita, taking her again by the arm, succeeded in setting her in motion. They entered the building where Lita lived, mounted the stairs in silence and went to Lita's room. Aurelia, who shared the room, being in the infirmary, secured them from interruption.

Mrs. Hazlitt walked at once to the window and peered out in all directions; but the window did not command that part of the grounds which lay between the chapel and the main gate. Finding the object of her hostile interest was not in sight, she turned back to her child.

"It's really too much," she said, "that I cannot have my one quiet Sunday a month with you. I never wanted you to go to boarding school at all. I only yielded because your coming here gave your father a place where he could see you without being obliged to come to my house— not pleasant for either of us. But it's a mistake to yield an inch to some people, as I ought to have known. I insist on my own Sunday. All other days are open to him, except this one, and so, of course, that's just the only one—"

"Only, mother dear, while he's been away I have been coming down to you in New York for most of my Sundays."

Mrs. Hazlitt had a way of opening her large black eyes until her curved lashes were flattened against her lids and looked as if they trimmed her eyes with black fringe. She did it now.

"And does he complain of that?" she asked. "Isn't it natural for a girl to spend her Sundays with her mother; or does he expect while he's away you and I—"

"No, no, mother. He doesn't complain. Father isn't a complainer."

"Lita! You hurt my feelings very much, criticizing me like that."

"Dearest mums, I didn't criticize you."

"You did! You said I was always complaining."

"No, dear, I only said that father did not."

This was so true that Mrs. Hazlitt could not deny it, and so with great quickness she shifted her ground.

"Isn't it something new," she said, "for you to feel it necessary to defend your father at every sentence?"

"I wasn't exactly defending him. I only—"

"My dear, you don't need to apologize for defending your father—very laudable, I'm sure. I feel deeply sorry for him myself—over forty, without a natural human tie. Only I do not feel called on to give up one of my few opportunities of being with you in order to suit his caprices."

"Is it exactly a—"

"It is exactly that. Rather late in the day for him to begin to discover the responsibilities of parenthood. Is he to have all the rewards?"

It did not seem a promising beginning; and Lita, in whom her mother's rapidly reflected changes of idea always set up a sort of baffled confusion, sighed. Her mother caught instantly that long-drawn-in breath and went through a complete change of mood—as rapid as her mental changes.

"Oh, well, of course you must lunch with him. I suppose that is what he wants, isn't it?"

Lita simply adored her mother when she was suddenly kind and reasonable like this. It was, the girl knew, a striking triumph of the maternal instinct over the hardly less fundamental human instinct to stick up for one's rights.

"Oh, mums, you are awfully good," she said.

This was not the right thing to say; perhaps nothing would have been.

"Don't thank me," her mother answered sharply, "as if I were doing you a favor. I didn't suppose you were so crazy to leave me. Oh, I know; and, after all, we have all the rest of our lives to spend together. Be sure to get back in time to walk to the train with me."

Lita promised to be back immediately after luncheon was over, and she added that she did really feel it was better to go to her father, as he had said he had something he wished to discuss with her.

At this, Mrs. Hazlitt, who, strictly against the rules of the school, had been sitting on Lita's bed, sprang up, and the girl at once began to smooth the bed. She was always destroying evidence of Mrs. Hazlitt's illegal conduct after one of her visits.

"Lita," exclaimed her mother, quite unconscious of any reproof in her daughter's action, "he's going to be married again! Oh! I suppose I should not have said that, but what else could he want to discuss? I do hope he is."

"Oh, I hope not!" said Lita, astonished to find how disagreeable the idea was to her.

"But don't you see how it would get him out of our way? He could hardly expect you to see much of a new bride, particularly the kind—Women pursue him so; they think that manner of his covers such a lot; they learn different. . . No, Lita, not that hat—like Tweedle-dee in the saucepan. If you come down to me next Sunday I'll get you one that matches the foulard."

Suddenly they began to talk about clothes, and spoke of nothing else until it was time for Lita to go.

She thought as she ran across the green that she of all people ought to understand why her parents couldn't get on. Sometimes her mother made her feel as if she were clinging to a slippery hillside while an avalanche passed over her; and sometimes her father made her feel as if she were trying to roll a gigantic stone up that same hill. But then, on the other hand, sometimes her mother made her feel gay and stimulated, and her father gave her calm and serenity. And, after all, she hadn't chosen them; and they had chosen each other.

Her father was already waiting for her in his little car, a runabout body on a powerful foreign chassis. Everything that Mr. Hazlitt had was good of its kind and well kept up. He was sitting in the driver's seat, reading the sporting sheet of a morning paper, his knees crossed and one elbow over the back of the seat. He looked young and smart. Other cars were waiting—closed cars full of heavy bald parents. Lita felt a glow of pride. To go out with her father was like going out with a dangerous young man. Fortunately the diversity of tastes between her parents extended to their places of lodging. Her mother always stayed at an old-fashioned inn near the school grounds, whereas her father, who motored the forty miles from New York, and so never spent the night, preferred to eat at the hotel in the nearest town.

She got in beside him and they drove for sometime in silence. Then he said, and she saw he had been thinking it over for sometime:

"Lita, I want to speak to you about interrupting. It's a habit a great many women allow themselves to form. It's not only rude, but it's extremely irritating—alienating, indeed." He went on to assert that such a habit might even wreck her married life. A man, he said, who was interrupted everytime he opened his mouth might get so that he never spoke at all; never told his wife things she ought to know.

Lita glanced at him sympathetically. Did the poor dear suppose she did not know just what he meant? She had suffered herself. Her mother often accused her of concealing things which she had tried repeatedly to tell; only her mother, with her mind running like a hound on someother idea, did not even hear. And yet on the other hand she had felt sympathetic when, not long before, her mother had delivered a short lecture on the treachery of silence; she had said—and quite truly—that a silence could be just as much of a lie as a spoken word. She wondered if she were a weak nature, agreeing with everyone who spoke to her.

At the hotel she found her father had ordered a special luncheon for her delight, composed of all the things he liked best himself. The regular hotel dinner, with its immense opportunities for choice, would have been a treat to Lita after the monotony of school fare; but she enjoyed the prestige that the special order gave them in the eyes of the dragoonlike head waitress, who never left their table. That was one of the amusing things about going out with her father. He had a quiet assumption of importance which made everyone think him important.

They had been at table several minutes before he spoke. He said, "If you take so much sauce you lose the flavor of the fish."

"I like the flavor of the sauce best," said Lita, and he smiled, a little sadly, as if he were at a loss to understand how his child could be such an utter barbarian.

Conscious that she had not quite so much time as he thought she had, she hurried to the point and asked him what it was he wanted to discuss. He seemed to be thinking deeply, which alarmed her; then he reached out and added a dash of pepper to his fish.

"Oh," he said, "I find I must go to Italy on business next summer. I wonder if you could arrange it with your mother so that you could go with me."

"Mercy!" exclaimed Lita. "I was afraid you were going to tell me you were going to be married again."

He looked up with a swift dark glance.

"Who put that idea into your head?" he asked.

"No one; it just occurred to me."

Where opposing affections exist, a lady, as much as a gentleman, is obliged to lie.

"That was your mother's idea," said her father, and gave a short, bitter laugh, as if human depravity could hardly go lower than to have made such a suggestion.

Well, Lita thought, perhaps her mother ought not to have said it; and yet, why not? Her father had remarried once. It made her feel old and cold, always to be obliged to weigh criticisms and complaints, to decide which of the two people she loved best in the world was right and which was wrong, every other minute. How she envied girls who could accept their parents as a unit!

Seeing her father's mind still occupied with his wrongs, she turned the conversation back to Italy. Of course, she would adore going—at least she would if her mother would agree to it.

"Of course, we could not go otherwise," said her father, and there was somehow in his tone the suggestion that he and his poor child were in the grip of an irrational and arbitrary power. After a moment he added, "And we'd stop in Paris on our way back and get you a lot of things." He smiled—he had a delightful, merry smile, quite at variance to his habitual blankness. "I don't suppose that idea is exactly repugnant to you?"

It wasn't, though Lita knew it was practically bribery. She adored shopping with her father. His method was simple. He went to the best shop and asked for their best things. If he liked them he bought them. If he didn't like them he went to the next-best shop. There was no haggling, no last-minute doubts whether, since the expense was so great, she really needed to get the things after all. Her father in Paris! It was a delirious thought.

"I should enjoy Paris with you, Pat," she said. He smiled with a faint suggestion that others had felt the same way. "If only mother approves."

"I don't see that there is anything to disapprove of, even for your mother, in a man's taking his daughter to Paris."

"What I mean is if she is really cordial about it. I could not go if she weren't cordial."

"Then," said her father, "we may as well give it up at once. For, of course, your mother won't be cordial. She won't want you to go. She never wants you out of her sight if she can help it."

"Father, mother isn't a bit selfish like that."

"I never said she was. It is natural she should want you to be with her. Please get it into your head, Lita, that I should never under any circumstances criticize your mother—least of all to you."

Lita looked at him reflectively. If he had been Aurelia she would have said "Bunk, my dear, and you know it." That was the way she and Aurelia carried on their relation—in the open. Candor cleared the air;

but older people, Lita had found, did not really want the air cleared. They could not stand criticism; perhaps that was why they were always insisting that they did not criticize, when as a matter of fact they never did anything else.

Luncheon pursued its delicious but somewhat leisurely way. Mr. Hazlitt lit a cigar and sent the coffee back to be heated. It was a pleasant moment. Lita was conscious that he was treating her more as an equal companion than ever before. She was enjoying herself, and yet in the back of her mind was a distressing awareness that time was passing and she ought to be getting back to school to her mother.

"The truth is," her father was saying, "that as one gets older one loses the power, or perhaps the wish, to make new friends; and one clings to the old ties. I hope you will arrange eventually, when you are twenty-one, to spend at least half the year with me. I shall be in a position then to make some long expeditions—China and Patagonia, and I should like you to go with me."

Lita's imagination took fire, but she said loyally, "But how about mother, Pat? I suppose she's lonely too."

Mr. Hazlitt laughed shortly.

"Your mother," he said, "unless she has changed very much, probably does not spend one waking hour in the twenty-four alone. I doubt if she ever loses the power of making new friends—quite indiscriminately. And, after all, I am only asking for half your time."

"But, father, suppose I should marry?"

Her father looked at her with startled eyes, as if she had suggested something unnatural and wrong.

"Marry!" he said. "I hope you have no such idea in your head."

She had not. Indeed her immunity from the crushes which occupied so much of the time and attention of her schoolmates occasioned her some concern. She feared her nature was a cold one. She disclaimed the idea of marriage, except as she had observed it in common.

"People do, you know," she said.

"A good many would be wiser if they didn't," said her father. "I am particularly opposed to young marriages."

He and her mother had married when they were young.

Presently she was obliged to tell him that she must go. He did not gainsay her decision, but she saw he took it as meaning that she had not really enjoyed herself. Yet when she tried to say she had—that she was sorry to leave him—it kept sounding as if she were saying it was a bore to go back and walk to the station with her mother. If only she could be loyal to one parent without being disloyal to the other!

She was a little bit late at the school. Her mother was just starting without her.

"Oh, I understand," she said, without listening to Lita's explanation. "Very natural. You were enjoying yourself; you don't need to explain."

Lita saw she was hurt but had determined to be nice about it.

They started on their walk. First they crossed the athletic fields; then their way would lie through the school woods, and then across stony fields, and then they would come out on the macadam road to the station—about three miles across country.

The Italian trip, which had seemed so simple and pleasant when her father mentioned it, now began to take on the appearance of a dark conspiracy. Lita thought that she would far rather give it up than mention it, only she had promised her father that she would speak of it that afternoon so that he might have plenty of time to make his arrangements. He was very particular about special cabins on a special boat. Oh, dear, with her mother's feelings already a little hurt, it wasn't going to be easy! Mrs. Hazlitt herself started conversation.

"And so you had a delightful lunch?" she said, trying to be nice, but also trying to find out what it was her child's father had wanted to discuss, for she was curious by nature.

"Yes, very nice. Pat's going to Italy next summer on business."

"Really?" said her mother, without special interest. "Some people's business does take them to the nicest places."

Lita suddenly wondered how it would work if she forced these insinuations of her parents to their logical conclusions.

"Don't you believe father really has business in Italy?" she inquired mildly.

"Of course he has if he says so. What funny things you say, Lita! Your father is one of the most accurate people I ever knew—if he makes an assertion. Well, if he goes to Italy that will leave us entirely free. I thought perhaps it would amuse you if I took a house at Southampton this summer. Of course, when I was young Newport was the place; but now I'm told the young people prefer—"

"But, mother," said Lita, and she felt just the way she did before she dived into cold water, "he wants to take me with him."

Mrs. Hazlitt merely laughed.

"A likely idea!" she said.

"And I told him I would ask you how you felt about it."

Her mother stopped short and looked at her. Then she said, and each syllable dropped lower and lower like pebbles falling down a well, "In fact—you want—to go."

It was hard to be truthful.

"Well, yes, in a way, I should like to go; at least I thought so when Pat spoke of it." She thought she ought to go as far as this, but even this moderate statement was fatal.

"You shall not go!" said her mother, her eyes beginning to enlarge as they did in moments of emotion until they seemed to fill her whole face. "I won't hear of it—or go—go if you want to. I never want anyone to stay with me as a duty."

"Mother dear, I don't care. I don't really want to go; it was just an idea."

"Do at least be honest about it. Of course you want to go, or you would not have promised to try to work me round to agreeing to it—conspiring together. No, of course I don't mean that. Nothing could be more natural at your age than to snatch at any pleasure that comes. I don't blame you—a child—but him—trying to steal you—"

Her nostrils began to tremble on her quick intaken breaths.

"Father did not mean—"

"Of course you don't think so; but you don't know him as well as I do," said her mother. "I suppose you've utterly forgotten how little he cared for you when you were a child; but now that all the care and responsibility is over—"

She simply could not go on.

Lita, a little constrained by this display of emotion, said, smiling, "It's nice to know I'm no care, mother." But as an effort at the light touch it was not a success.

Mrs. Hazlitt did not even hear her. She went on: "Now he's ready to charm you and tempt you away so as to leave me alone again. Oh, never love anyone, Lita, when you grow up! It's all pain. Be like your father; take what you want and go on your own horrible way, leaving destruction behind you." She covered her face with her hands, not because she was crying, but to hide the chattering of her teeth; and then as a new idea swept over her she dropped them again and continued: "It's all my own fault. I've been too absurdly honorable. I've brought you up to respect and admire him, when all the weapons were in my hands and I might just as well have taught you to despise him as he deserves.

I wish I had. Oh, how I wish I had! I've never said a word against your father, have I, Lita?"

"Never—never, dearest," said Lita. She thought to herself, "They are making me a liar between them, but I couldn't say anything else to her just now."

She was not a prig, but she could hardly help feeling that sense of superiority—of being in control of the situation—that the calm are so apt to experience in the presence of turgid emotions.

Mrs. Hazlitt suddenly turned back to her.

"But you don't really want to go with him?" she said as hopefully as if a minute before she had not considered the contrary as proved.

"No, mother, I don't."

"These silent people! Fortunately I know him like a book. He's probably been plotting this for months. I see what he's up to. He wants to get things so that by the time that you're twenty-one you'll be willing to spend some of your time with him; but you wouldn't do that, would you?"

"Nothing could ever come between you and me, mother. That's the solid comfort of a mo—"

"You don't answer what I say; you are keeping back some of your thoughts, just like your father. Oh, I couldn't bear it if you grew like him! No one is ever so candid as I am. What is in your mind?"

"Nothing, mother. It crossed my mind that I might marry some day."

"Marry!" Her mother's tone, given the difference of sex and temperament, was identical with her father's; as if marriage were a crime other people's daughters might commit, but not her lovely child. "What in heaven's name are you talking about, Lita?"

"Well, mother, you were mar—"

"And do you quote my case? Marriage! No, not until you are twenty-five at least. Don't mention the word to me!"

At least there was one subject on which her parents were in hearty agreement—the first, as far as she could remember, that she had ever found. They did not want her to marry. But, she reflected, as she joggled home alone on the back seat of the school flivver, was it entirely interest in her welfare that made them opposed? Wasn't it rather that they needed her to fill the gap in their lives that their own separation had made? This, she thought, was the real objection to divorce—that it made parents too emotionally dependent on their children. Suppose she died. She considered the possibility steadily. Why, yes, if she died they would probably come together in their grief.

She saw a little picture of herself in the infirmary, with her parents standing hand in hand at the foot of the bed. And yet one really could not commit suicide in order to reconcile one's parents.

Well, Italy was now out of the question; Italy was canned. She must write to her father immediately that she could not go, and she must do it so as not to make her mother seem selfish, and so as not to hurt her father's feelings. Some letter, she thought. She saw herself walking the deck of an enormous steamer, hanging on his arm, ordering meals in amusing restaurants, the Paris shops gleaming with hats and jewels and beaded bags and fans, all for her. Of course it was natural that she wanted to go. . .

The car stopped at the door of the main school building, and she sprang out, free at last to give her attention to Aurelia. Strangely enough, though she did not love her friend so much as she did her parents, she worried more about her, as one equal about another.

The infirmary, a neat white cottage, was set in a remote corner of the grounds. As Lita bounded up the steps she met Miss Barton coming out.

Every head of a school, perhaps every head of an institution, perhaps everyone in the world, acquires an artificial manner to serve as a method of holding off crises. Some adopt the genial, some the meditative, some the stern. Miss Barton had chosen the intellectually airy. As a problem was presented to her she would say "Ah, yes," with a faint, calm smile, as if that special problem were so easy and familiar she might float away to something more stimulating without remembering to give you the answer. She was a tall, good-looking woman, pale eyed, pale skinned, with thick, crinkly gray hair, parted and drawn down to a knot at the nape of her neck; it looked exactly like a wig, but wasn't. She stopped Lita.

"Oh," she said with her habitual gay casualness, "we have been looking for you. Don't be alarmed, but it seems that Aurelia has appendicitis."

"Yes I felt pretty sure she had," answered Lita.

Miss Barton did not think it worth while to contradict this absurd assertion. She merely smiled on one side of her face and replied that the doctors themselves had only decided it fifteen minutes before. It appeared that Aurelia was eager to see her friend before the operation.

"She's in Room 11," said Miss Barton. "They will operate as soon as they can get things ready. Don't alarm her. There is no risk nowadays, nothing to be excited about."

"Is she excited?"

"I think not."

"Of course she isn't."

It is hard sometimes to be patient with older people, playing their own rôles so busily they lose all sense of other individualities. Aurelia, Lita imagined, was probably the calmest person in the infirmary.

In Room 11 she found her roommate lying on her side, very pale, with her dark hair dragged back and tightly braided. The nurse was moving in and out and the two girls were practically alone, while the following dialogue took place.

"Pain?"

"Oh, my!"

"Poor kid!"

"Lita, in my shoe box there are five pictures of Gene Valentine, and a note—"

"From him?"

"No, dodo, from me—a rough draft. Get them, will you?"

"You bet!"

"Thanks."

Then the nurse came in to say that everything was ready, and Lita was hurried out of the room. She kept telling herself that there was nothing to worry about, but her heart was beating oddly.

In the hall a young man was standing; or rather, from Lita's point of view, an older man, for he must have been twenty-eight or nine. He was attired in a long white robe rather like a cook—or an angel. The sight of him dressed thus for his work upset Lita and made her feel like crying; in fact she did cry.

"Don't you worry," said the young man in a deep voice—a splendid, rolling, velvet sort of voice. "We've got the best man in the country to operate; there's no danger."

"Is that you—the best man in the country?"

He laughed.

"To be candid, no," he said. "I'm Doctor Burroughs' assistant. He's the best there is. There is nothing to cry about."

"If people only cried when there was something to cry about," said Lita; and added in an exclamation of the deepest concern, "Oh, goodness!"

Her tone alarmed the young man.

"What is it?"

"I haven't got a handkerchief."

He lifted his apron and from the pocket of his blue serge trousers he produced an unfolded handkerchief, which he gave her.

"I have a little sister just about your age," he said.

Lita's face was in the handkerchief as she asked. "How old?"

"Let me see," said the doctor. "I think she must be twelve."

A slight sound that might have been a sob escaped from Lita, and the doctor was so moved with compassion that he patted her on the head. Then the door of Room 11 opened and his professional duties called him away.

A moment later he came out, bearing Aurelia away to the operating room, and Lita went into Room 11 to wait. He promised as he passed to come and tell her as soon as it was over.

She felt perfectly calm now as she sat grasping his handkerchief in her hand. It was fine and embroidered in two letters—L. D. She ran over the L names and found she liked nearly all of them—Lawrence, Lionel, Leopold—not so good, though Leo was all right—Lewis—oh, of course, it was Lewis! She said the word aloud.

How still the house was! Now they were probably giving Aurelia the anæsthetic; now—

There was no use speculating about what D stood for. He thought she was twelve, did he? She put her hand up to where his had rested on the top of her head. She could not begin to make hers cover the same area. He must have a large hand. Well, that was all right; he was a large man. She could see his face before her, smooth as to skin and rather jutty as to outline of brows and jaw, and his heavy, thick, short, black hair, almost like an Indian's in texture. And she had thought that she preferred blond men. L. D.—Lita D. . . She wondered if she ought to go immediately and hunt up those photographs of Aurelia's. What a time it would make if they should be found before she got there! How long would this take—an hour? Would he really come back himself, or would he send that light-hearted, gray-haired nurse who looked like Marie Antoinette? If he patted her on the head he might even— Lawrence—Leonard—

Suddenly he was in the room again, smelling horribly of disinfectants.

"It's all right—all over," he said. He began to pluck ineffectually at the back buttons of his white robe. "Help me, there's a good child," he said, stooping so that she could reach.

She undid the buttons, the garment slipped to the floor, and he stood revealed as a normal young man in his shirt and dark blue serge trousers. He began rolling down his shirt sleeves, talking as he did so.

"Your friend has good nerve—brave and calm. Your sister? No? What's your name?"

"Hazlitt."

Too kind to smile at this infantile assumption of importance, his eyes did laugh a little, but he said, "I meant your first name."

"Lita. What's yours?"

"Luke— Well, Lita, I'm going to write to Effie about you. Wait! Where are you off to in such a hurry?"

She could not tell him that she was going to destroy the patient's compromising correspondence.

She said mysteriously, "I must go. You've been so kind. Good-by." For one tense moment she thought he was going to kiss her.

Evidently there is such a thing as thought transference, for as she drew back she heard him saying, "No, certainly not. I should not dream of kissing a lady of your mature years."

"You never kiss ladies of mature years?" murmured Lita in the manner of a six-year child.

"Well, I know how Effie feels on the subject. She boxed the ears of our local congressman for a salute which he offered merely as a vote getter. It was a terrible shock to him."

"You have a shock coming to *you*," she answered gently, and left the room.

She had a shock of her own on entering her bedroom, for Miss Jones, the house mistress, was already busy with Aurelia's bureau drawers. Had she or had she not lifted the top of the shoe box? It was necessary to act quickly; but fortunately Miss Jones was young and pleasant and easy to get round. If it had been Miss Barton— The school often commented with a sort of wondering irritation on the fact that in dealing with girls Miss Barton was not absolutely an idiot.

"Halloo, Jonesy dear," said Lita with a soft friendliness which in pupils is somewhat like the bearing of gifts by Greeks. "She's all right. The operation's over, the doctor told me."

Miss Jones was winding pink ribbon on a card, and answered, "Oh, isn't he wonderful? Of all the great men I ever met Doctor Burroughs inspires—"

"It wasn't Doctor Burroughs. It was the other one, his assistant— what's his name? It begins with a D."

But Miss Jones didn't know anything about the assistant, and drew Lita's attention from a subject tolerably absorbing by asking if she knew where Aurelia kept her bedroom slippers.

"Look here, Jonesy," said Lita. "Who is that queer-looking man—like a tramp—on the piazza downstairs?"

"I'll run down and see," said Miss Jones.

She was small, but there was something about her manner which would have made anything but a mythical tramp tremble.

When she had gone Lita opened the shoe box and found five large photographs of Eugene Valentine lying on top of the shoes: one in the aviator's uniform of his new play; one in his coronation robes in his last success, The King is Bored; and the other three just Eugene Valentine, with the light shining on the ridges of his wavy light hair. He was an awfully good-looking man, Lita thought—if you liked blonds. She laid the photographs under the paper in the bureau drawer Miss Jones had finished tidying. The draft of the letter had slipped down among the shoes, and Lita had only time to thrust it into the pocket of the coat she was wearing before Miss Jones was back again, saying that the tramp must have gone away.

Supper that evening was exciting. The great Doctor Burroughs had driven magnificently back to town in his car before Aurelia was fairly out of the anæsthetic; but he had left his assistant behind him—a clever young fellow. Miss Barton murmured she hoped he was tactful, discreet; one had to be careful in a school—parents, you know. Doctor Burroughs assured her she need give herself no concern; Doctor Dacer was quite safe—minded his own business—no trouble with the nurses or anything like that—just the sort of young man to leave in a girls' school. Even the wisest may be betrayed into sweeping statements when in a hurry to get away to Sunday dinner.

Lita, as chairman of the self-government committee, sat at the head of one of the senior tables—a conspicuous position. The girls were all in their places before Miss Barton came in with the tactful and discreet young fellow. It was the school's first view of him, and Lita could hear the comments of her peers rising about her:

"Looks a little like Doug."

"Isn't Aurelia the lucky stiff?"

"What are the symptoms of appendicitis? I feel them coming on."

She tried not to look at Miss Barton's table, and when she did she met his eye. He nodded and smiled with open friendliness; and bending toward Miss Jones, with his eyes still on hers, asked quite obviously for details about his little friend. Lita saw the smile fade from his face as he received them. Then a quite different smile flickered across his face; the smile of a man who says to himself, "To have even mentioned kissing the chairman of the self-government committee!"

As they were all moving out of the dining room again, Miss Barton called Lita to her.

"You will be glad to know," she said, "that Doctor Dacer says Aurelia will be up within two weeks—no complications—no danger. This is Lita Hazlitt, Doctor Dacer, Aurelia's best friend."

The doctor showed some of his advertised caution by merely bowing, but Lita answered, "Oh, yes, Doctor Dacer was so kind this afternoon." And looking up at him she asked, "Have you written to Effie yet?"

"Not yet," he returned politely; but below the level of the teacher's eyes a clenched fist made a distinctly menacing gesture in Lita's direction, and the corner of Lita's mouth, which occasionally created a dimple, just trembled. The doctor turned to Miss Barton, and it would be hard to imagine anything more professional than his manner as he said, "My patient seems to be very dependent on Miss Hazlitt. She was just asking for her. I think it would be a good idea if Miss Hazlitt could be in and out of the infirmary a good deal during the next few days."

"Of course, of course," said Miss Barton, who, though trained to distrust girls, was not trained to distrust doctors. "Aurelia is so alone, poor child." And lowering her voice as she moved away, with the doctor bending politely so as not to miss a syllable, Lita could hear a murmur:

"These terrible divorces! Do you know that over twenty of my girls—"

Lita found herself excused from sacred reading that evening so that she might sit with her friend.

Yet oddly enough, when she reached the infirmary the white-haired nurse seemed surprised to see her, and said that the doctor had given the patient something to make her sleep before he had gone to supper, and that she ought not to wake until morning—at least they hoped not.

But at that moment Dacer came out of another room, where he had evidently been smoking a pipe, and said, "Oh, well, stick round a little. She might wake up."

The nurse gave him a sharp look; and then, being really discreet and tactful, retired into Room 11 and shut the door. Lita and the doctor were left facing each other in the hall.

"Let's go out," he said, "where I can smoke. It's a good sort of evening—with a moon."

"Mercy!" answered Lita. "How do you think a girls' school is run? I couldn't do that."

"I thought the chairman of the self-government committee could do anything."

"On the contrary, she has to be particularly careful, and not go about exposing herself to being patted on the head."

"She was lucky worse than that didn't happen, masquerading as an infant." And then, without the slightest pause, but with a complete change of tone, Lita heard him saying: "No, I'm sorry; but I think it would be better not tonight. . . Ah, Miss Barton, I was just saying to Miss Hazlitt that as the patient had fallen asleep it would be better not to disturb her again tonight."

"Of course," said Miss Barton, who, it appeared, was coming upstairs behind Lita's back. "I think if you ran back to the study, Lita, you'd get in for the end of the reading."

And as she turned obediently away she heard Miss Barton suggesting that if Doctor Dacer found the infirmary dull, the sitting room in her cottage was at his service. No, Doctor Dacer had a good deal of work to do. Lita smiled to herself. He had not seemed so busy a few minutes before.

She had never been in love—never even deeply interested before. She had looked with surprise and envy on her classmates; not only Aurelia, with her devouring passion for Valentine; but Carrie Waldron, the senior president, who worshiped a dark-eyed motion-picture actor; and Doris Payne, who loved a great violinist to whom she never expected to speak. The authorities were terribly down on this sort of thing; but Lita, who knew more about it than the authorities, was not sure. Would Carrie be studying Spanish at odd moments so as to know more about her idol's great bull-fighter part—would Doris work so hard at her music—would Aurelia be learning Romeo and Juliet by heart as she did her hair in the morning—Romeo was a part Valentine was always contemplating—if it were not for love? More, would Miss Barton's course in English constitutional history be so interesting if Miss Barton did not feel—as the school had discovered—a romantic passion for Oliver Cromwell? Certainly not!

Her mother thought these excitements vulgar. She said if girls must be silly, why not be silly about people in their own class of life?

But Lita explained that the boys they knew were not so thrilling. Had her mother, she asked, never bought the picture of an actor? "Never!" said her mother with conviction; but Aunt Minnie, who happened to be there, said, "Nonsense, Alita! You had a picture of Sothern as the Prisoner of Zenda." Mrs. Hazlitt said that she hadn't, and that was entirely different anyhow.

The only result of the conversation was that Mrs. Hazlitt began to suspect Lita of some such ill-bred passion—most unjustly. The whole subject had had merely a theoretical interest for Lita. She was too practical to be fired by these intangible heroes—dream, dead or dramatic.

But now, even that first Sunday, as she stepped out of the infirmary into the bare March moonlight, she found that real life could hold the same thrill for her that dreams did for these others.

"And that," she said to herself, "is where I have the best of it."

II

LITA HAD DEVELOPED A TECHNIC by which she slept through the rising gong and for the next twenty-five minutes, allowing herself thus exactly five minutes to get up, dress and reach the dining room. But the morning after her friend's operation she woke with the gong, and five minutes later was on her way to the infirmary, first tying her tie and then smoothing down her hair as she went.

As she ran up the stairs of the infirmary, a voice—whose owner must have recognized the almost inaudible patter of her feet—called to her from the small dining room of the cottage. She put her face, flushed with running, round the jamb of the door and saw Doctor Dacer seated at breakfast. The nurse was toasting bread on an electric toaster, and he was spreading a piece, just finished, with a thick crimson jam. "Damson," Lita said to herself.

He looked at her.

"Youth's a great thing," he said.

"So the old are always saying," Lita answered. "But there's a catch in it; they get back at you for being young."

"Does that mean you think I'm old?" Dacer asked patiently; and the nurse with the white hair exclaimed to herself "Goodness!" as if to her they both seemed about the same age.

Lita cocked her head on one side.

"Well," she said, "you are too old to be my equal—I mean contemporary. I mean contemporary," she added as they both laughed. Dacer, with a more complete answer, gave her the piece of toast he had been preparing. It was delicious—cool and smooth and sweet on top, and hot and buttery below. Lita consumed it in silence, and then with a deep sigh as she sucked a drop of jam from her forefinger, she said, "How noble that was! Sometimes I'm afraid I'm greedy."

"Of course you are," said Dacer, as if greed were a splendid quality. "Sit down and have some coffee. . . Have you been introduced to Miss Waverley? She hates men."

"Goodness!" said Miss Waverley, glancing over her shoulder, as if it were mildly amusing that a man should think he knew anything about how she felt.

"Or is it only doctors?" Dacer went on.

"Men patients are worse," said Miss Waverley.

"Don't go away," said Dacer to Lita. "You are always going away."

"I came to see Aurelia."

"I know, but it's customary to discuss the case first with the surgeon—in some detail too. Sit down."

But she would not do that; her first duty was to her friend. She knew Aurelia would want to know that the photographs and the letter were safe. She stayed by her bedside until it was time to leap downstairs and run across the campus to the dining room, her appetite merely edged by the toast and jam.

Monday was a busy day for Lita. Immediately after luncheon her committee met and went over the reports of the monitors for the week; and then there was basket ball for two hours, and then study. The tennis courts were near the athletic field, and as Lita played with the first team she could hear a deep voice booming out the score as Doctor Dacer and Miss Jones played set after set. Miss Jones had been tennis champion of her college the year before. Lita sent out a young scout to bring her word how the games were going, and learned that Dacer was winning. He must be pretty good, then—Jonesy was no slouch. She would have taunted him in the evening, when she went to say goodnight to Aurelia, if he had let himself be beaten by Jonesy.

Every Monday evening Miss Fraser, the English teacher, read aloud to the senior members of her class. Miss Fraser was something of a problem, because she was so much more a lover of literature than a teacher. She inspired the girls with a fine enthusiasm for the best; but in the process she often incited them to read gems of the language which their parents considered unsuited to their youth. Shakspere she read quite recklessly, sometimes forgetting to use the expurgated edition. When Miss Barton suggested pleasantly that perhaps Antony and Cleopatra was not quite the most appropriate of the plays, Miss Fraser answered, "Don't they read worse in the newspapers in bad prose?"

At present she was conservatively engaged in reading Much Ado About Nothing. No one could object to that, she said. She made it seem witty and contemporary.

Lita slipped over to the infirmary between supper and the reading to bid Aurelia goodnight. Dacer wasn't there. She stayed, talking a few minutes with Aurelia, who was well enough to hear about the tramp and the bedroom slippers and a little school gossip. Lita asked casually where the doctor was, but no one seemed to know.

When a little later she entered Miss Fraser's study she found to her surprise that he was there, settled in a corner. Miss Fraser explained that Doctor Dacer was the son of an old friend of hers; he had been kind enough to say that it would be a pleasure to him to stay and hear the reading. She need not have felt under the necessity of apologizing to the six or seven members of her class. They felt no objection to his presence.

Lita was knitting a golf sweater for her father. She could do it at school, but not at home, for her mother was so discouraging about it. She had already objected to its color, shape and pattern; had felt sure that Lita's father wouldn't appreciate the sentiment, and wouldn't wear anything that did not come from a good shop. Probably after all Lita's trouble he'd give it to his manservant. But Lita did not think he would.

The nice thing about knitting is that it leaves the eyes disengaged—at least to an expert, and Lita was expert. She resolved that she would not look at Dacer; and did not for the first half hour or so, for she had a comfortable knowledge that he was looking at her. Then, just once, their eyes met. It was while Miss Fraser was reading these lines:

> *But nature never fram'd a woman's heart*
> *Of prouder stuff than that of Beatrice:*
> *Disdain and scorn ride sparkling in her eyes,*
> *Misprising what they look on; and her wit*
> *Values itself so highly, that to her*

All matter else seems weak.
She cannot love—

Holding her glance, he seemed to nod his head as if to say that was a perfect description of her. Could he mean that? Did he mean that? She averted her eyes hastily, and when she looked back again he had folded his arms and was staring off over everybody's head, very blank and magnificent, unaware of the existence of little schoolgirls. Had she offended him?

She decided that the next morning at the infirmary, while she was eating his toast and jam, she would ask him a pointed question about the character of Beatrice. She gave a good deal of time to framing the question—wasted time, for when she reached the infirmary she found he had gone—had taken a late train to New York the night before. Lita remembered he had looked at his watch once or twice toward the end of the reading.

"Yes," said the nurse cheerfully, "we're doing so well we don't need him." It was the second nurse. Miss Waverley had gone with the doctor.

Lita's frightened eyes sought Aurelia's, who framed the words: "Back Thursday."

She framed them as if two—almost three days were nothing. Lita, who knew no more of the Einstein theory than the name, discovered that time was relative; that Tuesday morning took what in old times she would have considered several weeks in passing; and that each study period—in the words of William James—lay down like a cow on the doorstep and refused to get up and go on. The truth was that time had never been time to Lita; it had been action. Now it was emptiness, something to be filled; and yet she couldn't fill it; it was a bottomless abyss. Worse still, she couldn't concentrate. She went to the blackboard to do an original—a simple thing she would have tossed off in a minute in old times—and couldn't think how to begin; she, the best geometer in the class. This was serious, and it was queer. Lita couldn't, as she said to Aurelia, get the hang of it. Time being her problem—this sudden unexpected accumulation of time on her hands—she might have been expected to spend it doing the practical, obvious things that had to be done. Not at all. She was incapable of exertion. She could not study; and even the letter to her father, saying the Italian trip was impossible, was never written.

She had a letter from him Wednesday morning in which he assumed that she had not been able to bring her mother to any conclusion. He said he would call her up when she came to town on Friday. Perhaps she would dine with him on Saturday, and do a play. Ordinarily this would have seemed an agreeable prospect; but now, since it was farther away than Thursday, it had no real existence.

Late Wednesday afternoon her unalterable decision not to discuss Doctor Dacer with anyone broke down, and she told Aurelia the whole story. It took an hour—their meeting, everything that he had said, done and looked, and all that she had felt. She paid a great price, however, for this enjoyment—and she did enjoy it—for afterward the whole experience became more a narrative and less a vital memory.

Thursday morning was the worst of all. Thursday morning was simply unbearable, until about noon, when she heard the whistle of the first possible New York train. After that things went very well until about five, when she had a moment to run over to see Aurelia and heard that the doctor had not come—had decided not to come until the next day, Friday.

As far as she was concerned, he might as well not have come at all. All her joy in the anticipated meeting was dead; but this might possibly have reawakened, except that on Friday she did not have a minute until the three-o'clock train, which she was taking to New York. Of course, she could develop a cold or some mysterious ailment which would keep her at school over Sunday, even in the infirmary; but deceit was not attractive to her; though, as she would have said herself, she was not narrow-minded about it.

The girls of Elbridge Hall were not supposed to make the trip to New York by themselves; but sometimes a prudent senior—and who is prudent if not the chairman of the self-government committee?— might be put on the train at Elbridge by a teacher and sent off alone, on the telephoned promise of a parent to meet her on her arrival at the Grand Central.

When, under the chaperonage of Jonesy, Lita stepped out of the school flivver at the station she saw that Doctor Dacer was there before her. He must have come up in a morning train, seen his patient and walked to the station. Wild possibilities rose at once in the girl's mind. Could he have known from Aurelia? Could he have arranged— No, for he took no interest in her arrival; hardly glanced in her direction. He was smoking, and when the train came he got into the smoking car without so much as glancing back to see where Jonesy was bestowing Lita.

The train, which was a slow one, was empty. Lita settled herself by a window and opened her geometry. She said to herself:

"I simply will not sit and watch the door. If he means to come he'll come, and my watching won't change things one way or the other."

She set her little jaw and turned to Monday's lesson: "To prove that similar triangles are to each other as the squares of the medians drawn to their homologous sides." The words conveyed absolutely nothing to her. She read them three times. It wasn't that she couldn't do the problem—she couldn't even think about it. She drew two similar triangles. They seemed to sit side by side like a cat and a kitten. She gave them whiskers and tails. Then, annoyed with herself, she produced a ruler and constructed a neat figure. She tried reading the theorem again, this time in a conversational tone, as if it were the beginning of a story: "Similar triangles are to each other—"

The door opened, letting in the roar of the train and a disagreeable smell of coal smoke.

"I will not look up," thought Lita; "I will not! I will not!" And raising her eyes she saw that Dacer was there. She smiled not so much in greeting as from pure joy.

He hadn't wasted much time. He took her books and bag from the seat beside her and put them on the rack. Then he sat down and said, "Isn't it dangerous to let such little girls travel by themselves?"

She found speech difficult between her heart's beating too fast and her breath's coming too slow, but she did manage to say, "What does Effie do?"

"Just what you do—she expects me to be on hand to look out for her."

"I didn't expect you."

"No? Can it be you are not such a clever girl as teacher always thought?"

"I thought you were spending the night at Elbridge."

"So did I when I arrived, but my plans changed. I found that it would be better for me to take the three-o'clock to town and go back on Sunday afternoon, by the—what is the train that we take back on Sunday?"

It was almost too serious for jests, and Lita said in a voice that just didn't tremble that she took the 4:08.

Life is not often just right, not only in the present, but promising in forty-eight hours to be just as good or better. Lita spent two wonderful hours. First they talked about Aurelia—her courage, her loneliness, her parents, divorce in general—and then Lita found herself telling him the whole story of her own position in regard to her parents. Even to Aurelia, with whom she talked so frankly, she had never told the whole story—her own deep emotional reactions. She found to her surprise that it was easier to tell a story of an intimate nature to this stranger of an opposite sex than to her lifelong friend. He understood so perfectly. He did not blame them; if he had she would have felt called on to defend them; and he did not blame her; if he had she would have been forced into attacking them. He just listened, and seemed to think it was a normal and deeply interesting bit of life.

He interrupted her once to say, "But you must remember that they are people as well as parents."

It seemed to her an inspired utterance. She did not always remember that. She offered the excuse: "Yes, but I don't mind their being divorced. Only why do they hate each other so?"

"How do you know they hate each other?"

Lita thought this was a queer thing to say after all that she had told him—almost stupid. She explained again: They were always abusing each other; nothing the other did was right; neither could bear her to speak well of—

"They sound to me," said Dacer, "as if they were still fond of each other." Then, as Lita just stared at him, he went on: "Didn't you know that? The only people it's any fun to quarrel with are the people you love."

"Oh, no."

"Well, I'm glad you haven't found it out as yet, but it's true."

"I never quarrel," said Lita.

"You will some day. I expect to quarrel a lot with my wife."

"I shall never quarrel with my husband."

"No? Well, perhaps I'm wrong then."

She was angry at herself for glancing up so quickly to see what he could possibly mean by that except—he was looking at her gravely.

"Look here!" he said. "That's a mistake about Italy. You don't want to go to Italy next summer."

She was aware of two contradictory impressions during the entire journey—one that this was the most extraordinary and dramatic event, and that no heroine in fiction had ever such an adventure; and the other that it was absolutely inevitable, and that she was now for the first time a normal member of the human species.

Nothing in the whole experience thrilled her more than the calm, almost martial way in which he said as they were getting off the train at the Grand Central, "Now we'll get a taxi."

She was obliged to explain to him that they couldn't; her mother would be at the gate waiting for her—she always was.

Only this time she wasn't.

Meeting trains in the Grand Central, though it has not the phrenetic difficulty of meeting trains in the Pennsylvania Station, where you must watch two crowded stairways and a disgorging elevator in three different directions, is not made too easy. To meet a train in the Grand Central you must be in two widely separated spots at the same time.

Mrs. Hazlitt, approaching the bulletin board through devious subterranean routes, was caught in a stampede of those hurrying to meet a belated Boston express; and when at last she wormed her way to the front she saw that the impressive official with the glasses well down on his nose and the extraordinary ability for making neat figures had written down Track 12 for Lita's train. She turned liked a hunted animal; and at the moment when Lita and Dacer were emerging from the gate Mrs. Hazlitt was running from a point far to the west of Vanderbilt Avenue to a track almost at Lexington. It was five o'clock, and many heavier and more determined people were running for their trains, so that she had a good many collisions and apologies before she reached the gate where her daughter ought to have been.

The last passenger, carrying a bunch of flowers and a cardboard box tied up with two different kinds of string, was just staggering through on oddly shaped flat feet. Everyone else had disappeared. Mrs. Hazlitt questioned the gateman. Had he seen a small young lady all alone who seemed to be looking for someone? The gateman said that he could not say he had, but would not care to say he had not. He possessed to perfection the railroad man's art of not telling a passenger anything he doesn't have to tell. His manner irritated Mrs. Hazlitt.

"I suppose you know," she said, "that you have horrible arrangements for meeting trains."

"If some of us had our way we wouldn't have any arrangements at all," answered the gateman.

This shocked Mrs. Hazlitt; it seemed so autocratic. She opened her eyes to their widest and felt she must argue the matter out with him.

"Do you mean," she asked, "that you would not let people meet trains?"

"I would not," said the gateman calmly, and having locked his gate he went his way.

This had taken a few minutes, and by the time Mrs. Hazlitt had gone back to the Vanderbilt Avenue entrance and found her car and driven home, Lita was already in the library—alone.

One of the disadvantages experienced by people who express themselves quickly is that while they are explaining how everything happened the silent people of the world are making up their minds how much they will tell. Mrs. Hazlitt was talking as she entered the room.

"I'm so sorry, my dear," she was saying. "Don't let's ever tell Miss Barton. I wasn't really late—at least I would not have been if I had not had to run miles and miles, knocking down commuters as I went. And do you know what a gateman said to me, Lita, when I found I had missed you? That people oughtn't to meet trains. I could have killed him. I don't suppose you were frightened though. I suppose you took a taxi?"

"Yes," said Lita.

She had had every intention of telling her mother everything— well, certainly that she had met Doctor Dacer on the train and that he had been kind enough to see her home; but the words did not come instantly, and as she paused, her mother rushed on to something else—clothes, and what Lita wanted to see if they went to the theater the next day. The moment for telling slipped away from her in the most unexpected way; it was getting farther and farther; in fact it was nothing but a speck on the horizon.

They had an amusing dinner together. One of the pleasantest features in her parents' divorce was that Mrs. Hazlitt felt not the least restraint about discussing the Hazlitt family.

"My dear," she would say, with her eyes dancing, "don't tell me you never heard about why your Uncle Elbert was driven out of Portland."

Lita enjoyed these anecdotes extremely. Sometimes they contained illuminating phrases: "Of course, your father and I preferred to be alone." "Naturally I knew just how Jim—your father—felt about it, but—"

When her mother was like this Lita was content that her father and the whole world should remain outsiders. Her mother was a sufficient companion.

When they were back in the library after dinner her father telephoned to her. It was about Italy. She took up the receiver with a sinking heart. Now she wished she had written to him. Her mother was holding the paper as if she were reading it, but Lita knew that she couldn't help hearing the faltering sentences she was murmuring into the mouthpiece:

"Yes, Pat, I spoke to her, and I'm afraid we can't. I mean that, under the circumstances—" She heard the paper rustling to the floor, and her mother standing beside her whispered to her: "Don't be so timid; don't say you're afraid."

Then both parents were talking to her at once, one over the wire and one in her ear. Now, it is possible to listen while you talk yourself, but it is not possible to listen to two people at once.

Her father was saying: "Of course, if you don't want to go say so, but if you do, and will put the matter as I suggested—"

And her mother was whispering sibilantly, "You're giving the idea you wish to go—so unjust to me. Say straight out you won't leave me."

It was one of those minutes that epitomized her life, and her nerves were distinctly on edge as she hung up the receiver, to find that her mother was only waiting for this, to go over the whole matter more at length.

"There are times, my dear," she was saying, "when it is really necessary to speak out, even at the risk of hurting a person's feelings. I do hope you are not one of those weak natures who can never tell a disagreeable truth. It will save your father future suffering if you can make him understand once and for all he cannot come in between us— not because I forbid it, but because you won't have it."

The evening never regained its gayety.

The next morning—Saturday—was devoted entirely to clothes, and Lita now discovered a curious fact. She found she knew exactly how Dacer liked her to dress. In their few interviews they had never mentioned clothes, and yet she did not buy a hat or reject a model without a sure conviction that she was following his taste. Heretofore her main interest in the subject had been a desire to knock her schoolmates in the eye.

She thought of an epigram: "Women dress for all women—and one man."

The morning saw a triumph of her diplomacy too. She and her mother were going to the theater together that afternoon. Coming down in the train, she had learned that Dacer was taking Effie and some of her friends to the matinée to see Eugene Valentine's new play, The Winged Victory. It had not been easy to steer Mrs. Hazlitt toward

ALICE DUER MILLER

this popular success; she was displeased with anything that fell short of the Comédie Française. Lita was obliged to stoop to tactics suggested by Aurelia. She intimated very gently that when her father took her to the play he never cared what it was so long as she was amused, and so she wouldn't bore her mother with the Valentine play: she'd wait until she and Pat were going on a spree—that very evening, perhaps—

Mrs. Hazlitt came to terms at once and sent for the tickets.

They came in a little late. The play had already begun, but Lita's first glance was not at the stage. Yes, he was there—three nice little girls in a row in the front of the box, and he in the back—but not alone. A woman was whispering in his ear. Who was she? His fiancée? His wife? Had he said anything which actually precluded the idea of his being married? "I expect to quarrel a great deal with my wife." That did not say more than that he had not quarreled with her so far. These two were certainly not quarreling. She sat in great agony; not of spirit only, for gradually a distinct physical ache developed in her left side. She tried to glue her eyes to the stage, and did not hear a word, except an occasional murmur from her mother: "What a silly play!"

The lights went up at the end of the act. Lita saw that the woman was rather fat and not at all young—thirty at least—and yet she knew that these sophisticated older women— There was something sleek and sumptuous about this one, all in black velvet and diamonds and fur. A slight respite came to her when Dacer went out to smoke a cigarette. Did this indicate indifference or merely intimacy? The white-skinned woman moved to the front of the box and began making herself agreeable to the children, particularly to the girl Lita had picked out as Effie—a regular sister-in-law-to-be manner. She had looked forward to the theater as a good time to tell her mother all about it, with a casual "Oh, do you see that man over there—" She was suffering too much to permit it. She became aware that her mother felt something tense and portentous in the air; and she said suddenly, with a sound instinct for red herrings, that she thought Valentine the handsomest creature that she had ever seen. Her mother's reaction to this took up most of the entr'acte.

Doctor Dacer never saw them at all. Mrs. Hazlitt was an adept at getting out of a theater and finding her car before anyone else. She and Lita were on their way uptown before the little girls in the box had sorted out their coats and hats. A good many people, mostly men, came in to tea; and when they had gone it was time for Lita to dress to go and dine with her father. Dine! She felt she would never be able to eat again—a very curious feeling.

When Mrs. Hazlitt went to her room Margaret was as usual waiting to help her dress, but it was not usual for Margaret to wear such a long face. She had entered the family as Lita's nurse, but was now Mrs. Hazlitt's maid and the pivot on which all domestic machinery revolved.

As she unhooked Mrs. Hazlitt's dress her solemn voice came from the middle of Mrs. Hazlitt's back: "I think you ought to know, mum, that when I was brushing that heavy coat of Miss Lita's this afternoon I found something in the pocket."

"Goodness, Margaret! What?"

Margaret fumbled under her apron and produced a folded, typewritten sheet a little grimy about the edges. Mrs. Hazlitt seized it and read:

> *Dear Eugene Valentine:*
>
> May I not tell you what an inspiration your art is to me in my daily life? I think I have every photograph of you that was ever published, and one I bought at a fair with your signature. Only this is not my favorite. I like best the one as a miner from The Emerald Light. It is so strong and virile. Oh, Mr. Valentine, you cannot guess how happy it would make me if you would autograph one of these for me! I am not at present living in New York, but I am often there for week-ends, and could easily bring one of these pictures to the theater after a matinée, if that would be easiest for you.
>
> I shall not attempt to tell you what your art means to me, and how you make other men seem, and I fear they always will seem like they was pigmies beside you.
>
> I take the great liberty of inclosing my own picture in case it would interest you to see what a great admirer of yours looks like.

Being merely a rough draft, it was unsigned.

Of all the possibilities that crossed Mrs. Hazlitt's mind on reading this document, the possibility that her daughter had not written it was not one. Several suspicious circumstances at once popped into her head—Lita's insistence on going to Valentine's play; her admiration of him; her tentative suggestion about marriage; her alternate high spirits and abstraction.

"And who was he?" Margaret went on. "That young fellar brought her home yesterday?"

"A man brought her home yesterday?"

"Yes—the two of them in a taxi."

"What did he look like?"

"I couldn't see him very good; but I heard him say 'Until Sunday' as he got back into the taxi; and when I opened the door for Miss Lita you could see she was smiling all over her face, but not letting it out."

Ah, how well, in other days, Mrs. Hazlitt had known that beatific state!

She walked to her door and called, "Lita! Lita!"

Probably if one read the memoirs of Napoleon, the dispatches of Wellington and the commentaries of Cæsar one would find a place where the author asserts that the best general is he who takes quickest advantage of chance. Lita, entering her mother's room with her head bent over a fastening of her dress, was wondering what made some fasteners cling like leeches and others droop apart like limp handshakes. For the first few minutes she had no idea what her mother was talking about. She was prepared to feel guilty—she was guilty, but she had written no letter.

"Writing a letter like that—a vulgar letter—and making me take you to his play—and coming home with him, when I was actually waiting at the gate for you. Perhaps you were not even on that train at all—so terribly deceitful—as if I were your enemy instead of your mother. I felt there was something queer about you at the play! An actor! I wish you knew something about actors in private life. And Valentine of all people! A man—"

Mrs. Hazlitt paused. She knew nothing about Valentine's private life; but she thought it was pretty safe to make that pause as if it were all too awful to discuss.

"Your father must be told of this. It will shock him very much."

That was the phrase that gave Lita her great idea. Not since she was four years old had she heard the words "your father" spoken in that tone. Perhaps after all, it was not necessary to die in order to reconcile your parents; perhaps it was enough to let them think you were undesirably in love. She had a moment to consider this notion while her mother, in a short frilled petticoat, with her blond hair about her shoulders, was running on about what Mr. Hazlitt would say to this man.

Lita said at a venture, "Mr. Valentine doesn't even know my name. He won't have any idea what father is talking about."

"Indeed?" cried Mrs. Hazlitt. "Your father is not a man who talks without contriving to make himself understood. And as to Valentine's not knowing your name, you'll find he knows it—and the amount of your fortune, too, probably. Little schoolgirls have very little interest for older men, I can tell you, unless— And such a letter too. 'Like they was pigmies.' If you must be vulgar, at least try to be grammatical."

"Shall you see my father when he comes for me?"

"Of course I shall not see him; but I shall take care that he knows the facts." At the same time, Lita could not help noticing that Mrs. Hazlitt refused to wear the garment Margaret had left out for her, and put on, with apparent unconsciousness, a new French tea gown in mauve and silver. "He will tell you better than I can what sort of a man this Valentine is."

"But, mother, is father's judgment of men to be depended on? You said about his lawyers that he had the faculty of collecting about him the most inefficient—"

"I never said any such thing—or rather, it was entirely different. How can you speak like that of your father? But it's my own fault, treating you as if you were a companion instead of a silly child."

This was war. Lita withdrew into herself. Parents, she reflected, did not really quite play the game; they couldn't belittle a fellow parent one day, and the next, when they needed to use force, rush away into the wings and dress him up as an ogre. After all the things her mother had said about her father, how could she expect him to inspire fear? And yet Lita knew that she was a little afraid.

Then Freebody the butler came up to say that Mr. Hazlitt was waiting in his car for Miss Hazlitt. Freebody had been with the Hazlitts before their divorce, and when the split came had preferred to remain with Mrs. Hazlitt, although he had been offered inducements by the other side. In her bitterness of spirit she had felt it a triumph that Freebody had chosen her household. She had particularly valued his reason for staying with her. He had said he did not care to work for stage people. This was wonderful to quote. It let people know that her husband's second wife had been an actress, and moreover a kind of actress that Freebody did not care to work for; and it could be told so good-temperedly, as if it were a joke on Freebody. She had always felt grateful to him.

Now she sealed the incriminating note in another envelope and gave it to Freebody.

"Give this to Mr. Hazlitt," she said, "and tell him it was found in the pocket of Miss Lita's coat"; and she added, when he had gone down again, "You can explain the rest yourself."

"No, mother," said Lita; "if you want any explaining done you must do it yourself."

Mrs. Hazlitt was still protesting against this suggestion when Freebody came back and said that Mr. Hazlitt was in the drawing-room, and would be very much obliged to Mrs. Hazlitt if she could arrange to see him for just five minutes. There was a pause; Mrs. Hazlitt and Lita looked at each other; and Freebody, just as much interested as anyone, looked at no one. Then Mrs. Hazlitt said they would both go down.

And so for the first time since she was five years old Lita stood in the room with both her parents—her mother trembling so that the silk lining of her tea gown rustled with a soft, continuous whispering like the wind in dead leaves, and her father, white and impressive, with his crush hat under one arm and the open letter held at arm's length so that he could read it without his glasses. Something hurt and twisted came to rest in Lita by the mere fact that the three of them were together.

Her father spoke first, and his voice was not quite natural, as he said, "It was kind of you to come down, Alita. I know it is exceedingly painful to you—"

"I've done a good many painful things in my life for Lita."

"I know, I know," he answered gently; "and this not the least. But this letter—I don't exactly understand it."

"Have you read it?"

"Not entirely."

"Well, read it—read it," said Mrs. Hazlitt, as if he ought to see that he couldn't understand anything until he had read it; but everytime he began to read it she began to explain all the hideousness of Lita's conduct; and when he looked up to listen to her she said, with a sort of weary patience, "Won't you please read the letter? Then we can discuss it."

At last he said quietly, "Alita, I cannot read it while you talk to me."

She did not answer. She moved her neck back like an offended swan, and glanced at Lita as much as to say, "You see the sort of man he is?"

She did, however, remain silent until he had finished, and looking had said, "But this isn't even good grammar—'Like they was pigmies.' Don't they teach her grammar at this school?"

Alita Hazlitt was one of those people who, when blame is going about, assume it is intended for them and consider the accusation most unjust.

"Well, really," she said now, "it wasn't my wish that she should go to boarding school. It has turned out exactly as I prophesied it would. Common girls have taught her to run after actors, and inefficient teachers have failed—"

"I don't remember your prophesying that, Alita."

"You mean to say I did not?"

"I mean to say I have no recollection of it. I do remember that you said it would make it easier for me to kidnap her. I shall never forget that."

"You cannot deny that I was opposed to school. I only yielded to your wishes—such a mistake."

"You have not many of that kind to reproach yourself with."

Lita, who had felt a profound filial emotion at seeing her parents together, was now distressingly conscious that they had never seemed less her parents than at this moment. They seemed in fact rather dreadful people—childish, unjust, lacking in essential self-control. The last remnant of her childhood seemed to perish with this scene, and she became hard, matured and to a certain degree orphaned.

"What I am trying to say," Mr. Hazlitt went on, "is that we can hardly attribute this unfortunate episode entirely to the influence of the school. I mean that if there had not been some inherent silliness in the child herself—"

This was too good a point for Mrs. Hazlitt to let slip.

"It was not from me," she said, "that Lita inherited a tendency to run after people of the stage."

"We need not discuss inherited tendencies, I think."

Mrs. Hazlitt laughed.

"Ah, that is so like you! We may criticize the child or the school or my bringing up, but the instant we begin to talk about your shortcomings it is discovered that we are going too far."

"Alita," he said, "I came here in the most coöperative spirit—"

"And do you make it a favor that you should be willing to try to save your child?"

ALICE DUER MILLER

That was unjust of her mother, Lita thought. Her father was trying to be nice. It was her mother who kept making the interview bitter, and yet in essentials her mother had behaved so much better. Why did she suffer so much in the atmosphere of their anger? Why did she wish so passionately that they should treat each other at least fairly? She couldn't understand.

"You have not met me in a coöperative spirit," her father was saying, "and I see no point in my staying. Goodnight."

"And you're going—just like that—without doing anything at all?"

"Of course, I shall write to Miss Barton—and if you are not able to take Lita back to school tomorrow I'll go myself."

Lita noticed that though an instant before her mother had reproached him with indifference, she treated his last suggestion as if it were impertinent.

"I think I shall be able to take my daughter safely to school," she said. "But you must see this man; that I cannot do."

"I shall do nothing so ridiculous," said Mr. Hazlitt. "Valentine! Why, a man like that gets a basketful a day of letters from idiotic women of all ages! He's bored to death by them."

"I have yet to find a man who is bored by the adoration of idiotic women," said Mrs. Hazlitt, and there was no mistake in anybody's mind as to what she meant by that.

A discussion on the relative idiocy of the sexes broke out with extraordinary violence. Lita's conduct was utterly forgotten. She might have slipped out of the room without being noticed, except that her father was standing between her and the door. She tried to remember Dacer's saying that quarreling meant love, and found to her surprise that that idea was almost as shocking. Could it be that she did not want her parents to have any emotions at all?

When her father had gone, her mother burst into tears.

"I am so sorry," she said, "that you should have seen him like that—at his very worst."

Lita had just been thinking how much the better of the two he had appeared. She felt as hard as a stone. She had no wish to be continually appraising her parents; they left her no choice. Her childish acceptance of them had been destroyed, and at the moment her friendly emotion towards them as companions and human beings had not yet flowered. Instead of wanting to tell her mother about Dacer, she wanted to tell Dacer about her mother.

She saw that her whole scheme about Valentine had been ridiculous—a complete failure. She ought to clear that up at once, but she did not feel up to explaining it; an explanation with her mother involved so much. Mrs. Hazlitt would give those she loved anything in the world—except her attention. It was necessary to hold her attention with one hand and feed her your confidence with the other. Lita was too exhausted to attempt it that evening. She would do it the next day, of course.

The next morning—Sunday—Mrs. Hazlitt awoke with a severe headache. Though she insisted on Lita's remaining in sight—for fear that she would rush to the arms of Valentine—it was made clear that no friendly intercourse between parent and child was possible. Lita felt herself to be the direct cause of the agony of mind which had led to the headache.

After luncheon, looking like carved marble, Mrs. Hazlitt got up and announced her intention of escorting Lita back to school. The girl saw that her mother was not well enough to make the double journey, and suggested that it would be better for her father to go with her. Mrs. Hazlitt treated this proposal with the coldest scorn.

"I think we will not trouble your father further," she said.

At times like this she used a flat, remote voice; as dead, Lita thought, as a corpse talking on a disconnected telephone. In old times it had nearly broken her heart when her mother spoke to her in that tone. Today it had lost its power.

They drove to the station in silence, every jar of the car sending a tremor through Mrs. Hazlitt's eyelids. In the train, she put Lita's knitting bag behind her head and shut her eyes. Lita, sitting in silence beside, felt so wooden—inside and out—that, she said to herself, not even the appearance of Doctor Dacer would make any difference to her. But when, before they were out of the tunnel, he did pass through the car—not stopping, just raising his hat—she found it did affect her.

Her mother opened her eyes.

"Who's that man?" she said in an almost human tone.

"I think he's one of the surgeons who is taking care of Aurelia," Lita answered, and instantly regretted the "I think." It was positively deceitful, where she had intended to be merely noncommittal. But all the relations of her life seemed to have gone wrong.

She had not done any of her work for the next day; not the original in geometry or the sonnet she should have learned by heart; in fact she had not opened a book. She couldn't concentrate her mind now on mathematics or poetry, but she might do some of the collateral reading for Greek History. She slipped the book out of its strap and opened it.

"Of Lycurgus the lawgiver, we have nothing to relate that is certain and uncontroverted—" Lita thought: that's at least a candid way to begin a biography. The door opened, letting in the roar of the train and the smell of coal smoke, and Lita's nerves remembered it, as if only once before in her life had she ever known a car door open, and looked up— to see the conductor. She dropped her eyes and went on: "For there are different accounts of his birth, his death—" The door again; this time a passenger in search of a seat. She made a vow to herself to read three pages without looking up—and did. "Endeavoring to part some persons who were concerned in a fray, he received a wound by a kitchen knife, of which he died, and left the kingdom—"

She was aware that something in blue serge was stationary beside her. She looked slowly up. Yes, there he was.

She introduced him to her mother. The seat in front of them was now free, and Dacer, turning it over, sat down. Mrs. Hazlitt was not sorry to show that her coldness concerned her daughter only. She was very willing to talk agreeably to a stranger. The conversation was carried on between them as if Lita were too young to be expected to take part. She was not sorry, and went on glancing at a sentence here and there: "He set sail, therefore, and landed in Crete—" "—in which the priestess called him beloved of the gods, and rather a god than a man."

At this she really could not help looking at Dacer, and finding his eyes on her, she said, "I saw you at the theater yesterday."

He was interested.

"I didn't see you."

"Oh, yes, we were there," said Mrs. Hazlitt languidly. "Such a poor play! And as for Valentine—these popular actors in America—"

"He was thought very handsome and dashing, in our box," said Dacer.

And then Lita was surprised to hear her own voice saying, "Was that lady your wife?"

He stared at her for a second as if he had not heard, or could not understand what he seemed to have heard, and then answered quietly, "No, I don't care for them by the cubic foot."

Never had such a perfect reply been made, Lita thought. It reconstructed their relation and the whole world, and yet it took place so gently that her mother had hardly noticed that they had spoken to each other. Life was simply immense, she said to herself; she had been quite wrong about it before.

Then presently Dacer drew from Mrs. Hazlitt the admission that she had a wretched headache—hadn't slept—had had a disagreeable day—so foolish, but she was affected by scenes—

"Everybody is, you know," said Dacer.

She should not have come on such an expedition. The idea of her driving four miles out to the school in a jiggling car—and right back again—was absurd. He spoke almost sternly. He had a time-table in his pocket; a train left for New York five minutes after their train arrived at Elbridge; Mrs. Hazlitt must take that back, go straight to bed; he would give her a powder. Of course he would see Miss Hazlitt safely to the school—yes, even into Miss Barton's presence. He wrote his prescription. Lita saw that her mother was going to obey.

As they got out at the station they saw the New York train already waiting. Dacer put Mrs. Hazlitt on it; and Lita, watching them, saw Mrs. Hazlitt turn at the steps and give him some special injunction. Well, she probably would not confide to him so soon the scandal of the letter to Valentine; and if she did, it would be easy to explain. Dacer's face was untroubled as he returned to her.

"She's all in," he said.

A sharp self-reproach clutched at Lita's heart, the capacity for emotion having unexpectedly returned to her.

"Did it really do her harm to come out here?"

"It really is better for her to go straight home," he answered, as if admitting other motives had entered into his advice.

They got into the school flivver, which was waiting for them. Rain had just stopped and the back curtains were down. It was dark.

As they wheeled away from the station lights Lita heard him saying, "Didn't you know I wasn't married?" She did not immediately answer. Her hand was taken. "Didn't you know?" he said again.

A strange thing was happening to Lita. She formed the resolution of withdrawing her hand; she sent the impulse out from her brain, but it seemed only to reach her elbow; her hand, limp and willing, continued to remain in his.

They spoke hardly at all. The near presence of Matthew, the driver, a well-known school gossip, made speech undesirable. Besides, it wasn't necessary. Lita was perfectly content with silence as long as that large, solid hand enveloped hers.

As they turned in at the school gate he said, "You'll come over to see Aurelia this evening, I suppose."

She knew it wouldn't be possible, and was obliged to say so. And he was going back to town by a morning train. There was a pause.

As they got out he said, "Do you ever get up very early—as early as six?"

"I could always make a beginning," said Lita.

And then, true to his promise, he turned the chairman of the self-government committee over to the keeping of Miss Barton herself.

One excellent way of waking early is not to sleep at all. Lita hardly slept and was out of bed in time to watch the slow but fortunately inevitable spreading of the dawn. The new day was evidently going to be one of those days in late March when, though the earth has no suggestion of spring, the sky and the air are as vernal as May. Lita could see a light in the upper story of the infirmary. Dacer's perhaps.

It was not yet six when she stole downstairs and across the green. She had a good reason for being anxious about Aurelia—the stitches had been taken out of the wound the night before. That's what she would say if anyone asked her. But no one was awake, except far away in the school kitchen. The door of the infirmary was locked, but as she pressed noiselessly against it a figure faced her on the other side of the glass—Dacer. He opened the door and came out. It shut behind him, and as the night latch was still on, they were locked out. So they sat down on the narrow steps of the cottage, each with a pillar to lean against, and for the first time looked long and steadily at each other, as people who have met by deliberate acknowledged plan.

"Do you like the early morning?" he asked.

"I never did before," she answered.

He smiled at her.

"Do you realize," he said, "that in this lifelong friendship of ours that is the first decent thing you have ever said to me?"

Why, it was true! To Lita it had been so clear that she was more interested than he was; more eager; but it was true, she had given him none of those poignant, unforgettable sentences which he had left with her, to go over in his absence. She smiled, too—very slowly.

"Perhaps it won't be the last," she said.

At half past seven Dacer went in, and a few minutes later Lita arrived at Room 11 to inquire after her friend. When it was time to go, she shook hands with Doctor Dacer in the presence of Aurelia, Aurelia's mother, who had just arrived, and the trained nurse.

It was the last possible meeting before the Easter holidays.

III

IMMEDIATELY AFTER BREAKFAST LITA HAD geometry, and then a study period. During this she received a message that Miss Barton wished to speak to her. Such a message was not necessarily alarming; as chairman of the self-government committee she was consulted on many school problems. It was known that Miss Barton relied more on her judgment than on that of the senior president. Still, with a poor classroom record for the past week, and that unlicensed hour and a half on the infirmary steps, Lita did feel a trifle nervous; not that she could care very much about such minor matters. And then there was Matthew and the flivver—

The head mistress was sitting at her desk in her study, with its latticed windows and the etchings of English cathedrals on the walls. Her head was slightly on one side, which meant, according to school lore, that she was going to be particularly airy. She was.

"Oh, well, come, my dear Lita," she said. "This is really going rather far—a bit thick, as our little English friend would say."

"But what is it, Miss Barton?" Lita breathed, with all the pearly innocence of young guilt.

"Oh, dear, dear!" said Miss Barton. "So we have nothing on our conscience!"

"I have a great many things," said Lita quietly. She knew just how to talk to her chief—if that would do any good.

"One asks oneself whether girls are worth educating at all if this is the way the more intelligent ones expend their time and energy." And Miss Barton handed Lita the crumpled but familiar letter to Valentine. "I've had a sharp note from your father this morning, and I must say I don't blame him—really I don't. The grammar would be a sufficient humiliation to any school, even if the letter were addressed to your grandmother. And I may tell you that five different photographs of Mr. Valentine have been discovered hidden about your room—most ingeniously, it is true, but quite against our rules. Really, it's a question whether the school can keep on if this sort of thing is general."

Lita listened in what appeared to be the most respectful silence. Her relief was intense. Also she was trying to remember what Miss Barton said word for word so as to repeat it to Aurelia, to whom, after all, it justly belonged. Aurelia did a wonderful imitation of the head mistress, and could make use of every phrase; she was always on the lookout for material.

Lita was dismissed with a warning that she was to be kept in bounds until the holidays, and all her mail, outgoing and incoming, would be watched. This was rather serious, as Dacer had distinctly intimated that he intended to write. Still, a way could probably be found— She would speak to Aurelia about it.

She did not see Aurelia until the late afternoon. Dacer, as she expected, had gone; but he had left a message for her, Aurelia said—a very particular message.

With what extraordinary rapidity does the human imagination function! Between the time Aurelia announced the fact that a message existed and the giving of the message, Lita had time to envisage half a dozen possibilities, from the announcement of his immediate return to an offer of marriage.

The message was this: "He said to tell you that he had no idea you were so fond of the stage, or he would have behaved very differently. Do you understand what that means?—for I don't."

It meant, of course, that Miss Barton had told him about Valentine; had possibly even shown him the letter. It was just the sort of thing that she might do. Lita could almost hear her describing the comic complications of a head mistress' life: "This note, for instance, discovered in the pocket of one of my best girls; not even English; that hurts us most."

Why did Aurelia do such silly things—write such silly letters? Then, her sense of justice reasserting itself, she admitted it was not her friend's fault that the authorship of the letter had been mistaken. She was conscious of a physical nausea at the idea that Dacer was going about in the belief that she, Lita Hazlitt, had written thus to another man.

In the first few minutes she sketched an explanatory letter to him, and then remembered that her mail—in and out—was watched. That wouldn't do. In fact, there was nothing to do but to wait for two interminable weeks to pass and bring the Friday of the Easter holiday. Once in the same town with him, she could make him listen to her. There was nothing agreeable in life except the recollection of a large hand on hers, and even that memory was beginning to take on mortality.

She had not even the attentions of her parents to console her—not that forty thousand parents would have made up to her for the estrangement of Dacer. Her mother wrote conscientiously, but coldly. If she had seen her mother Lita would have told her everything, but the next Sunday was Mr. Hazlitt's official visiting day.

He came, but he came in a somewhat disciplinary mood. He gave Lita a long talk on how men felt when women forced attentions upon them. Lita did not dare take the risk of telling him; she had so little control over him that he might possibly tell the whole story to Miss Barton and involve Aurelia. At the same time she did not want him to find it out for himself by a futile visit to Valentine. Before he left she asked him point-blank if he contemplated such a step.

"Of course not," he answered.

And at almost that exact moment Freebody was ushering Valentine into Mrs. Hazlitt's library. For Mrs. Hazlitt was not a woman to let the grass grow under her feet, where her maternal obligations were concerned. The more she thought the matter over the more obvious it became that one or the other of Lita's parents must see Valentine and let him know that, however silly and forthputting the child had been, she was not without conventional protection. Of course, this was her father's duty; but since men as fathers were complete failures, all the disagreeable tasks of parenthood devolved inevitably on mothers. After Dacer had put her on the train the Sunday before, she had gone home and taken the powder he gave her and slept through a long night; and when she waked the next morning she had seen her duty clearly—to interview Valentine herself. It was a duty which implied a reproof to her former husband.

She looked for Valentine's name in the telephone book, but of course he was not there. Then she called up the theater where he was acting, and they refused to give her his address, but said a letter directed to the theater would reach him. Mrs. Hazlitt was in no mood to brook the mail's delays, and telegraphed him that it was necessary that she should see him for a few minutes at anytime or place convenient to him, and signed her name with a comfortable conviction that all New York knew just who Alita Hazlitt was.

Now Valentine, like most people busy with a successful career, was utterly uninterested in conventional social life; he hardly ever opened his mail, rarely answered telegrams; and if, by mistake, he did make a social engagement, he always told his secretary to call the people up and break it. In the ordinary course of events Mrs. Hazlitt's telegram would have been opened in his dressing room, and would have lain about for a day or two until Valentine thought of saying to someone who might know, "Who is this woman—Alita Hazlitt?" And then it would have dropped on the floor, and would eventually have been swept up and put in the theater ash can.

But, as it happened, Valentine had always cherished a wish to play the balcony scene in Romeo and Juliet before he was too old to wear a round-necked doublet; and a charitable institution, of which Mrs. Hazlitt was a most negligent trustee, had made a suggestion that Valentine should help them out in a benefit they were about to give. So Valentine, remembering her name on the letterhead of the institution, jumped at the conclusion that she had been selected to clinch the arrangement.

And so not more than three or four days went by before he answered her telegram by calling her up on the telephone, and it was arranged that he was to come and see her on Sunday at five.

She felt nervous as the time approached. She kept saying to herself that she had no idea how to deal with people like this. So awkward for a woman alone; but she was alone—utterly alone. She had become rather tearful by the time Valentine was announced. She waited a moment to compose herself and became even more unnerved in the process.

When she went down she found him standing by one of the bookcases, reading. She saw with a distinct pang that he was a handsomer man off the stage than on, with his fine hawklike profile and irrepressibly thick, furrowed light hair. He slid a book back into place as she entered, with the soft gesture of a book lover.

"I see you have a first edition of Trivia," he said. "I envy you."

Mrs. Hazlitt, who had thought up a greeting which was now rendered utterly impossible, was obliged to make a quick mental bound. She had never opened her edition of Gay, which she had inherited from her grandfather, and had never suspected it of being a first.

She said, "Oh, do you go in for first editions?"

"Not anymore," answered Valentine. "I've become more interested in autographs and association books. I have a wonderful letter of Gay's from—from—oh, you know, where he was staying when he wrote the Beggar's Opera—that duke's place—well, it will come to me."

But it never did come to him—not, at least, until he went home and looked it up—because, glancing at his hostess, he saw in those anxious, dark-fringed eyes that she wasn't a bit interested in his Gay letter; and so, with that tact that all artists possess if they will only use it, he said gently, "But it wasn't about autographs that you wanted to see me, was it? It's about your benefit."

"The benefit?"

"No? Well, what is it then?"

"Oh, I hoped you would understand without my being obliged to dot all the *i*'s."

She said this with a great deal of meaning. Leaning forward on her elbow, in her mauve and silver tea gown, behind her silver tea tray, she looked very charming. Valentine thought that he had never known a woman who combined such perfection of appointments with such simplicity of manner. He had a strong instinct for the best in any art. It struck him that for a certain sort of thing this was the best.

She went on: "Perhaps you will think I should not have sent for you; but what could I do? I am so alone. My husband and I, as you perhaps know, are divorced."

Valentine achieved just the right sort of murmur at this, indicating that he personally could not regret the fact, but found it of intense interest.

Mrs. Hazlitt hurried on: "I feel I must apologize for my silly child— so vulgar and absurd, though I suppose girls must think they're in love— not that I mean it's absurd to think—I mean in your case it's natural enough—your last play—so romantic, dear Mr. Valentine—only, would you mind telling me just how it was you brought my daughter home a week ago Friday?"

Valentine emerged from this like a dog from the surf, successive waves had passed over him without his having had any idea what it meant.

"I don't think I have the pleasure of knowing your daughter," he said.

"Ah, not by name!"

She was ready for him there. She rose, and taking a silver-framed photograph from the table she thrust it into his hands.

He studied it and said politely, "What a charming little face! How like you, if I may say so!"

"Don't you recognize it? Hasn't she sent it to you? Hasn't she written you letters?"

"Possibly," said Valentine, and he added apologetically, "You know, I can't read all my letters. The telegrams I do try to manage, although—"

　　　　　　　　ALICE DUER MILLER

Mrs. Hazlitt could not pretend to be interested in how Valentine managed his telegrams.

"You mean you didn't bring Lita home last Friday—a week ago?" she said, and her eyes began to get large.

Valentine leaned back and looked at the ceiling, stamped one foot slightly on the floor and crossed the other leg over it. This seemed to help him think, for almost immediately he said:

"We were putting in our new villain"; and when he saw that Mrs. Hazlitt did not grasp the information, he added, "We were rehearsing all that afternoon."

Of course, she told him the whole story, and heard in return many interesting and surprising incidents of a popular actor's life. He was extremely interesting and sympathetic; so different from what she had expected—delightful. She felt she had made a real friend. In fact, she had promised to have tea with him at his apartment the following Thursday. She was so glad he had not said Friday. Lita would be back for her holidays on Friday, and somehow it would be hard to explain after all she had said against actors; though, of course, Lita herself would be called on to explain how she had allowed—and who was the man who had brought her home? Thursday would be safe, though; and she did want to meet this new Spanish actress Doria for whom the party was given. Valentine had assumed that Mrs. Hazlitt spoke Spanish, and when she insisted that she did not he was perfectly tactful. His own, he said, was getting rusty; but Doria was all right in French. He said he would come for her himself on Thursday. She thought that very kind.

She had a flurried, excited feeling when he had gone that she was entering upon a new phase of life. She had had a delightful afternoon. But the mystery of Lita's conduct was deeper than ever. Who was the man? Had there been a man at all? She sat down to write to her child, demanding to know the truth; but was interrupted by the entrance of Freebody with a long, narrow box which looked as if it might contain a boa constrictor, but did actually contain a dozen long-stemmed roses, with Valentine's card.

Mrs. Hazlitt tore up her letter. After all, it would be better to wait until Friday, and when Lita returned they could have a long, clear explanation.

But, as things turned out, Lita came back on Thursday. A little girl in one of the younger classes contrived to catch a light case of measles, and the school was hurried home a day ahead of time. It was generally mentioned that the child deserved a tablet in the common room; and she did actually receive a laurel wreath tied with red, white and blue ribbon, and bearing the inscription, "*Dulce et decora est* to get measles for the good of your schoolmates."

The New York girls came back unheralded, for the school did not have time to telephone every parent. Miss Jones went about in a bus dropping the girls at their places of residence.

Lita, for the first time in her life, hoped that her mother would not be in. She wanted to be free to telephone Doctor Dacer without comment. She knew her mother would disapprove of her telephoning. She had had other glimpses of the last generation's method of dealing with romantic complications. They had strange old conventions about letting the advances come from the masculine side, or at least of maneuvering so that they appeared to. Subtle, they called it. Lita thought it rather sneaky.

She learned from Freebody at the door that her mother was dressing and was to be out to tea, but was to be home to dinner. Lita walked straight to the library, and having looked up Dacer's number called the office. The office nurse answered. Yes, the doctor was in. Who wished to speak to him? Miss Hazlitt? Just a minute. There was a long silence. What would she do if he refused to speak to her? Go there?

"Oh, Doctor Dacer, I wanted to tell you that Miss Barton told you something that wasn't true, though she thought it was. You know what I mean. . . I want to see you, please. I wish you would. . . Now; the sooner the better. . . Yes; good-by."

She hung up the receiver with a hand not absolutely steady. He was coming at once. She took off her hat and dropped it on the sofa and stood still in the middle of the floor. If only her mother would keep on dressing for half an hour or so! It couldn't take him very long to get from his office in Sixty-third Street near Park— Now he was putting on his hat, now he was in the street, now he was coming nearer and nearer every minute—

Exactly eleven minutes by the watched clock after she had hung up the telephone receiver the doorbell rang. The doorbell could just be heard in the library by straining ears.

And then Freebody said from the doorway, "Doctor Dacer to see you, miss."

Dacer was standing now in the doorway, looking at her darkly. Severity was evidently going to temper his justice.

"Well?" he said.

The main thing was that he had come.

"Didn't you think I could write a better love letter than that?" she began.

"Unfortunately I have had no opportunities of judging."

"What does a head mistress know about girls?"

"She tells a pretty well-documented story."

It came over Lita that they were quarreling—almost—and that she liked the process, but liked it only because she knew it must come out right. Her case was so clear.

"The letter and the photographs belonged to Aurelia," she said. "I hid them for her when she was taken ill. That was why I was in such a hurry to go that first day—when you patted me on the head. And if they told you about a mysterious man who brought me home in a taxi—that was you, and—"

"You never wrote to Valentine?"

"Never!"

He took a step toward her.

"Never sent him your photograph?"

"No!"

He took another step.

"Never saw him except on the stage?"

"No!"

Another step would bring him to her; and what, she wondered, would happen then?

What happened was that the door opened and Freebody said, "Mr. Valentine."

And there he was, the man himself, more beautiful than the posters.

Never before had the chairman of the self-government committee found herself deserted by the powers of speech and action. She stood helplessly staring at the great artist before her. And even then the day might have been saved if Valentine had not been so kind, so determined to put everything straight.

"Ah," he said, supposing he had to do with an embarrassed child, "you are Miss Hazlitt, and very like your picture. I should know you anywhere."

"You've seen my picture?" said Lita, with a sort of feeble hope that the question would convey her complete innocence to Dacer. She could hear her own voice twittering high and silly like a hysterical bird.

"Yes, indeed," said Valentine; and the voice, which was only kind, sounded in Dacer's ears significant. "This one, isn't it? Photography"— he turned politely, including Dacer in the conversation—"is only just getting back to where it was in the days of the daguerreotype. How wonderful they were! So soft—"

"Photography has always had its uses, I believe," answered Dacer in his deepest voice. He made a slight bow in the general direction of Lita. "Good-by, Miss Hazlitt," he said, and each word came with a terrible distinctness. "If you and I don't meet for sometime, you'll remember me to Aurelia, I hope. She seemed to me a singularly candid, truthful nature. I admire that."

He bowed also to Valentine, and was gone. Something about his manner struck Valentine as peculiar. He feared that he had interrupted one of those conversations that do not bear interruption—an impression somewhat confirmed when Miss Hazlitt snatched her hat from the sofa and ran out of the room without a word.

Left alone, Valentine returned to Trivia; but he began to be nervous about the time. He did not want Doria to arrive at his apartment before he and Mrs. Hazlitt got there; so that when Alita came down, apologizing for being late, but in the tone of the habitually late, as if no one really expected you to be on time, he hurried her grimly downstairs.

Freebody was waiting in the hall to open the door, and told her of her daughter's return. She showed a disposition to stay and argue the matter with him. How could it be, when she was not to come till the next day? But Freebody wouldn't argue, and Valentine was firm—they must go.

"Tell Miss Lita I'll be back before seven," said Mrs. Hazlitt, and let herself be hurried out to the car.

Freebody stared at her. Did not she know that Miss Hazlitt had just torn out of the house like a little mad witch?

Lita had moved fast, but an angry man faster. As she left the house she could see him swinging on the step of a moving Madison Avenue car. As it was a southbound car, she hoped this meant that he was going back to his office.

She had seen the address only once, when she looked up his number in the telephone book; but it was indelibly impressed on her mind, although the date of the Battle of Bosworth Field, which she had spent so much time memorizing, always escaped her. In her hurry she had forgotten not only her gloves but her purse, so that she was obliged to walk the eight or nine blocks. Walk? She almost ran, crossing all necessary streets diagonally, dodging in and out between motors. Suppose he should go out again before she got there! It was terrible!

Doctor Burroughs' office was in an oyster-colored apartment house. In a window on the ground floor she read the blue porcelain name of Doctor Burroughs—very large; and Doctor Dacer—very small. She entered a hall that was low and decorated in the style of a Florentine palace. Miss Waverley, with her white hair brushed straighter than ever, answered the door.

"Have you an appointment with the doctor?"

She spoke very politely, but there was a hint that without an appointment—

"I think he'll see me for a minute," said Lita.

She was far from feeling certain of this; and if he refused, she did not know exactly what she could do except sit on the doorstep.

She was shown into the waiting room. A complete silence fell upon the room—the house—the city. Then a returning rustling of starched skirts in the narrow passageway was heard. The doctor would see her. She was led down the long corridor to a small room filled for the most part by a desk. A door was standing open into a larger room beyond, which was lined with white tiles and decorated with glass cases along the walls in which hideous instruments were displayed as if they were objects of art. The nurse having ushered Lita into the first room, retired to the second, where she remained without shutting the door between, and could be heard moving about and doing something with instruments that made a soft, continual clinking.

Dacer rose slowly from his desk, on which cards in several colors were strewn.

He said in his deep voice, "Yes, I thought it might be you."

"Doctor Dacer—" Lita began. Her throat was dry.

"Oh, don't explain," he said. "What's the use?"

For the first time she saw that she had no explanation whatsoever to offer. She could only say, "I haven't any idea why that man suddenly appeared at the house." It sounded feeble, even to her.

"Perhaps to inquire about Aurelia," answered Dacer, and permitted himself a most disagreeable smile.

"That's not funny," said Lita.

"It's not original. I got the main idea from someone else."

"Doctor Dacer, I never saw Mr. Valentine—nor wrote to him. The only explanation I can think of is—"

Miss Waverley entered.

"Mr. Andrews on the telephone, doctor."

Dacer snatched up the telephone as if it were a captured standard, saying as he did so, "Perhaps while I'm telephoning you'll be able to think of the explanation."

But she wasn't able to think at all. She could just stare at him.

"Yes," she heard him saying, "there is a—someone is here at the moment, but I shall be free directly." He hung up the receiver and replaced the telephone on the desk. "Well," he said, "have you got something good ready for me?"

She had one small idea.

"Can't you see that if things were as you think I would hardly have left Mr. Valentine to follow you, at once?"

"Oh, quite a time has gone by!"

"Because I had to walk—I had no money with me. Walk? No, I ran!"

He was affected by the picture of her running after him through the streets, and she pressed on: "Doctor Dacer, I want to tell you why I let my parents and Miss Barton and everyone think that letter to Valentine was from me."

He sat down, shrugging his shoulders as if it were useless but he would not forbid it.

Truth in detail is almost inimitable. Lita told her story in great detail—Aurelia's request—the hidden photographs—the story of the tramp—the letter thrust into her pocket and discovered by Margaret—the identical expressions of her parents on the subject of her marriage and her own sudden inspiration that here, at least, was one topic on which they agreed.

"You see," she said eagerly, "it was only a few hours before that my father had said just the same thing—that I must not think of marrying for years; and then my mother—"

"You had sounded both your parents on the subject of marriage?"

Lita looked at him. His face was like a mask.

"I had happened to mention in the course of conversation—"

"You are thinking of getting married, Miss Hazlitt?"

"No, Doctor Dacer."

"No? The idea has never crossed your mind?"

"No—at least not in connection with—no."

Someone had told her that blushing could be prevented by a sharp pinch in the back of the neck. It was a lie. She felt as if she were being painted in a stinging crimson paint, while Dacer continued to regard her with a cold, impassive stare. He rose and shut the door between the two offices.

"Am I to understand," he said, "that you have never considered the possibility of marriage?"

She shook her head. She felt as if she were drowning.

"Then consider it now," he said, and took her up in his arms, her toes dangling inches from the floor.

Miss Waverley entered again. The apartment was well built and the doors opened without any preliminary creaking.

"Doctor Burroughs on the telephone, doctor," she said.

There was nothing to do but to let Lita slide to her feet and to take up the telephone from the desk. It was all very well for him, with his attention immediately occupied; but Lita was left alone to encounter the blank self-control of Miss Waverley's expression as she again shut the door behind her. Dacer was giving his chief an account of a professional visit, and was about to receive instructions. Lita heard him say, "Yes, I'll hold the wire."

In the pause that followed, Lita whispered, pointing toward the door, "She saw!"

"Unless stricken with blindness."

"She took it so calmly."

"Nothing in her life."

"I mean as if it happened everyday."

Dacer shouted, still holding the telephone to his ear, "Miss Waverley!" Miss Waverley returned, and Dacer went on, "Have you ever found a lady in my arms before?"

"No, not in yours, doctor," said the nurse, as if she would not wish to be pressed about some of the people she had worked for.

"Thanks," said Dacer. "Miss Hazlitt thought you were not quite enough surprised."

"I wasn't surprised at all," answered Miss Waverley, and as Dacer was obliged to turn back to the telephone and take down some directions in writing she added, "He's been so absent-minded lately—since Elbridge—forgetting everything if I didn't follow him up."

Dacer had finished telephoning.

"Miss Hazlitt and I are going to be married," he said. "Get me a taxi, will you?"

"Not now!" said Lita.

He laughed.

"No, not tonight," he answered. "I've got to see a patient in Washington Square. You'll go with me and wait in the cab. Then we'll dine somewhere—and not get you back until late. We'll test this theory of yours that parents can be reconciled through anxiety."

"Oh, I couldn't!" said Lita. "It would drive my mother mad!"

"Or to your father."

"It would hurt her terribly."

"I'm a surgeon. I know you've got to hurt people sometimes for their own good. My bag, please, Miss Waverley. My book—thanks. Good-by."

A moment later they had gone, and Miss Waverley was left alone, tidying the office for the night. She shook her head. Her thought was: "And they expect us to respect them as if they were grown men." She sighed. "And the grown-up men aren't any better," she thought.

In the meantime the pleasure of Mrs. Hazlitt's afternoon had been spoiled by the idea that Lita was sitting at home, waiting for her. Hers was a nature most open to self-reproach if no one reproached her.

She returned about seven, eager to do her duty. She came running upstairs, calling to her daughter as she ran, and felt distinctly foolish when Freebody said coldly that Miss Hazlitt had not yet come in.

"Hasn't come in?" cried Mrs. Hazlitt, and looked very severely at him over the banisters.

Freebody had been with her long enough to have learned to withstand the implication that anything he told her was his fault. He moved about, putting the card tray straight.

"Miss Hazlitt went out before you did, madam."

"Alone?"

"After the other gentleman left. Not Mr. Valentine."

"There was no other gentleman but Mr. Valentine."

Freebody, in his irritating way, would not argue with her. She had to begin all over again in order to elicit the facts—a gentleman had come to the house soon after Miss Hazlitt's arrival, and just before the arrival of Mr. Valentine. When he left, Miss Hazlitt had gone directly— Freebody would infer that she had been trying to catch up with him.

"Did she?" asked Mrs. Hazlitt.

"Ah, I couldn't say, madam."

Mrs. Hazlitt was really alarmed. This was the other man—the real danger. By half past eight she was convinced of disaster. She called up her former husband at his club. He had gone out to dinner. How characteristic!

No one in the club seemed to know where he was dining; but the telephone operator was ill-advised enough to say that if they did know they were not allowed to give out the information.

Nothing annoyed Mrs. Hazlitt so much as a rule. The idea that the telephone operator of the club knew something which she wanted to know and would not tell her was an idea utterly intolerable. Was her child to be murdered—or worse—because the club had a silly rule? She ordered her motor and drove down to interview the starter. He fortunately had heard the address Mr. Hazlitt had given his chauffeur. It was that of a small restaurant famous for quiet and for good food.

A few minutes later Mrs. Hazlitt was standing in the doorway, fixing her former husband with a significant stare. He was half through dinner with a man from Baltimore. Baltimoreans believe that good food is only terrapin and canvasback; and that terrapin and canvasbacks can only be properly cooked in Baltimore, hence that no good food is obtainable outside of their native city. Hazlitt was in process of proving his friend wrong when he looked up and saw his former wife. He guessed at once that something had happened to Lita, and began to feel guilty.

Alita, in common with so many wives, had always possessed the power of making her husband feel guilty. In old times, with just a glance or an inflection of the voice she could make him feel like the lowest of criminals. And, rage as he might, he found this power had persisted. Love may not always endure until death do them part, but the ability of married people to make each other feel guilty endures to the grave—and possibly beyond.

Hazlitt sprang to his feet, thinking that he ought to have seen Valentine. It had been mere obstinacy on his part. If anything had happened to Lita as a result—

Presently they were driving back to the house in Mrs. Hazlitt's car, and so strong is the power of association that as they got out at the house Hazlitt found himself feeling for his latchkey, though it was thirteen years since he had had a key to that lock. Mrs. Hazlitt saw it and felt rather inclined to cry. She herself was not without a sense of guilt, for she had not told him about her interview with Valentine.

When he said repentantly that he ought to have seen the fellow she answered that she was convinced his first judgment had been correct— it wasn't necessary. He thought this very generous of her.

It was after nine when they entered the house. Still nothing had been heard of Lita. Activity for some common interest can make strangers friends and may keep enemies from open quarrels. Mrs. Hazlitt admired Hazlitt's methods—his instructions to his secretary—his possession of a friend in the police department. He complimented her upon the placing of her telephones, her pens and ink. He thought to himself as he looked about the room that she had always had the power to make the material side of life comfortable and agreeable; if only she had understood mental peace as well—

Their intercourse was impersonal, but not hostile. Hazlitt bore interruption calmly, and though she could not allow him to say that Lita resembled him in temperament, she contradicted him without insult. They came nearest to a disagreement over the question as to whether it was or was not a good rule that club employes should not be allowed to give information as to the whereabouts of the members.

"Are all the members' lives so full of secrets?" she asked, and she made the word "secrets" sound very sly.

Fortunately at that moment the doorbell rang, and Lita and Dacer entered.

"Where have you been?" asked her father angrily.

"Dining with Doctor Dacer," answered Lita. "He and I are engaged."

"Nonsense!" said Mrs. Hazlitt.

"My daughter is not old enough to know her own mind," said Hazlitt to Dacer.

"I know it all right," said Lita.

"Of course," said Dacer temperately, "we understand that we could not be married for sometime, but we wanted you to know—"

"Oh, that's what young people always say to begin with," Mrs. Hazlitt answered; "but the first thing you know they are sending out their wedding invitations."

Lita and Dacer looked a trifle silly. This had been exactly their idea— to get consent to a long, long engagement, and then by the summer to start a campaign for an early marriage.

Mr. Hazlitt rose and stood on the hearth rug—as if it were his own.

"You two young people realize," he remarked, "that I have never seen or heard of Doctor Dacer before, and that so far he has caused me nothing but anxiety."

"The whole thing has just been a web of deceit," said Mrs. Hazlitt.

"Until I know a little more about him, and until Lita is a year or so older and more mature, I should not be willing even to discuss an engagement, and I'm sure my wife agrees with me."

All four noticed that he had used the word without qualification, and all four successfully ignored the fact. Indeed anyone entering the room at that moment and seeing Mr. Hazlitt, so commanding on the hearth rug, and Mrs. Hazlitt in a chair beside the fire, looking up at him and nodding her head at the end of every sentence, would have supposed them a married couple entering upon middle age without a thought of disagreement.

The discussion followed good orthodox lines. The older people, Olympian above their distress, granted that in a year or so if all went well an engagement might be discussed; but at present none existed. The young people, really calm, knew that nothing but their own wills could change the fact that they were engaged at that moment.

When Dacer had gone home and Lita had gone to bed her parents outlined their campaign. Delay without definite commitment was the idea—it always is. In the meantime Hazlitt would have the young man thoroughly looked up. Mrs. Hazlitt wagged her head despondently.

"I'm afraid there's nothing really against him. Doctor Burroughs wouldn't have an assistant with anything actually criminal in his record."

Lita was to be allowed to see him occasionally. To write? No, they decided, after talking it over, that letters would be a mistake. The point was, Mrs. Hazlitt explained, that the child must be left perfectly free to change her mind. This might be just a fancy for the first man who had asked her to marry him. Mrs. Hazlitt supposed it was the first. Next winter Lita might meet a dozen men she preferred. She had a sudden idea: Perhaps it would be wiser if the girl did go to Italy with her father, to get her out of the way for a few months.

"I'm afraid you'd miss her dreadfully."

"I should cry all summer, but it doesn't matter."

"There's nothing that I can see to prevent your going to Italy yourself."

"It's not usual to go junketing about Europe with your divorced husband," she answered.

"It need not be known that we went together; we might meet by accident," said Mr. Hazlitt, at which his former wife laughed a little and said it sounded to her like a very improper suggestion, and he looked serious and blank and monumental.

The Italian trip was left in abeyance, but the other details were settled in a clear and definite manner. Dacer was to come to the house once a month, never to write; and there were to be no flowers or presents, or mention of an engagement. Certainly not! They parted gravely, like people who had had their last long talk.

But this campaign, like many others, worked better in theory than in effect. Dacer came the next morning, and again in the afternoon, and then again the next morning. Mrs. Hazlitt protested. She said three times in twenty-four hours was not occasionally. Dacer only laughed and said it seemed very occasional to him. The situation was made more difficult for her, too, by the fact that she really liked Dacer, and he and Lita were so friendly and seemed to value her company so much that she enjoyed herself with them more than was consistent in a stern, relentless parent. Besides, in old days she had told Lita a great many clever things she had accomplished in the management of her own parents when she had been first engaged; and Lita, horrible child, remembered every word, and would repeat them all to Dacer in her mother's presence.

Finding herself helpless, the second morning she telephoned to Hazlitt. She said she thought it was almost impossible to forbid a man the house partially; it ought to be one thing or the other.

Hazlitt said, "Let it be the other then; don't let the fellow come at all."

Hearing a note of pitiable weakness in her voice, he offered to come in himself.

He came that afternoon about three—an excellent time, for Lita was upstairs and Dacer was occupied with office hours. Mrs. Hazlitt sent Freebody to ask her daughter to come down, while she apologized to her former husband for troubling him again.

"But the fact is," she said, "turning a young man out of the house— that really is a father's job."

"Even if it isn't the father's house?"

"It's no affair of Doctor Dacer's whose house it is," answered Mrs. Hazlitt with dignity. "You see, a mother's relation with a daughter is too intimate, too tender—"

"I hope a father's may be both."

"I suppose it might, but it's not like a mother's. She respects you deeply, Jim. I've brought her up to that."

"Have you, Alita?"

A hint of skepticism in his voice wounded Mr. Hazlitt.

"Of course I have," she answered. "Why, what do you mean? Are you trying to suggest—how unjust! Lita," she added, as her daughter entered, "have I ever said a word that could in anyway reflect on your father? Haven't I always brought you up to respect him?"

Lita looked at them reflectively. She had, in her time, told a great many untruths for their sake. Now that she had them here together, she rather thought it would be a good idea to tell them the truth. As she paused, her mother repeated her question even more emphatically: "Have I ever said anything to prejudice you against your father?"

"Why, of course you have, mother," she said. Her father gave a short, bitter laugh, and she turned on him. "And so have you, Pat—only not so often as mother."

"How can you be so disloyal?" cried her mother, her eyes getting larger than ever.

"How can I be anything else? You two make me disloyal."

"Remember you are speaking to your mother," said Hazlitt protectingly.

"And to you, too, Pat," answered his daughter calmly. "You've each wanted me to hate the other one, and you've both been as open about it as you dared to be. It was always like giving mother a Christmas present if I said anything disagreeable about you. And your cold gray eye would light up, Pat, if I criticized anything about her."

"Divorced or not, we are your parents, please remember," said Hazlitt.

"You don't always remember it yourselves," the girl answered. "Parents! You seem sometimes as if you were just two enemies trying to injure each other through me."

Mrs. Hazlitt was already standing, and she drew a step nearer her former husband.

"Jim," she wailed, "aren't they terrible—these young people? And I thought she loved me!"

"I do love you, mother," said Lita; "I love you dearly—better than I love Pat, only I can't help seeing that he behaves better. Or perhaps not. Women understand the art of undermining better than men do. I think Pat did all he knew how. You both filled my mind with poison against the other, drop by drop. Oh, you don't know how dreadful it is to be poisoned all the time by the two people you love best in the world!"

Mrs. Hazlitt looked up into the face of her former husband, as to an oracle.

"Do you think it's our divorce she's talking about?"

"Of course it isn't, mother," Lita answered. "I see you had a perfect right not to be husband and wife anymore if you didn't want to be; but you couldn't change the fact that you are still my parents. You ought to be able to coöperate about me, to present a united front."

"You'll find we present a united front on this issue," said Hazlitt sternly. "I mean your engagement."

"Indeed?" said his daughter. "Let me tell you, I could separate you tomorrow on it. I'm an expert. I should only have to intimate to Pat that mother was getting to like Luke so much that behind his back—but I'm sick of being treacherous and untruthful. You two must face the fact that I love you both; that I like to be with both of you; and that I will not be made to feel lower than the wombat because I do love you both. Now, there it is; settle it between you."

After she had gone they continued to stare at each other, like the last sane people in a world gone mad.

"What," said her father, "do you gather that that incomprehensible tirade was all about?"

"I can't make out," answered her mother. "She never was like that before—so excitable and rude. And I need not tell you that it's all her fancy. I've been ridiculously scrupulous in never saying anything to her but what a girl ought to hear about her father—a fixed principle that our difficulties should not come between you and her."

"Of course, I know," he answered. "I know, because I know how absolutely without foundation her attack on me was. I've been most punctilious. To hurt a child's ideal of her mother! No, I have a good deal to reproach myself with in regard to my treatment of you, Alita; but not that—not that."

"I'm sure of it," and she gave him quite a starry glance. "The truth is, I've spoiled her, Jim. I've treated her too much as a friend—as an equal."

"It can't be done," said Hazlitt, shaking his head.

"It isn't possible to have an equal relation with the younger generation. You've got to go to your contemporaries for friendship, Alita. That was true since the world began; but these young people—"

Mrs. Hazlitt, who was still treating him as if he were an oracle, brightened at these words as if he were an oracle in excellent form.

"Yes," she said, "they are different, aren't they? I can't imagine my ever having spoken to my parents as Lita just spoke to us."

"Your mother! I should say not. One of the greatest ladies I ever met anywhere!"

"Wasn't mother wonderful?" murmured Mrs. Hazlitt, and there was a pause while they both reflected upon common memories.

Then she went on: "I must say I think you are very generous not to criticize me for the way I've brought Lita up. I feel humiliated."

"My dear Alita," said Hazlitt, "I never have criticized you, and I never shall."

"She hurt me terribly, Jim. She seemed so hard, so ruthless, so appraising of things that ought to be held sacred."

These words were faintly reminiscent to Mr. Hazlitt, and he summoned them up: "In short a little like me, after all."

"Perhaps a little bit. I know what you mean," answered his former wife; and then, as he laughed at this reply, she saw that it was funny, and she began to laugh too. But laughter was too much for her strained nerves, and as she laughed she also cried, and the most convenient place to cry on was Hazlitt's shoulder. They clung together, feeling their feet slipping on the brink of that unfathomable abyss—the younger generation.

THE AMERICAN HUSBAND

Princesses are usually practical people, but we Americans, whose ideas of princesses are founded rather on fairy tales than on history, allow ourselves to be shocked and surprised when we discover this trait in them.

The Princess di Sangatano was practical; she was noble, dignified, unselfish, patient, subtle, still extremely handsome at thirty-nine, and—or but—practical. She had just married her young daughter excellently. She had not done this, however, by sitting still and being dignified and noble. She had done it by going pleasantly to the houses of women whom she disliked; by flattering men in whom even her subtlety found few subjects for flattery; by indorsing the policy of a cardinal, of whose policy as a matter of fact she disapproved. Nor did she feel that her conduct in this respect was open to criticism. On the contrary, there was nothing which the princess viewed with a more satisfactory sense of duty done than the marriage of her daughter.

And now she was beginning to recognize that her son must be launched by similar methods. The launching of Raimundo was something of a problem. He had much to recommend him; he was good-looking, gay and sweet-tempered; he loved his mother, and was not naughtier than other boys of his age; but he lacked the determined industry likely to make him successful. It was impossible to consider a learned profession for him, and even for diplomacy, in which the princess could easily have found him a place, Raimundo was a little too impulsive. And so his mother, working it out, came to the conclusion that a business—a business that would like to own a young prince and would need Raimundo's knowledge of Italians and Italy—would be the best chance; and so, of course, she thought of America—her native land. Yes, though few people remembered the fact, the princess had been born in the United States. She had left it as a small child, her mother having remarried—an Italian—and she had been brought up in Italy thenceforth. By circumstance and environment, by marriage and religion and choice, she had become utterly an Italian. She betrayed this by her belief that America—commercial America—would respect and desire a prince. And hardly had she reached this conclusion when she met Charlotte Haines.

They met quite by accident. The princess during a short stay in Venice was visiting her mother's old friend, the Contessa Carini-Bon.

The Carini-Bon palace, as all good sightseers know, is not on the Grand Canal, but tucked away at the junction of two of the smaller canals. It is a late Renaissance palace, built of the white granite that turns blackest, and it is decorated with Turks' heads over the arches of the windows, and contains the most beautiful tapestries in Italy. The princess, who since the war did not commit the extravagance of having her own gondola in Venice, had walked to the palace, through many narrow streets over tiny bridges, and under porticos, and having arrived at the side door was standing a minute in conversation with the concierge—also an old friend—discussing his son who had been wounded on the Piave, and the curse of motor boats on the Grand Canal, and the peculiar habits of the *forestieri*, and other universal topics, when she saw, across the empty courtyard, that a gondola had appeared at the steps.

It was a magnificent gondola; the two men were in white with blue sashes edged with gold fringe; blue ribbons fluttered from their broad-brimmed hats; their oars were striped blue and white; and the gondola itself shone with fresh black paint relieved here and there by heavy gold. In the front there was a small bouquet of roses and daisies in the little brass stand that carried the lamp by night. Out of this, hardly touching the proffered arm of the gondolier, stepped a pretty woman, her white draperies and pearls contrasting with her smooth dark hair and alert brown eyes. She asked in execrable Italian whether it were possible to "visitare" the *palazzo*. The concierge, in that liquid beautiful voice which so many Italians of all classes possess, replied that it was utterly impossible—that occasionally, when the contessa was not in Venice, certain people bringing letters were permitted, but at present the contessa was at home.

The lady did not understand all of this, and was not at her best when crossed in her pursuit of ideal beauty and without a language in which to argue the point. She kept repeating "*Non è possible?*" and "*Perche?*" and never appearing to understand the answer, until in despair the concierge looked pathetically at the princess. Following his glance Charlotte, bursting with a sense that she was somehow being done out of the rights of an American connoisseur, broke into fluent French. Was it, she asked, really impossible to see the tapestries? How could such things be? She was told they were the best tapestries in all Italy; tapestries were her specialty. She knew herself in tapestries.

The princess courteously repeated the concierge's explanation; and so these two women, born not two hundred miles away from each other in the state of Ohio, stood for a few minutes and conversed in Venice in the language of the boulevards. Perhaps it was some latent sense of kinship that made the princess feel sorry for Charlotte. She told her to wait a moment, and went on up to see the contessa.

When the first greetings were over she explained that there was a very pretty young American woman downstairs who was bitterly disappointed at not being able to see the tapestries.

"Good," said the contessa. "I'm delighted to hear it." She was very old and wrinkled and bright-eyed, and she had a habit of flicking the end of her nose with her forefinger. "These Americans—I hear their terrible voices all day long in the canals. They have all the money in the world and most of the energy, but they cannot have everything. They cannot see my tapestries."

"And that is a pleasure to you?"

The contessa nodded. "Certainly. One of the few I have left."

The princess sighed. "I am more of an American than I supposed," she said.

The contessa hastened to reassure her: "My dear Lisa! You! There is nothing of it about you."

The princess was too remote from her native land to resent this reassurance.

She continued thoughtfully: "There must be. I am a little bit kind. Americans are, you know. If anyone runs for the doctor in the middle of the night at a Continental hotel it always turns out to be an American. The English think they are officious and we Italians think they are too stupid to know when they are imposed upon, but it isn't either. It's kindness. The English are just, and the French are clear-sighted, but Americans are kind. You know I can't bear to think of that young creature loving tapestries and not being able ever to see yours."

"My dear child, if you feel like that!" The contessa touched the bell, and when in due time Luigi appeared, she gave orders that the lady waiting below was to be allowed to see the tapestries in the dining room and the salas. "But not in here, Luigi; no matter how much she gives you—not in here—and let her know that these are much the best ones. So, like that we are all satisfied."

An evening or so after this the two women met again; this time at a musicale given by a lady as international as the socialist party. Charlotte, still in spotless white and pearls, came quickly across the room to thank the princess, whom she recognized immediately. She said quite the right things about the tapestries, about Venice, about Italy; and the princess, who was susceptible to praise of the country which had become her own, was pleased with Charlotte.

"One is so starved for beauty in America," Mrs. Haines complained. "I'm like a greedy child for it when I come here; you can form no idea how terrible New York is." The princess dimly remembered rows of chocolate-colored houses—the New York of the early '90's. She was ready to sympathize with Charlotte.

"Why don't you come here and live—such beautiful old palaces to be had for nothing—for what Americans consider nothing," she suggested.

Charlotte rolled her large brown eyes. "If only I could; but my husband wouldn't hear of it. He actually likes America. Italy means nothing to him."

Lisa was destined to hear more of Charlotte's husband before she took in the fact that he was the president of the Haines Heating Corporations. It made a difference. It wasn't that she didn't really like Charlotte—Lisa would never have been nice to her if she hadn't really liked her; but neither would she have been so extremely nice to her if Haines had not been at the head of such a hopeful company. It was a wonderfully lucky combination of circumstances.

And to no one did it appear more lucky than to Charlotte, to whom the princess seemed so well-bred, so civilized, so expert and so wise— the living embodiment of all that Charlotte herself wished to become.

And then she knew Venice so wonderfully; she was better than any guidebook. She knew of gardens and palaces that no one else had heard of. She knew of old wellheads and courtyards. A few people went to see the Giorgione in the Seminario, but only the princess insisted on Charlotte's seeing the library, with its row of windows on the Canal, and its beautiful old books going up to the ceiling, and the painted panel that looked like books until, sliding it, you found it was the stairway to the gallery—all these delights Charlotte owed to her new friend.

And as the moon grew larger—on the evenings when Charlotte wasn't dining with Americans at the Lido or at that delightful new restaurant on the other side of the Canal, where you sat in the open air and ate at bare tables in such a primitive way—the two women would go out in Charlotte's gondola—sometimes through the labyrinth of the little canals, but more often the other way—past some tall, empty, ocean-going steamer anchored off the steps of the church of the Redentore—out to the Giudecca, where they could see the lighthouse at the entrance to the port, past a huge dredge which looked in the misty moonlight, as Charlotte said, like a dragon with its mouth open; on and on with their two gondoliers, to where everything was marsh and moonlight.

The princess had often noticed that Americans in Europe explained themselves a good deal. Perhaps citizens of a republic must explain themselves socially; after all, a princess does not need explanation. Charlotte on these evenings explained herself. Even as a child, she said, she had been reaching out for beauty—a less sophisticated person would have called it culture—when she had married she had thought only of the romance of it—she had been very much in love with her husband, ten years older than she, already successful; a dominating nature, she had not thought then that they were out of sympathy about the impersonal aspects of life—art, beauty. It was natural for Charlotte to slip into the discussion of her own problem—the problem of the American husband—so kind, so virtuous, so successful, but alas, so indifferent to the finer arts of living.

"What are we to do, we American women?" Charlotte wailed. "We grow up, we educate ourselves to know the good from the bad, the ugly from the beautiful—and then we fall in love and marry some man to whom it is all a closed book; who is sometimes jealous of interests he cannot share. Sometimes it seems as if we should crush all that is best in us in order to be good wives to our husbands. You Europeans are so lucky—you and your men have the same tastes and the same interests."

"At least," said the princess politely, "your men are very generous in allowing you to come abroad without them. Ours wouldn't have that for a minute."

Charlotte laughed. "Our men would rather we came alone than asked them to go with us. You can't imagine how bored my husband is in Europe. He speaks no language but his own, and instead of meeting interesting people he goes to his nearest office and entirely reorganizes it."

The princess had always wanted to know whether these deserted American husbands had other love affairs; or, rather, not so much whether they had them as whether they were permitted to have them. Here was an excellent opportunity for finding out. She put her question, as she felt, delicately, but Charlotte was obviously a little shocked.

"Oh, no!" she said quickly. "At least Dan doesn't. Dan isn't a bit horrid in ways like that."

Lisa felt inclined to disagree with the adjective. Human, she would have called it. At the same time she felt extremely sympathetic with Charlotte's situation. She knew how she herself would have suffered if she had married a competent business man who lived in a brownstone front with a long drawing-room like a tunnel, and talked nothing but business at dinner. She inquired whether Mr. Haines was in Wall Street, and heard that he was the head of the Haines Heating Corporations. Then making more extended inquiries in her practical Latin way, she saw that she had found the right opening for Raimundo.

Before Charlotte left Venice she invited the princess and her son to pay her a visit in New York that winter; she urged it warmly. For to be honest Charlotte was in somewhat the same position in regard to the princess that the princess was in regard to Charlotte. The fact that she was a princess warmed the younger woman's liking.

Lisa did not jump at the invitation. It was her duty to accept it, but she was not eager.

"I haven't crossed the Atlantic since I was eight years old," she said. "Besides, how would Mr. Haines feel about us? If Italy bores him, wouldn't two resident Italians bore him more?"

"You would start with the handicap of being my friends," Charlotte answered, "but he'd be perfectly civil, and in the end he would learn to appreciate you. He's not a fool, Dan. He's wise about people, if he can only get over his prejudices. But he'd be away most of the time. He always goes to California in January to look after his oil wells or something."

It was not quite the princess' idea that Dan Haines should be away all the time. He must see Raimundo, and be charmed by his youth and gayety, while she, the princess, would provide a background of solidity and Old World standards. She talked the matter over with her son—a thin, eagle-nosed boy of twenty. He was enthusiastic at the prospect, but more, his mother feared, because he had fallen in love with Charlotte's niece, whom he had met at the Lido, than because he took his future in the Haines Heating Corporations seriously. Nevertheless Charlotte's invitation was accepted.

Yet many times before January came she woke up in the night, cold with horror at the idea of this journey to an unknown land. She had hardly been out of Italy for twenty years. And even after she had actually sailed, walking the inclosed deck at night, while Raimundo was playing bridge, she shrank from the undertaking. She was very lonely, the poor princess. She and the prince had had their own troubles and disagreements, but these had gradually passed, and she had come to look forward to his companionship for her old age—a quiet prospect of settling their children and bringing up grandchildren, and making two ends meet at the dilapidated Sangatano villa. And then he had failed her; he had died during the war; and the princess had found that all her little world died about the same time. The old circle in Rome was gone, ruined, embittered, changed and scattered. The pleasant clever friendly educated group of her friends were a group no longer. And she was changed too. The war—or, rather, the aftermath of war—had brought out in her something different from her beloved country of adoption. She was not willing to sit down and lament the passing of her own order. She could not weep because the peasants no longer rose as you passed their houses. She had even a suspicion that the new order was not so terrible, and this put her old friends out of sympathy with her. They remembered that she was, after all, an American. Perhaps it was as well she was going away that winter, for she was very lonely at home.

Her steamer chair was next that of an American gentleman, a short, fat, round-faced man, who bore out her theory that Americans were kind, by the most careful and unobtrusive attention. The name of Haines was introduced into the conversation, and evidently inspired the fat man's interest. She asked if he knew Mr. Haines. No, not really. She saw that he would like to have been able to say that he did. He knew a great deal about Haines, which he was more than ready to tell. Haines was a man whom many people thought dangerously liberal in his ideas of handling his labor, and yet ultra-conservative in his investments. His ideas worked out, though—a brilliant man—creative—and then the usual story of having begun life on nothing.

"Really?" murmured the princess, not at all surprised, because she supposed all rich Americans began life on nothing.

Still, she was glad of this increase in her knowledge of her host. He was evidently one of these tremendous commercial powers. Charlotte's account had hardly prepared her for this, but then, she supposed Charlotte lived so surrounded by these vigorous fortune-makers that she had lost her sense of proportion about them. The possibility pleased the princess. After all, there were other heads of large industries besides Haines.

She conveyed her extended hopes to Raimundo when about noon he appeared on deck, having had already a game of squash, a swim, and a turn on deck with a very pretty opera singer.

"This is a great opportunity, Raimundo," she said, "if you take it in the right way."

"Oh, I shall take it right," said the boy, sitting down beside her and studying his long, slim foot in profile. "I shall, of course, make love to the beautiful Charlotte."

"You will do nothing of the kind."

"For what are we crossing the ocean?" replied her son. "Oh, I have read transatlantic fiction. American men do not mind your making love to their wives—because it saves them the time it would take to do it themselves; and then also it confirms their belief that they have acquired a valuable article."

"You must not talk like this, even to me," said his mother. "You are quite wrong. Charlotte, like most of the American women I have met, is extremely cool and virtuous."

"Of course," said Raimundo, "you offer them only a dumb doglike devotion." And looking into her face he sketched a look of dumb doglike devotion at which she could not help laughing.

Charlotte was at the wharf to welcome them, accompanied by a competent manservant to do the work of the customs. Mr. Haines, it appeared, was in California. The princess expressed polite regret at hearing this.

"Oh, he'll be back," answered his wife, and if she did not add "quite soon enough" her tone conveyed it, and Raimundo darted a quick impish glance at his mother.

As they waited while the princess' maid put back the trays of the trunks Lisa tried to convey her admiration of the harbor. Of course a great deal has been written about the approach to New York by sea, but as the princess, like most Europeans, had never read anything about America, it all came as a great surprise to her. It seemed to come as a surprise to Charlotte too.

"Beautiful?" she said incredulously. "After Venice?"

"Different," answered the princess.

"I should say it was different," said Charlotte. "There—I think those horrible men have finished mauling your trunks, and we can go."

It was on the tip of Lisa's tongue to say that she found the American customs officials perfectly civil, and that her experiences on European frontiers had been much more disagreeable, but as she began to speak she was suddenly conscious that Charlotte did not really want to think well of her native land, and she stopped.

"Oh, I say," cried the little prince as they came out of the cavelike shadow of the pier into the cloudless light of the winter day, "what a jolly day! I shan't be responsible for anything I do if you have many days like this."

"Oh, we have lots of these," returned Charlotte, signaling to her footman. "We have nothing else—no half lights, no mists, no mystery." And they got into her little French town car and started on their way uptown.

The princess stared out of her window in silence, noting the disappearance of the chocolate-colored houses, the beauty of the shops—and yes, even of the shoppers. But her son was not gifted with reticence. If his impressions had been disagreeable he might have been silent, but as they were flattering he saw no reason for suppressing them. He thought Fifth Avenue wonderful.

"And, my eye," he kept saying—an expression he had learned early in life from an English groom—"what a lot of pretty girls, and what a lot of cars! I did not know there were so many motor cars in the world."

Charlotte smiled as if she knew he meant to be kind, and suddenly laying her hand on the princess' knee, she said, "Oh, I'm so afraid you're going to hate it all, but you don't know what it means to me to have you here."

The princess was touched.

Yet it must be owned that Lisa found the next few weeks, confusing—confusing, that is, if Charlotte were to be regarded as the starved prisoner of an alien culture. They were agreeable weeks; Raimundo was in the seventh heaven. He dined, danced, lunched, and danced again. He went into the country and tobogganed, and learned to walk on snowshoes. When asked how he was enjoying America he always made the same answer: "I shall never go home. My eye! What girls!"

His mother enjoyed herself more mildly, and with certain reservations. Erudite gentlemen were put next to her at dinner—a Frenchman who was a specialist on Chinese porcelains; a painter of Spanish birth; and several English novelists and poets who were either just beginning or just completing successful lecture tours of the United States; interesting men, in one way or another, yet—and yet—the princess asked herself if she had crossed the wide Atlantic simply to see this pale replica of a civilization she already knew.

And something else puzzled and distressed her. Her friend Charlotte seemed to her the freest of created beings—freer than any woman the

ALICE DUER MILLER

princess had ever known, to make of her life anything she wanted to make of it. But Charlotte's life seemed to lack purpose and dignity. Charlotte liked to feel that learned men came to her house, but her state of nerves did not always allow her to listen to what they said. Serious books were on her table, and sometimes in her hands, and yet her day lacked those long safe hours of leisure in which such books are read.

There was no doubt that a realer, more vital Charlotte appeared buying a new hat or playing a game of bridge or asking someone to dinner, than the Charlotte who lamented the lost beauty of an old world. And yet she wasn't just a fraud.

She was not an early riser, and if toward eleven o'clock the princess penetrated to Charlotte's bedroom, overlooking the park, she would find her still in bed—a priceless Italian bed—said to have been made for Bianca Capello—propped by lace pillows, and reading a fashion paper. And something else worried the princess—the house, the way it was managed. It was comfortable, well heated—too well; there was always delicious food and too much of it, but Charlotte lived in her house as in a hotel. If butchers overcharged or footmen stole, Charlotte's only feeling was that they were tiresome dishonest people with whom she wished to have nothing to do. Abroad, she said, one's servants did not do such things.

The princess disagreed. They did not have the same opportunities, she said; the mistresses were more vigilant. The extravagance of the Haines household actually hurt her, coming as she did from a group where extravagance had ceased to be possible. But Charlotte would not admit that she had any responsibility.

"Really, dear Lisa," she said almost crossly, "I have better things to think about than housekeeping."

Well, the princess wondered what those things were.

As the days went by and as small party succeeded small party, Lisa noted that she met no American men—or hardly any—at Charlotte's house, and she asked finally why this was.

"Do they work so hard they can't dine out?"

"No—or, rather, yes, they work hard; but that's not why I don't ask them. They're so uninteresting—you would be bored to death by them."

"I'd rather like to try," said the princess mildly.

Charlotte contracted her straight eyebrows in thought. "I'll try to think of some not too awful," she said.

And a few evenings afterward the princess found herself next to a nice little chattering gentleman who spoke Italian better than she did, and made lace with his own hands. On the other side was a former ambassador—a charming person, but of no nation or age. She had known him in Paris for years. She sighed gently. She wanted to meet a financial colossus. She liked men—real ones.

Needless to say that in the Haines house she had her own sitting room—a delightful little room hung in old crimson velvet, with a wood fire always blazing on the hearth. The first day when Charlotte brought her into it she apologized for a picture over the mantelpiece.

"The things one puts in the spare room!" she said. "My husband bought that picture at an auction once, because it reminded him of the farm he was brought up on. I didn't dare give it away, but there's no reason why you should be inflicted with it." And she raised her arm to take it down.

"No! Leave it; I like it," said the princess. "It's delightful—that blue sky and clouds."

She was quite sincere in saying she liked it. She did. Often she would look up from her book and let her eyes fall with pleasure on the small green and blue and white canvas, and wonder in what farming district Mr. Haines had been brought up—and in what capacity.

The New York climate affected the princess' ability to sleep. She read often late into the night. One night—or rather morning—for it must have been three o'clock—she was interrupted by a visit from her son. He often dropped in on his way to bed to sketch for her the strange but in his opinion agreeable habits of the American girl. But this evening he did not burst out into his usual narrative. He entered silently, and stood for some seconds silent.

Then he said "Our host has returned."

"Oh," said the princess with pleasure, for, after all, this was the purpose of the long excursion.

"How unexpected!"

Her son gave a short laugh. "I believe you," he said. "Unexpected is just the word. It sometimes seems as if, in spite of all that has been written on the subject, husbands would never learn the tactlessness of the unexpected return."

"Raimundo, what do you mean?" asked his mother with a sinking heart.

The boy hesitated. "The lovely Charlotte," he said, "is all that you told me she was—cool and virtuous—so much so that it never occurs to her that others may be different. Tonight I brought her home from a dull party. We got talking; we sat down in the drawing-room. The back of a lovely white neck bent over a table was so near my lips—and the husband enters."

"Was there a scene?"

"Oh, no. It was worse. We chatted *à trois* for a time."

The princess drew a long breath. "Perhaps he did not see; but really, Raimundo—"

"Oh, he saw," said the prince. "He maneuvered the suspicious Charlotte off to bed, and then he suggested without a trace of anger or criticism that I should leave the house in the morning; and really, my dear mother, I'm afraid I shall have to do it. I'm so sorry, I know you'll feel annoyed with me, but it is hard to remember that no woman means anything here. I just manage to remember it with the girls; but the married women—well, one can't always be so sure; not so sure, at least as one is with Charlotte. There was no excuse for me—none."

"You're an awkward, ungrateful boy," said his mother, with an absence of temper that made her pronouncement more severe. "I think I shall go downstairs now myself and have a talk with Mr. Haines."

"You'll do the talking," answered her son. "He isn't exactly a chatty man."

But the princess was not discouraged. She could not see that she could do any harm to Raimundo's prospects, since evidently all was now lost, and she felt she owed it to Charlotte to repair, if she could, any damage the boy's folly had occasioned.

The lights on the stairs and corridors were all going; they were controlled by switches working, to the princess' continual surprise, from all sorts of unexpected places. She had no difficulty in finding her way to the drawing-room, on the second story, where Raimundo told her the interview had taken place.

As she opened the door she saw that a tall thin man in gray morning clothes was standing alone in the middle of the room, with his hands in his pockets and a cigar stuck in the corner of his mouth, quite in the American manner. He was pale, pale as his blond smooth hair, now beginning to be gray, and everything about him was long—his hands, his jaw, his legs like a cavalryman's. He was turned three-quarters toward the door, and he moved nothing but his eyes as the princess entered.

There was always something neat and finished about the way Lisa moved, and the way she held herself, the way she put her small steady feet on the ground; and this was particularly evident now in the way she opened the door, moved the train of her long tea gown out of the way and shut the door again. She did all this in silence, for it was her theory to let the other person speak first. It was a theory that she had had no difficulty in putting into practice during her stay in America, but it was now forced upon her attention that Haines had the same theory, for he remained perfectly silent, and something told her that he was likely to continue so. The fate of interviews is often decided thus in the first few seconds.

She spoke first. "I am the Princess di Sangatano," she said.

He nodded.

"My son has just told me about the incident of this evening."

He nodded again, and then he said, "You want to discuss it?"

His voice was low and not without a nasal drawl, but the baffling thing about it was the entire absence of any added suggestion of tone or emphasis. There were the bare words themselves and nothing more— no hint as to whether he himself wished or didn't wish to discuss it— approved or didn't approve of her intention.

"Yes, I do," she replied.

"Better sit down then."

The princess did sit down, folding her hands in her lap, drawing her elbows to her side, and sitting very erect. She did not say to herself, like Cleopatra: "Hath he seen majesty?" but some such thought was not far from her.

For twenty years she had been acknowledged to be an important person, and this had left its trace upon her manner. She knew it had.

"Are you very angry at this silly boy of mine?" she said.

Haines shook his head—that is to say, he wagged it twice from side to side.

"Not at Charlotte, I hope?"

Another shake of the head.

The princess felt a little annoyed. "Then what in heaven's name do you feel, if anything?" she said.

"I feel kinda bored," he answered; and as Lisa gave an exclamation that expressed irritation and lack of comprehension he added, again without any added color in his voice: "How did you expect me to feel?"

"Oh, either more or less," answered Lisa. "Either you should be furious and shake Charlotte until her teeth rattled, and fling my boy into the street, or else you should be wise enough to see it doesn't make the least difference—and be human—and sensible—and—and—"

"—and give your son a job," said Haines quietly.

The princess was startled. She drew herself up still more. "I have not asked you to give my son a job," she said.

He took his cigar out of his mouth, and she noticed that his strange long pale hands were rather handsome.

"Look here," he said, "answer this honestly: Didn't you have some such idea in your head when you decided to come here? Look at me."

She did look at him, at first rather expecting to look him down, and then so much interested in what she saw—something intense and real and fearless—that she forgot everything else—forgot everything except that she was thirty-nine years old, and had lived a great deal in the world and yet had not met very many real people, and now— Then she remembered that she must answer him.

"Oh, yes," she said; "I had it in mind."

"Well," said Haines, "that's what bores me." He began to walk up and down the room, somewhat, Lisa thought, as if he were dictating a letter. "Poor Charlotte! She's always making these wonderful discoveries—and they always turn out the same way—they always want something. You— why she's been talking about you—and writing about you. You were the most noble, the most disinterested, the most aristocratic— She would hardly speak to me because I asked her why you were making this long journey. For love of her society, she thought. She thinks I'm a perfect bear, but, my God, how can a man sit round and see his wife exploited by everyone she comes in contact with—from the dealer who sells her fake antiques to the grandee who offers her fake friendship?"

"I can't let you say that," said the princess, too much interested to be as angry as she felt she ought to be. "I have never offered anyone fake friendship."

"I didn't say you had."

"Pooh!" said she. "That's beneath you. You should at least be as honest, as you ask other people to be."

This speech seemed to please him—to please him as a child might please him. He came and sat down opposite to her, looked at her for a moment and then smiled at her. His smile was sweet and intimate as a caress.

"Come," he said, "I believe you're all right."

"I am," she answered. "Even a little bit more than that."

He sat there smoking and frankly studying her. "And yet," he said after a moment, "they're mostly not—you know—Charlotte's discoveries. They're mostly about as wrong as they can be."

"And they kinda bore you?" said the princess, to whom the phrase seemed amusing. He nodded, and she went on: "A good many things do, I imagine."

"Almost everything but my business. You don't," he added after a second; and there was something so simple and imperial in his manner that she did not think him insolent; in fact, to tell the truth, she was flattered. "You might tell me something about yourself," he added.

The princess was too human not to be delighted to obey this suggestion, and too well-bred to take an unfair advantage of it. She talked a long time about herself, and then about the Haines Heating Corporations.

And then they talked about him. In fact they talked all the rest of the night—as continuously as schoolgirls, as honestly as old friends, as ecstatically as lovers; and yet, of course, they were not schoolgirls or old friends, and even less lovers. They were two middle-aged people, so real and so fastidious in their different ways that they had not found many people whom they liked; and they had suddenly and utterly unexpectedly found each other.

They were interrupted by the entrance of a housemaid with a broom and a duster. She gave a smothered exclamation and withdrew. Haines looked at his watch. It was half past seven.

He got up and pulled the curtains back. A pale clear pink-and-green winter morning was just beginning to shine upon the park, glittering in snow and ice.

"At home," said Lisa, "I should consider what we have just done as rather irregular."

"In this country," he answered, "you can do anything if you have sufficient integrity to do it."

"How can I tell whether I have or not?" she asked.

He smiled again. "I have enough for both," he answered. "Luckily or unluckily"—and he sighed as he repeated it—"luckily or unluckily."

"Oh, luckily; luckily, of course," said Lisa, though there was just a trace of annoyance in her voice that this was so clear. She held out her hand.

"Good-by," she said.

He took her hand, and then from his great height he did something that no one had ever done to the princess before—he patted her on the head. "You're all right," he said, and sighed and turned away—as it were, dismissing her.

She went upstairs to her own room—which seemed altered, as backgrounds do alter with changes in ourselves. It was no longer a room in Charlotte's house but in Haines'; and she was leaving it, leaving it in a few hours. She did not debate that at all. She was going with her son, but there was something that must be done before she went— something that she must do for this new friend of hers whom she would never, probably, see again.

She did not have much time to think it over, for when her breakfast tray came in, as usual, at nine, Charlotte came with it—striking just the note the princess hoped she wouldn't strike—apology.

"I suppose your son told you what happened last night. So silly. I'm so ashamed."

"Ashamed?" said the princess, and she noted that her tone had something of the neutrality of Haines' own. She had copied him.

"Ashamed of Dan," answered Charlotte. "That's so like him—not to understand—just to take the crude view of it. I haven't seen him since, but I know so well how he would take a thing like that. As a matter of fact, I must tell you, Lisa—though I promised that I wouldn't— Raimundo was asking my help. He wants to marry the little Haines girl; he wants me to bring you round. He knows you hate everything American—"

"I don't hate everything American," said the princess, and again her voice sounded in her ears like Haines'.

"This girl, you know, is Dan's niece, and exactly like him. And now I'm afraid that will do for her, as far as you're concerned. Of course you must hate Dan—the idea of him—and if you saw him—well, you will see him at dinner tonight."

The moment had come. The princess shook her head.

"No," she said, "I shan't be at dinner tonight."

Charlotte looked at her and then broke out into protest: "No, no, you mustn't go. Let Raimundo go, if he must, but not you. Don't desert me, Lisa, because I have the misfortune to be married to a man who does not understand. Oh, to think that anything should have happened in my house that has hurt your feelings! I shall never forgive Dan— never! But don't go—for my sake, Lisa."

"It's for your sake I'm going, my dear."

"I don't understand."

"I know you don't, and it is going to be so difficult to explain." The princess rose and, going to the looking-glass, stared at herself, pushed back her hair from her forehead, and then turned suddenly back to her friend. "I suppose I seem to you a terribly worn-out old creature."

"My dear!" cried Charlotte. "You seem to me the most elegant, the most mysterious, the most charming person I ever knew."

Lisa could not help smiling at this spontaneous outburst. "Then," she said, "let me tell you that the most charming person you ever knew has fallen in love with your husband." Charlotte's jaw literally dropped, and the princess went on: "Yes, last night when Raimundo came and told me what had happened, I went downstairs. I wanted to do what I could to protect you from his thoughtlessness. I went down expecting to see the kind of man you have painted your husband. Oh, Charlotte, what a terrible goose you are!"

Even then Charlotte did not immediately understand. She continued to stare. At last she said, "You mean you liked Dan?"

"I did much more than that. I thought him the most vital, the most exciting, the most romantic figure I had ever seen."

"Dan?"

The princess nodded. "The power of the world in his hands—and so alone. I said just now I had fallen in love with him. Well, I suppose at my age one doesn't fall in love, even if one talks to a man all night—"

"You and he talked all night?"

"All night long—all night long."

Charlotte looked quickly at her friend, blinked her eyes, looked away and looked back again. It was not for nothing that her black eyebrows almost met—a sign, the physiognomists tell us, of a jealous nature.

The whole process of her thought was on her face. She had never been jealous of her husband in all her life before—but then, she had never before brought him face to face with perfection. She summed it up in her first sentence.

"Dan is no fool," she said. "He felt as you did?"

The princess smiled. "Ah, Charlotte!" she said. "An Italian woman would not have asked that. You must find that out for yourself."

There was a short silence, and then Charlotte got up and walked toward the door.

It was evident that she was going to find out at once. But the princess had one more salutary blow for her. She was standing now with her elbow on the mantelpiece and her eyes fixed on the little spare-room picture, and just as Charlotte reached the door Lisa spoke.

"Oh!" she said. "One other thing. Don't despise this little picture that your husband bought. It's the best thing you have."

This was a little too much. "Not better than my Guardis," Charlotte wailed, for she would never think of disputing the princess' judgment.

"The Guardis are like you, Charlotte," said the princess; "they are excellent copies. But this little picture is original—it's American—it's the real thing."

DEVOTED WOMEN

N an felt a sense of drama as she rang the bell of her friend's house. The houses in the row were all exactly alike, built of a new small dark-red brick, and each was set on a little square of new turf, as smooth and neat as an emerald-green handkerchief. To make matters harder, the house numbers were not honest numerals, but loops of silver ribbon festooned above the front door bell, so that Nan had almost mistaken the five she was looking for for the three next door.

She had not seen her friend for four years; and four years is a long time—a sixth of your entire life when you are only twenty-four. It seemed to her that they had been immensely young when they had parted; and yet she had never been too young to appreciate Letitia— even that first day back in the dark ages of childhood when they had found their desks next to each other at school. Even then Letitia had been captivating—lovely to look at, and gay; and, though it seemed a strange word to use about a child in short dresses, elegant. She came of the best blood in America; indeed, in the American-history class it was quite embarrassing because so many of the statesmen and generals whom the teacher praised or condemned were ancestors of Letitia's. She was a red-gold creature with deep sky-blue eyes, and, at that remote period, freckles, which she had subsequently succeeded in getting rid of.

She had charmed Nan from the first moment—none the less that Nan understood her weaknesses as well as her charms. No one could say that Letitia was untruthful; to lie was quite outside her code; but if at seven minutes past eight she was late, she said it was barely eight o'clock, and if you were late she said it was almost a quarter past. Someone had once observed to her mother that Letitia distorted facts, and Mrs. Lewis, had replied, after an instant of deliberation, "Well, undoubtedly she molds them."

She molded them particularly in conversation with the opposite sex; she could not bear any competition as far as her admirers were concerned. Strangely enough, though Letitia was much the prettier and more amusing of the two girls, she was always a little jealous of Nan, whereas Nan was never at all jealous of her. Letty herself explained the reason for this once in one of her flashes of vision: "It's because whatever you get from people is your own—founded on a rock, Nan;

but I fake it so—I get a lot that doesn't belong to me—and so I'm always in terror of being found out."

After their schooldays the girls had seen a great deal of each other. Nan's father was a professor in a small college, and it was pleasant to be asked to stay with the Lewises in their tiny New York flat. It was also agreeable to Letitia to be invited to share in commencement festivities with their prolonged opportunities to fascinate. Then Nan's father had accepted an appointment in China; but the separation did not lessen the intimacy—perhaps it even increased it; you can write so freely to a person living thousands of miles away. Letitia had written with the utmost freedom to her friend, who at that distance could not in anyway be regarded as a competitor.

Letitia always described the new people she was seeing, and Nan noticed that the first mention of Roger in her letters had in it something sharply defined and significant:

"I sat next the most romantic-looking boy I ever saw. No, my dear, no occasion for excitement; he must be years younger than I am; but the most beautiful person you ever saw—hollow-cheeked, broad-browed like that picture you adore so of Father Damien, oh perhaps I'm thinking of an illustration of Rossetti; and he can talk, too, I promise you. He's an experimental chemist in some great manufacturing company, which at this age—"

In the next letter it appeared that he wasn't really years younger—hardly a year; in fact, nothing to speak of. Letitia began to write a good deal about the scientific point of view—its stimulating quality—its powers of observation—its justice—"almost as just as you are, Nan."

Nan waited for each letter as if it were the next installment of a serial. She had seen Letitia through a good many such affairs, and she knew that before long her friend would stage a quarrel. It was a good way, Letty said, of finding out how much he cared; although, as a matter of fact, Nan noticed that she never precipitated it until she was sure the unfortunate man in question cared enough to be at a disadvantage.

But in Roger's case, when she had said sadly, "I'm afraid, Mr. Rossiter, that this means our friendship is ended," he had answered without a word of pleading, "Yes, I'm quite sure it does."

Letitia, a little startled, had asked, "What? You wish it too?"

"No," he had said; "but the fact that you do ends it automatically."

She had some difficulty in extricating herself from her own ultimatum. Naturally, her respect for him increased.

"I'm almost glad you are not here, Nan," she wrote. "He is so honest he could not help loving your honesty. I feel as if together, somehow, you would both find me out."

She inclosed a little photograph of him to show Nan what a splendid-looking person he was; but it was not his beauty she dwelt upon, but his straight, keen eyes and the fine firmness of his mouth— not the determination of the self-conscious bulldog, which so many people assume in a photograph, but just a nice steely fixity of purpose. Yes, Nan, far away in China, with plenty of leisure for reflection, found that for the first time she envied her friend.

A little later a real honest quarrel was reported. Letitia, habitually unpunctual, was three-quarters of an hour late for an appointment, and he simply had not waited for her. Under her anger Nan could catch her admiration for the first man who had dared not to wait.

"I explained to him that I could not help it, and all he said was: 'You could have helped it if I had been a train.' Of course, everything is over—he does not know how to behave."

No letter at all came in the next mail, and the announcement of her engagement in the one following:

"Fortunately—and wonderfully—mamma likes him, for, as you know, it would have been awfully hard to marry a man if she hated him."

It would indeed; or, rather, Nan thought, it would have been difficult for Letitia to fall in love with a man Mrs. Lewis did not approve of, for she had a wonderful gift of phrase—just, but cruel—by which budding sentiments could be cut off as by a knife. Nan had seen her more than once prune away a growing romance from Letitia's life with a deft, hideously descriptive sentence. Each time Nan had been in complete sympathy with her.

She usually did agree with Mrs. Lewis, who was the most brilliant woman she had ever known—and almost the most alarming. She saw life not only steadily and whole, and in the darkest colors, but she reported most frankly on what she saw. Frauds, or even people mildly artificial, dreaded Mrs. Lewis as they did the plague. Letitia herself would have dreaded her if she had not been her daughter. It said a great deal for Roger Rossiter's integrity that his future mother-in-law liked him. It also said something for his financial situation. Mrs. Lewis had always intended her child to marry someone with money.

"It is not exactly that I'm mercenary," she said. "I don't want Letitia to be specially magnificent; but I want her to have everything else, and money too. Why not?"

So when Nan heard the marriage had actually taken place, she felt pretty sure Roger must have enough to support Letty comfortably. It was really astonishing, she thought, how much she knew about him, this man she had never seen, more than she knew about lots of people she saw constantly. And so, as she rang the bell of his house, she had something of the same excitement that she might have had on seeing the curtain rise on a play about which she had heard endless discussion. At last she was going to be able to judge it for herself.

A Swedish maidservant came to the door—a nice-looking woman with an exaggerated opinion of her own knowledge of English. She almost refused Nan admittance—just to be on the safe side; but Letitia's cheerful shout intervened.

"Is that you at last, Nan?"

The two girls were quickly clasped in each other's arms—not so quickly that Nan did not see that Letitia was lovelier than ever—happier—more alive—more golden.

It was about noon when Nan arrived. She was to stay not only for luncheon but for dinner, so as to see Roger, who never got home until five o'clock, and possibly later today, for he had been in Albany the night before and might find extra things waiting for him at the office when he returned to it. Both mothers were motoring from town for lunch—in Mrs. Rossiter's car—so that the only time the friends could count on was now, immediately, this hour and a half. Letitia was awfully sorry, but she didn't see how she could have arranged it differently.

Nan smiled at that well-remembered phrase of her friend's. As a matter of fact, she was not sorry the mothers were coming. She was curious to see Roger's mother, who, for a mother with an only son, had behaved with the most astonishing cordiality about the marriage. A well-to-do widow, she had given Roger a good part of her income. Letty's letters had referred to her as an angel; and Nan was always eager to see Mrs. Lewis at anytime. Only she and Letty must waste no time, but set immediately about a process known to them as catching up. This meant that they each asked questions, listening to the answers only so long as they appeared to contain new matter, and then ruthlessly interrupting with a new question. Thus:

"Have you seen Bee since she—"

"Oh, I meant to tell you—she never did."

"Isn't that just like her? She always reminds me of—"

"Yes, you wrote me—Roger simply loved it. You knew that Hubert—"

"Yes, he cabled me. I thought it was you he—"

"So did I—so did he, for that matter—only mamma once said of him—"

"Oh, my dear, that heavenly thing about the scrubbing brush! Isn't she priceless—your mother? And she really likes Roger?"

"Crazy about him—thinks him too good for me."

And so they came to talk about the really important subject—Letty's marriage—Roger's wisdom and kindness and generosity. It amused and delighted Nan to hear her friend talking of men from the point of view of a person who owned one. Mrs. Lewis, who had long ago been obliged to part from an impossible husband, had always been a little more aloof from men, a little more contemptuous of them than of women; and Letitia, although her life was occupied with nothing else, had regarded them as an exciting, possibly hostile and certainly alien tribe. Now it was wonderful to hear her identify herself with a man's point of view— "We think—" "We feel—"

Not for a long time did the old remote tone creep in. They were speaking of men in general, and Letitia said suddenly:

"Tell me something, Nan—you have brothers—do you think the cleverest of them are a little silly about women?"

Nan's heart gave a leap. Letitia was looking intent.

"Running after women, you mean?"

"Oh, no!" Letty was quite shocked at the suggestion. "No, I mean believing everything they say. Roger repeats the most fatuous things women say to him, as if they had any importance."

Letitia twisted her eyebrows in distress only half comic.

Nan hesitated; she knew just the sort of thing Letitia must have in mind.

"Well," she said, "I think men often seem rather naïve—particularly scientific men."

"Yes," Letty agreed quickly, "and of course Roger has always been so busy. He has never gone about much; but still, he'll say driving home, 'Did you ever think, Letty, that I was a specially dominating sort of person? Mrs.'—somebody or other whom he sat next to—'said I was the kind of man who if I couldn't dominate a woman might kill her.' That old stuff, Nan, that we've all used and discarded. Or he'll look in the glass and say, 'Honestly, I can't see that my eyes—' It makes me feel ashamed, Nan."

Oh, dear, Nan thought, she could have made Letty understand, if she had had brothers, that these were a man's moments of confidence, attaching and friendly, like the talk she and Letty were having at that moment. It wasn't fair to judge a man by such moments anymore than to judge girls by silly giggling confidences to one another. Yes, that was it—men let down the bars of their egotism to the woman they loved, and maintained a certain reserve with their men friends, while women, just the other way—

"Oh, mercy, Nan, you're so just!" Letitia broke out. "If you were in love with a man, you'd want him to appear well all the time."

There was a ring at the bell and the sound of a motor panting at the door. The two mothers had arrived, and the subject of man's gullibility had to be dropped, as the two friends hurried downstairs.

As they went Nan whispered, "Do the mothers like each other?"

Letitia smiled, shaking her head.

"No; but they think they do."

No two women of the same age and country could have been more utterly different than the two mothers. Mrs. Rossiter, who must have been rather pretty once, was still ruffled and jeweled like a young beauty; and her diction, though not exactly baby talk, had in it a lisp somewhat reminiscent of the nursery. There was a lot of gentle fussing about her wrap and gloves and lorgnette and purse—and a photograph of Roger she had been having framed for Letty, and a basket of fruit she had brought from town. The little hallway was quite filled with the effort of getting her settled. Mrs. Lewis, on the contrary, who not only had been but still was as beautiful as a cameo, was also as quiet as a statue, watching with a sort of icy wonder the long process of unwrapping Mrs. Rossiter.

"Your dear little house," Mrs. Rossiter was saying, trying to blow the mesh veil from between her lips, while she undid the pin at the back of a frilled hat which would have looked equally well on a child of seven. "It is a dear little house, isn't it, Miss Perkins? But you must let me call you Nan. We all call you Nan—even Roger. He's so excited about your coming home. He said to Letitia only yesterday, 'I feel as if I had known Nan all my life.' Didn't he? You'll let me go up, dear, won't you? One does get a little bit grubby motoring, doesn't one?"

She was led upstairs by her daughter-in-law.

Mrs. Lewis patted the hair behind her ear with a brisk gesture.

"I don't confess to any special grubbiness," she said with her remorselessly exact enunciation. "Well, Nan, that's what sons do to their mothers; almost consoles me for never having had a son. Letty thinks she's perfection—that's marriage, I suppose. How do you think Letty seems?"

"Wonderful—wonderfully happy, Mrs. Lewis."

"She ought to be. Roger is a very splendid person."

"You really like him?"

"Yes," said Mrs. Lewis as one facing a possible charge of sentimentality; "yes, I really do."

"No criticisms at all?"

"Oh, come, Nan," answered the older woman, "remember who it is you're talking to. When you find me without criticisms you'll find me in my grave. I have endless criticism of him—of that cooing aged seraph who has just gone up to powder her elderly nose—even of my own daughter; but still, I do say that Roger is a fine man as men go—and that is saying a good deal."

It was saying more than Nan had ever expected to hear Mrs. Lewis say of her son-in-law, and she was content.

Presently the nose powderer came down, still cooing, and they went in to luncheon. It was a pleasant meal. The little room was full of sunlight; the Swede, though a poor linguist, was a good waitress; the food was excellent, and the talk, though not brilliant, for it was absorbed by Mrs. Rossiter, was kind and friendly; and Nan had been so many years away that she enjoyed just the sense of intimacy. They were talking about Roger—his health—how hard he worked.

"I really think," said his mother, shaking her head solemnly, "that you and he ought to go abroad. I think it's your duty."

"I'm not sure Roger means to take a holiday at all, Mrs. Rossiter," answered Letitia. "You see, he did take two weeks in the winter when we were married."

"If that may be called a holiday," said Mrs. Lewis. No one noticed her, and Mrs. Rossiter pressed on:

"Not take a holiday! Oh, Letty, he must! You must make him! He'll break down. Remember, he's only twenty-four. The strain at his age— You agree with me, don't you, Mrs. Lewis? If you had a son of twenty-four, you would not want him to work steadily all the year round?"

"If I had a son," replied Mrs. Lewis, "I should be surprised if he ever found a job. The men of my family have always been out of a job."

There was a ring at the front door and the Swede went to answer it.

"Now that Meta is out of the room, Lett," said her mother, "might I suggest that you never allow her to answer the telephone? She always begins the conversation by stoutly denying that anyone of your name lives here."

Mrs. Rossiter gave a little scream of laughter and a gesture of her hand with the fingers self-consciously crooked.

"Oh," she exclaimed, "how perfect that is! How exact!"

Mrs. Lewis looked at her coldly, as much as to say she had not intended to be, and, as a matter of fact, had not been so humorous as all that.

Then Meta returned to the room, and with the manner of beaming surprise which never left her—except on the rare occasions when she simply burst into tears—she announced that there was a policeman in the hall, come after Mr. Rossiter. At least, this was what she seemed to say; but there was enough doubt about it to keep the two mothers fairly calm, while Letitia ran out of the room to find out the truth.

"Do you suppose he's met with some horrible accident?" Mrs. Rossiter asked tremulously.

"More likely to have parked his car somewhere he ought not to have," answered Mrs. Lewis; but Letitia, knowing her well, saw that her secret thought was darker than her words. All three women remained silent after this, listening for some sound from the hall, until Letitia came back. She was holding herself very straight and her face was white.

She came straight to the table and said in a low firm voice, "There is some mistake, of course; but this man has come to arrest Roger."

"To arrest him!" cried his mother. "For what?"

"For murder," answered Letitia simply.

It is only men who break news with slow agony to women—women are more direct in dealing with each other.

Mrs. Rossiter gave a little cry, and then all four were silent, and in the pause Meta came in from the pantry and, deceived, by the quietness, began to clear the side table.

When they were in the sitting room, with the door shut, Letitia told them as much of the story as she had been able to get from the policeman. According to his account, Roger had been not in Albany the night before but in Paterson—yes, he did sometimes go there for the company; but he never stayed there overnight. He had gone to a cheap dance hall—no, not at all like Roger, though he did love dancing—and afterward had gone to supper with a man and woman. She was a concert hall singer, or something of the kind. There had been a row. The man had first gone away in a fury and then put his pride in his pocket and had come back—had drunk a cup of coffee of Roger's brewing—and had dropped dead. The woman had confessed—

"It obviously isn't true," said Nan, and somehow her voice seemed to ring out too loudly.

"Of course not," answered three voices in varying tones; and none of them had the trumpet ring of complete conviction. Nan stared from one to the other, and saw that each was busy with a plan to save him. Well, that perhaps was love—to be more concerned with the dear one's physical safety than with his moral integrity. When the first shock was over, when they had had time to think, they would see as clearly as she did that the whole thing was utterly impossible.

But they were not thinking it over. They were talking about telephoning his office—whether it would be wise, whether the telephone wires could be tapped. Mrs. Rossiter was pleading that something should be done at once, and blocking every action that Letitia suggested. It was finally decided to telephone his office. The telephone was upstairs in her bedroom, and as Letitia opened the sitting-room door she revealed the policeman on a hard William-and-Mary chair in the hall. He had taken off his cap and showed a head of thinning fuzzy blond hair. He looked undressed, out of place, menacing. Mrs. Rossiter was upset by the sight and began to cry. Mrs. Lewis, who hated tears, cast a quick look at her and followed her daughter out of the room.

Nan, left alone with Roger's mother, felt the obligation of attempting comfort. She patted her shoulder.

"Don't cry, dear Mrs. Rossiter. It will turn out to be some stupid mistake."

"Oh, of course, of course, it's a mistake!"

Mrs. Rossiter wiped her eyes bravely and put her handkerchief away. "But he works so hard, Nan; up at seven and never back at home until six—drudgery—and he's so young—so terribly young never to have any fun."

And, more touched by her word picture of facts than by the facts themselves, the tears rose again in her eyes.

"Some people would think it quite a lot of fun to be married to Letitia," said Nan gently.

But Mrs. Rossiter only shook her head, repeating, "It's all my fault—all my fault!"

"How can it be your fault, Mrs. Rossiter?" Nan asked a little sharply.

Mrs. Rossiter glanced over her shoulder to be sure no one had reëntered the room while her nose was in her handkerchief.

"He never was in love with Letitia—not really, you know—not romantically," she said. "And when a young, ardent boy like Roger is tied for life—to an older woman—whom he doesn't really love—what can you expect?"

This view of the case was so unexpected to Nan that she could hardly receive it.

"Letitia believes he loves her," she said.

"Does she?" answered Mrs. Rossiter in a tone that made the question a contradiction. "Or does she only try to believe it? Or it may be she doesn't know what it is to have a man really in love with her. These modern girls—"

"More men have been in love with Letitia than with any girl I ever knew," said Nan firmly. "And unless your son has definitely told you that he does not love her—"

"Of course he hasn't done that," returned his mother, more shocked at the idea than she had been at the suggestion of murder. "He's loyal, poor boy. It wasn't necessary for him to tell me. I know my son, Nan, and I know love. There wasn't a spark—not one—on his side at least. But she never let him alone; everyday a telephone or a letter, or even a telegram. He was touched, I suppose, by her devotion. That isn't love, though. I might have saved him. I ought to have spoken out and said, 'Dear boy, you do not love this woman.' I did hint at it several times, but he pretended to think I was in fun. Nan, they were like brother and sister— or, no, more like an old married couple—no romance. If they had been married twenty years, you would have said, 'It's nice to see them so companionable.' Now it's only natural that love should come to him in some wild and terrible form like this—an outlet—the poor child." There were steps in the hall, and she added quickly, "But, of course, I would not have them know I thought the thing possible."

The footsteps belonged to Letitia. She entered, bringing word that Roger had not been at the office; he had been expected about noon from Albany—yes, they had said Albany, but it was only a clerk. They had been expecting to hear from him, but knew nothing of his whereabouts. Letty was too young to look aged by anxiety, but she looked like a water color in process of being washed out. Not only her cheeks but her hair and eyes, and even her skin, seemed to have lost their color. Nan had never seen her friend suffering. She had seen her angry or jealous or wounded, but never like this. Her heart went out to the girl. She managed to get Mrs. Rossiter away to telephone to her son at his club, on the unlikely possibility that he might have stopped there. Left alone with Letty she said:

"My dear, I know just how ugly and painful this is; but do remember that in a few hours it will all be explained and you will be telling it as an amusing story."

"I know, of course," said Letitia, as if she were listening to a platitude; and then she added, "Did you happen to bring any money with you? You see, the banks are closed now."

Nan could hardly believe her ears.

"Yes," she said, "I have; but why should you need it just now?"

"I shan't need it, of course," said Letitia hastily; "but in times like this you think of all sorts of possibilities. If we did have to leave the country at a second's notice—"

Her voice died way under Nan's look of disapproval.

"Would you go with him if he did?" said Nan, wondering how a woman could love a man so much and understand him so little.

"Go with him!" cried Letitia. "I'd hang with him if I could! Oh, Nan, you don't know what it is to love a person as I love Roger! I believe I could be perfectly happy exiled, hunted, poor, in some impossible South Sea island, if I could only have him all to myself. While I was upstairs I put a few things in a bag; I brought it down and left it in the hall, and I thought that you could take it with you when you go. That couldn't excite any suspicion, and then if I have to leave in a hurry—"

Nan could not let her go on like this.

"Letitia," she said in a sharp tone, as if rousing a sleeper, "you simply can't talk like that. You must believe in your husband's innocence. Your face alone would hang him."

"I do believe in it," answered Letitia; "only I can't help seeing some terrible coincidences. There is no one in the world knows more about poisons than Roger does. He is always talking about the Borgias and what they used. And after all, Nan, I was brought up to face facts. There is a streak of weakness in Roger where women are concerned—a certain vanity."

"There is in every man."

"And then, Nan, I love my mother-in-law; but I can't help seeing she did not bring him up right. She spoiled him; not that she made him selfish or self-indulgent—no one could do that to Roger; but she did give him too much confidence in his own ability to arrange any situation. He jumps into anything— Oh, can't you see how he might easily be led on to do something like this?"

"No," said Nan; "no. I'm not his Wife—I never saw him, but I feel sure he did not do this."

Perhaps her manner was more offensive than she meant it to be; but for some reason Letty's rather alarming calm suddenly broke into anger.

"That's impertinent, Nan," she said. "Why should you always think you understand better than anyone else? He's my husband. If you had any delicacy of feeling, you'd admit that if anyone knew the truth about him, I do—not you, who never saw him. It's easy enough for you to come preaching the beauty of perfect faith. Don't you suppose I'd believe in him if I could?" And so on and on. It was as if she hated Nan for believing in him when she didn't.

Nan let her talk for a few minutes, and then at the first pause she got up and walked to the door. "I think I'll go and sit with your mother," she said.

"Don't tell her what I've been saying—don't tell her that I have doubt of Roger."

"You know I would not do that, Letty."

"I don't know what you'd do in your eternal wish to know more about people than anyone else knows."

Nan left the room with a heavy heart. Did she want to be omniscient? Was it impertinent to be surer of a man's innocence than his wife was? Well, if he were innocent, Letitia would never forgive her—that was clear.

She found Mrs. Lewis alone in an upper room. She was standing looking out the window, her arms folded, her body tilted slightly backward, while she crooned sadly to herself. As Nan entered she shook her head slowly at her.

"The poor child," she said.

"Roger or Letty?"

"Oh, both; but, of course, I was thinking of my own."

"Mrs. Lewis, do you believe he's guilty?"

"No, my dear—nor innocent. I don't believe anything. I simply don't know. When you get to be my age, Nan, you will understand that anything is possible; the wicked do the most splendid things at times, and the virtuous do the most awful. I don't know whether Roger did this or not. He may have. It may even have been the right thing to do, although poison—well, I'm surprised Roger descended to that."

With this point of view Nan had some sympathy, although she felt obliged to protest a little.

"You said he was the finest man you had ever known."

"I thought so—I think so still—but what does one know about such people? An utterly different class, a different background. I'm as good a democrat as anybody, but there is something in tradition. Oh, I see you don't know. Well, the father was a plumber. Yes, my dear, little as you might think it, that ruffled marquise downstairs is the widow of a plumber. How do we know what people like that will do or not do when their passions are roused? It nearly killed me to have Letitia marry him."

"I thought you liked the marriage, Mrs. Lewis."

"That's where I blame myself, Nan. I let it get out of my control. I hesitated. I admired the man. He had plenty of money; and of course the mother was delighted to get such a wife for her son, and made it all too terribly easy. And then he was mad about Letty."

"Wasn't she mad about him too?"

Mrs. Lewis shook her head.

"Not at first; but he was always there—always writing and coming. I don't suppose I ever came into the flat in those days without finding a message that Letty was to call—whatever his number was—as soon as she came in. He's a determined man and he meant to get her."

"She is tremendously in love with him now."

Mrs. Lewis sighed.

"Ah, yes, now, poor child—of course. Don't betray me, Nan. Don't let those two downstairs know that I have a doubt. She's a sweet creature— the plumber's widow—though to me irritating; and she wouldn't doubt anyone in the world, let alone her darling son; and, of course, Letitia does not think it possible that her husband can have killed a man, especially for the sake of another woman."

"Have you ever heard a suspicion that there was another woman?" Nan asked.

"No; but then I shouldn't be likely to. We three women are the last people in the world to hear it, even if it were notorious."

Nan was obliged to admit the truth of this; and presently Mrs. Lewis, fearing that her absence might appear unfriendly, decided to go back to the sitting room.

　　　　　　　　ALICE DUER MILLER

Nan said she was coming, too, but stood a minute staring at the carpet. What was it, she wondered, made her so passionately eager that Roger should be innocent? Was it love of her friend, or pride of opinion, or interest in abstract truth, or interest in a man she had never seen? She had a strange feeling of a bond between her and Roger. As she went slowly down the stairs, her eye fell again upon the police officer, shifting, patient, but uncomfortable on the William-and-Mary chair. A sudden inspiration came to her. She asked to see the warrant.

Well, it was just as she thought—not for Roger at all, but for a man whose last name was Rogers, who lived in a house two away. The number wasn't even right; but that was more the fault of the real-estate company than of the police department. She took the officer outside and showed him his mistake, and finally had the satisfaction of shutting the door forever on that blue-coated figure.

She turned toward the sitting room. To break good news is not always so easy, either. She thought of those three doubters, each one trying to show the others how full her heart was of complete confidence.

Nan opened the door, went in, shut it behind her and leaned on the knob.

"Now, you three," she said, "you've been wonderful in bad times; try to be equally calm in good." They looked up at her, wondering what good news was possible, and she hurried on: "The policeman has gone. The warrant was not for Roger at all."

There was a pause, hardly broken in any real sense by the sound of Mrs. Rossiter repeating that she had always known it could not be true—had always known it could not be Roger.

"Still," said Mrs. Lewis with an amused sidelong glance, "it is a comfort that now the police know it too."

But Nan's eyes had never left her friend's face. Letty did not say a word. She rose and stared straight at Nan, looking at her almost as if she were an enemy. Nan knew that Mrs. Rossiter would forget that she had ever doubted her son—had already forgotten and was crooning her faith and joy. Mrs. Lewis had nothing to forget. She had merely expressed an agnostic attitude; but Letitia had revealed to Nan the very depths of her estimate of her husband—and she had been wrong and Nan right. She would never forgive that.

Except for this change in the relation between the two younger women, in five minutes it was as if the whole incident had never occurred. Mrs. Rossiter was again the devoted mother-in-law, Letitia the happy bride, and Mrs. Lewis was saying, "Which brings us back to the point I was making when the fatal ring came—it is a mistake to let Meta answer either the door or the telephone."

In a little while Mrs. Rossiter announced that she must be going, and Nan was not surprised when Mrs. Lewis, who had had a few minutes alone with her daughter, suggested that Nan should go back with them and spend the night with her.

"But I promised Letty—" she began, and then glancing at her friend she saw that she was expected to accept.

Letitia spoke civilly, kindly, as if she were doing everyone a favor.

"Oh, I let you off," she said. "Mamma is all alone, and I know how you and she enjoy picking all the rest of us to pieces."

Nan hesitated rebelliously. It seemed hard that she was not to see Roger just because she had understood him too well.

She said, "But I want so much to see Roger."

Mrs. Lewis glanced at her. It was not like a girl to be so obstinate. Of course, poor Letty wanted her husband to herself after a shock like this.

"Roger will keep," she said firmly.

She went into the hall and picked up her scarf from the companion chair to that on which the policeman had sat. As she did so her eye fell upon a bag standing as if ready for a journey.

"Is that your bag, Nan?" she asked, trying to remember if the plan had ever been that Nan was to spend the night.

"No," said Letitia in a quick sharp voice; "that's something of mine."

And then, without the least warning, the front door opened and Roger himself walked in—walked in without any idea that he had been a murderer, arrested, extradited, defended and freed since he had last seen his own house.

He was just as Nan knew he would be. She didn't care anything about his mere beauty. It was that fine firm mouth of his—just like the photograph. How could anyone imagine that a man with a mouth like that—

He greeted his wife, his mother, his mother-in-law casually, and came straight to Nan.

"So this is Nan—at last," he said, and he stooped and kissed her cheek.

Well, Nan said to herself, she had a right to that; but she saw Letty's brow contract; and Mrs. Lewis, who perhaps saw it, too, hurried her toward the car. Roger protested.

"But you're not taking Nan! I came home early especially to see her. I did not even go back to the office for fear of being detained." But, of course, his lonely protest accomplished nothing, and as he opened the front door for the three departing women, he asked, "When am I to see you, Nan?"

Nan looked up at him very sweetly and said "Never." She said it lightly, but she knew it was the bitter truth. She knew Letitia. Letitia would never permit a second meeting.

Just as she got into the car she heard him call, "Oh, isn't this your bag?" and she heard Letty answer:

"No, it's mine. It represents one of Nan's abandoned ideas."

The Return to Normalcy

S trange, unnatural conventions were growing up about divorce, Cora reflected. The world expected you to appear as completely indifferent to a man when once your decree was granted as it had assumed you to be uniquely devoted to him as long as the marriage tie held. Here she was, sitting at her ease in her little apartment; she had bitten her toast, poured out her coffee, opened her mail—a dinner invitation, a letter from her architect about the plans for her new house, a bill for her brocade slippers, an announcement of a picture exhibition, and— As she moved the last envelope from its position on the morning newspaper her eye fell for the first time on the account of Valentine Bing's illness.

"It was said at the Unitarian Hospital, where Mr. Bing was taken late last night, that his condition was serious."

A sketch—almost obituary—of him followed: "Valentine Bing was born in 1880 at St. Albans, a small town on Lake Erie. He began life as a printer. At twenty-one he became editor of the St. Albans Courier. In 1907 he came to New York." She glanced along rapidly. "Great consolidation of newspaper syndicate features—large fortune—three times married—the last time to Miss Cora Enderby, of the prominent New York family, from whom he was divorced in Paris in October of this year." Nothing was said about the two other wives; that seemed natural enough to Cora. But it did not seem natural that this man, who for two years had made or marred every instant of her life, was ill— dying, perhaps; and that she like any other stranger should read of it casually in her morning paper.

She did not often think kindly of Valentine—she tried not to think of him at all—but now her thoughts went back to their first romance. In those days—she was barely twenty—she had been in conflict with her family, who represented all that was conservative in old New York. She had wanted work, a career. She had gone to see Valentine in his office, armed with a letter of introduction. He was a tall red-haired man, long armed and large fisted, with intense blue eyes, clouded like lapis lazuli; he was either ugly or rather beautiful, according as you liked a sleek or rugged masculinity. For an instant she had had an impression— the only time she ever did have it—that he was a silent being.

She had told her little story. "And as I really don't know much about writing," she ended, "I thought—"

"You thought you'd like to do newspaper work," he interrupted with a sort of shout.

He explained to her how newspaper writing was the most difficult of all—the only kind that mattered. What was the object of writing anyhow? To tell something, wasn't it? Well, in newspaper work— On and on he went, the torrent of his ideas sparkling and leaping like a mountain brook. She was aware that she stimulated him. She learned later that he was grateful for stimulation, particularly from women.

Almost immediately afterward, it seemed to her, he was insisting that she should marry him. At first she refused, and when her own resistance had been broken down her family's stood out all the more firmly.

They regarded two divorces and a vulgar newspaper syndicate as insurmountable obstacles. But a family had very little chance against Bing, and he and Cora were married within a few months of their first meeting.

On looking back at it she felt that she soon lost not his love but his interest. He would always, she thought, have retained a sincere affection for her if she had been content to remain the patient springboard from which he leaped off into space. But she wasn't content with any such rôle. She wanted to be the stimulus—the excitement of his life. And so they had quarreled and quarreled and quarreled for two horrible years which had just ended in their divorce.

And now he, so vital, so egotistical, so dominating, was dying; and she, the pale slim girl whose charm to him had been the joy of conquering her, was alive and well and happy. It would annoy Valentine to know that she was happy—fairly happy—without him.

She wondered whether she should call up the hospital, or go there herself to inquire about him. Wasn't it possible that he would send for her? After all, it was only the other day that she was his wife. And at that instant the telephone rang.

She heard a suave voice saying, "Is that Mrs. Bing? Mrs. Enderby-Bing? This is Doctor Creighton, at the Unitarian."

Half an hour later she was at the hospital. She had expected to be hurried at once to Valentine's bedside. Instead a little reception room was indicated. At the door a figure was standing, head raised, hands clasped behind the back. It was Thorpe, Valentine's servant.

"In here, madam," he said, opened the door for her, and closed it, shutting her in.

The sight of him destroyed the last remnant of Cora's self-control. He seemed like a little bit of Valentine himself. Thorpe had been with them on their honeymoon; she could see him waiting at the gate under the turquoise dome of the Grand Central Station, with their bags about his feet, and their tickets in his hand—so cool and competent in contrast to their own excitement that first day.

She hurried into the room. It is not to be expected that a hospital should waste sun and air on mere visitors, and yet the reception room, painted a cold gray and dimly lighted by a shaft, was depressing. Some logical interior decorator had hung one large Braun photograph on the wall. It was a copy of the Lesson in Anatomy.

Cora sat down and covering her face with her hands began to cry. A kind voice said in her ear, "I'm afraid you've had bad news."

Looking up Cora saw that a middle-aged woman was sitting beside her, a woman with comfortably flowing lines and large soft brown eyes and hair beginning to turn gray.

"I'm afraid my husband is dying," answered Cora simply. She thought it better not to mention divorce to a person who seemed like the very genius of the family.

"Why, you poor child," said the other, "you don't look old enough to have a husband."

"I'm twenty-four," replied Cora. "It's almost three years since I was married."

"Of course," said the other. "It's just because I'm getting old that everyone seems so young to me."

She smiled and Cora found herself smiling too. There was something comforting in the presence of the older woman; Cora felt assured that she knew her way about in all simple human crises like birth and illness and death.

Suddenly as they talked Cora saw the face of her companion stiffen; Thorpe was ushering in another woman, sleek headed, with a skin like white satin, wrapped in a mink cloak. Evidently the newcomer was painfully known to Cora's friend, though the mink-clad lady gave no sign. She sat down, holding the blank beauty of her face unruffled by the least expression; and as she did so Doctor Creighton entered.

"Mrs. Bing," he said. All three women rose. The doctor glanced at a paper held in the palm of his hand.

"Mrs. Johnson-Bing, Mrs. Moore-Bing, Mrs. Enderby-Bing."

Even in her wild eagerness to know what the doctor had to tell them of Valentine's condition Cora was aware of the excitement of at last seeing those two others. Phrases that Valentine had used about them came back to her: "A cold-hearted unfaithful Juno"—she in the mink coat. "She was so relentlessly domestic"—Cora glanced at her new friend. Yes, she was domestic—almost motherly. Cora's friendly feeling toward her remained intact; but toward Hermione—Mrs. Moore-Bing—who had so deceived and embittered Valentine, her hatred flamed as it had flamed when Valentine first told her the story.

How could she stand there, so calm, drooping her thick white eyelids and moving her shoulders about in a way that made you aware that under the mink coat they were as white as blanc mange. "She must know," Cora thought, "that I know everything there is to know about her. Valentine had no reserves about it. And Margaret, from whom she took him; and Thorpe, whose testimony in the divorce case—" Instinctively she took a step nearer to Margaret, as if wishing to form an alliance against Hermione.

Meantime the doctor was speaking rapidly, apologetically: "You must forgive me, ladies. I might have arranged this better, but time is short. You must help me. Mr. Bing's condition is serious—very serious. He keeps demanding that his wife come and nurse him. He believes we are keeping her from him. His temperature is going up, he is exciting himself more and more. We must give him what he wants, but—" The doctor paused and looked inquiringly from one to the other.

Mrs. Johnson-Bing smiled her quiet maternal smile. "Poor Valentine," she said; "he was always like that when he was ill."

There was a pause.

"But you don't help," said the doctor. "You don't tell me which one it is that he wants."

"Well," said Mrs. Moore-Bing in her cool drawl, "as I'm the only one who left him against his will I'm probably the only one he wants back again."

Cora would not even glance in the direction of such a woman. She had been kept silent heretofore by the trembling of her chin, but now she managed to enunciate: "Mr. Bing and I were divorced only a few months ago. Until October, you see, I was his wife."

The logic of this, or perhaps his own individual preference for a slim elegant young woman, evidently influenced the doctor. He nodded quickly.

"If you'll come with me, then—" he began, and turned toward the door, but there Thorpe was standing, and he did not move.

"If you'd excuse me, sir," he said, "am I right in thinking it will be bad for Mr. Bing if we mistake his wish in this matter?"

"Yes, I'd like to get it right," said the doctor.

"Then, sir, may I say it's not Mrs. Enderby-Bing that he wants, sir?"

"What makes you think that?" said Doctor Creighton.

"I could hardly explain it, sir. Twenty years of being with Mr. Bing—"

There was an awkward pause. The obvious thing to do was to ask Thorpe who it was Bing did want, and something in the poise of Thorpe's head suggested that he was just waiting to set the whole matter straight, when hurried footsteps were heard in the hall, and a nurse entered—an eager panting young woman. She beckoned to Creighton and they spoke a few seconds apart. Then he turned back to the group with brightened face.

"At last," he said, "Mr. Bing has spoken the first name. It is Margaret."

Cora caught a glimpse of Thorpe quietly bowing to himself—as much as to say, "Just what I had expected."

Mrs. Johnson-Bing rose.

"My name is Margaret," she said, and left the room with the doctor.

Hermione rose, too, hunching her cape into place. "Well," she said without taking the least notice of Thorpe, who was opening the door for her, "that's one chore you and I don't have to do. He was bad enough healthy—sick he must be the limit."

Cora did not so much ignore Hermione as she conveyed in her manner as she turned to Thorpe that everyone must know that whoever might be the object of Mrs. Moore-Bing's conversation it could not be herself.

"Tell me, Thorpe," she said, "what do you think of Mr. Bing's condition?"

"Mr. Bing is ill, madam—very ill," Thorpe answered immediately; "but not so ill as the doctors think."

"No?" said Cora in some surprise.

"No, madam. Mr. Bing, if I might use the expression, yields himself up to illness; this assists him to recover."

He opened the door for her at this point, and she went out of it.

She returned home not so emotionally upset but more depressed than before. There was a core of bitterness in her feeling that had not been there when she went to the hospital, and at first she found it difficult to discover the reason for this. Was it anxiety at Valentine's illness? No, for he was a little better than she had feared. Was it the realization that those two former wives, who had always seemed to her like shadows, were, in fact, living beings like herself? No, for they had turned out to be more unattractive, more utterly unsuitable to Valentine than she had imagined. It was true that her taste, her sheltered selectiveness—a passion which many well-brought-up women mistake for morality—was outraged at being in the same room with Hermione, but there was a certain satisfaction in finding her to be worse even than Valentine's highly colored descriptions of her. And as for Margaret, she felt no jealousy of her, even though she had been chosen. No one could be jealous of any woman so kind, so old and so badly dressed.

It came to her gradually as she moved about her room, unable to look at her plans, unable to read, unable to do anything but encourage the toothache at her heart, which was like a memory of all her later relations with Valentine. The reason was Thorpe—Thorpe's instant conviction that it was not she whom Valentine wanted. Why was he so sure? He had been right; Thorpe was always right. For twenty years he had made it his business to know what Valentine wanted. That was Thorpe's idea of the function of a good servant. He had always quietly and consistently followed his line, while the wives had followed others. Margaret had been concerned with what was best for Valentine; Hermione had thought entirely of what was most agreeable to herself; Cora had cared only to preserve the romance of her love. Thorpe's specialty was knowing what at the moment Valentine wished for, and then in getting it. Thorpe had survived all three.

Cora could understand a sick man having a fancy to be nursed by Margaret, but Thorpe's conviction that she, Cora, could not be the wife called for had a deeper and more lasting significance. That was the thought that made her heart ache.

She tried to take up her life where she had left it that morning, but everything had paled in interest—even her new house. She had bought a little corner of land, within the city limits but near the river, surrounded by trees. She saw wonderful possibilities—a walled garden and a river view within twenty minutes of the theaters. She recognized certain disadvantages—the proximity of a railroad track, and the fact that the neighborhood was still unkempt; she enjoyed the idea of being a pioneer. But now, though the plans were lying on the table, she did not open them. It was as if that hour in the hospital had married her again to Valentine, and there was no vividness left in the rest of life.

For ten days the bulletins continued to be increasingly favorable, and then—a sign that convalescence had set in—they ceased entirely.

Cora found the silence trying. With the great question of life or death answered there was so much else that she wanted to know—whether he had been permanently weakened by his illness; whether he would now be starting on one of his long-projected trips—to China or the South Seas. China had always fired his imagination. Twice during her short marriage they had had their trunks packed for China. Had he been softened, or frightened, or in anyway changed by the great adventure of almost dying?

There was one person who could tell her all these things, and that was Margaret. Without exactly formulating a plan Cora went to the hospital one day and inquired about him. The girl at the desk answered as if Valentine were already a personage of the hospital.

"He's getting along splendidly now. His wife's with him."

"I wonder," Cora heard herself saying, "whether Mrs. Bing would see me for a minute."

She retired, rather frightened at her temerity, to the reception room, where the Lesson in Anatomy still dominated the wall. "Margaret won't mind," she kept telling herself. "She's so kind, and, anyhow, she's more like his mother than his wife." It was on this maternal quality that Cora depended.

There was a footstep in the hall. A statuesque figure molded into blue serge stood in the doorway—bare-headed with shiny bronze-colored hair elaborately looped and curled. It was Hermione.

"You wanted to see me?" she asked in her drawling, reconstructed voice. She did not at once recognize Cora.

"No," said Cora, "I certainly did not want to see you. I thought it was Mrs. Johnson-Bing who was here."

"Margaret?" replied Hermione. She drooped her thick eyelids and smiled, as if the name itself were comic—she never broke her beautiful mask with a laugh.

"No, that didn't last long. He bounced Margaret as soon as he got over being delirious."

"And was it then that he sent for you?" asked Cora with an edge to her voice that a Damascus blade might have envied.

"As a matter of fact he didn't; it was Thorpe who sent for me," said

Hermione. "Thorpe had a wholesome recollection that I used to keep Val in order. Nice little job, keeping Val in order. Ever tried it? No, I remember Thorpe said that wasn't your line."

Cora would have given a good deal to know just how Thorpe had characterized her line, but not even curiosity could make her address an unnecessary word to the coarse, cold woman before her. She was not jealous as she understood the word, but the disgust she felt for Hermione included Valentine, too, and made her hate him for the moment with an intimate disturbing warmth.

Hermione went on: "And, after all, as I said to Val yesterday, what does it matter to me whether he gets well or not? It takes too much vitality—making him mind. I'm through. I'm off for Palm Beach tomorrow. Thorpe's taking him home."

"It's amiable of you—to come and go as Thorpe orders."

Hermione moved her eloquent shoulders. "Oh, Thorpe and I understand each other."

"I knew Thorpe understood you," said Cora insolently.

But the woman was insensitive to anything but a bludgeon, for she answered, "I understand Thorpe too. All he objects to is wives. He's like the—whatever it is, you know—that fishes in troubled waters."

Cora merely moved past her and went away. It wasn't until she was outside that she took in how pleasant had been the unconscious suggestion behind Hermione's last words. Thorpe objected to wives. That was why he had not sent for her—she wasn't a mother like Margaret; nor a vice, like Hermione. She was a wife. The story-teller, the magic builder of castles that is in everyone, suddenly made for Cora a splendid scene, in which she, reunited to Valentine, was dismissing Thorpe.

Ten days later she took title to her new property and her architects filed the plans. Both events were announced in the newspapers.

That very morning her telephone rang, and Thorpe's voice—a voice so associated with all her emotional life that her nerves trembled even before her mind recognized it—was heard saying, "I'm telephoning for Mr. Bing, madam. Mr. Bing would be pleased if you could make it convenient to stop in and see him this afternoon."

"Tell Mr. Bing I'm sorry. I can't," answered Cora promptly. She was not a Hermione to come and go at Thorpe's invitation. And then just to show that she was not spiteful she added, "I hope Mr. Bing is better."

"Yes, madam," said Thorpe, "he's better, but he hasn't thoroughly regained his strength. He tests it everyday."

Cora hung up the receiver. Her thought was, "He can't test it on me." She was aware of a certain self-satisfaction in having been able so firmly to refuse, to set her will against Valentine's. In old times she had been weak in yielding to every wish and opinion that he had expressed, until she had almost ceased to be a person. Of course in this case her ability to refuse had been strengthened by the incredible impertinence of allowing Thorpe to be the one to communicate Valentine's invitation. A few minutes later the telephone rang again. This time she let the servant answer it, and when the woman came to her with interested eyes and said that Mr. Bing was on the wire Cora answered without a quaver, "Say I'm out."

But she knew Valentine well enough to know she was not going to get off so easily as that. He kept steadily calling until at last, chance, or perhaps Cora's own wish, directed that he should catch her at the telephone.

He must see her; it was about this new house of hers. Her heart beat so she could hardly breathe, while Valentine ran on as of old:

"It's folly, Cora, absolute folly! Why didn't you consult me before you bought? You can't live there—the railroad on one side and a gas tank on the other. Besides, the railroad is going to enlarge its yards; in two years you'll have switching engines in your drawing-room."

On and on, giving her no chance to answer him, during the ten minutes he kept her at the telephone. Yet when she hung up the receiver she found she had spoken one important word: she had promised to come and see him late the following afternoon. She had made him beg; she had refused to come that day, she had put it off; she had, in fact, teased him as much as was consistent with ultimately agreeing to do what he wanted. Before she did agree the impertinence of Thorpe was explained. Valentine had simply told him to get her on the telephone. Of course he had meant to speak to her himself. Thorpe was an idiot—overzealous. Cora had her own view about that, but she let it pass. Thorpe feared her, and Thorpe knew what was to be feared. He knew that if she once entered that house she might never be allowed to leave it.

"No," she said to herself the next day, as she tried various hats, and with hands that shook a little put on the dangling earrings that Valentine had given her in Madrid, "it will be Thorpe who will leave."

If there was fear in Thorpe's heart he did not betray it when he opened the door and led her upstairs to the library. The room was empty.

"Mr. Bing has been expecting you for sometime, madam," he said.

The slight reproach was agreeable to Cora. She had waited long enough for Valentine in old times, and sometimes he had not turned up at all.

The room was familiar to her. They had not been much in New York during their brief marriage, but she had spent part of the previous winter in this house. She had left her own imprint in the decorations. Valentine used his house as he might use a hotel—asking nothing but that it should be convenient for the purposes of his stay. Cora had been greeted on her first arrival by hideous tasseled gold cushions and imitation Japanese lamp shades; remnants, she believed, of Hermione's taste. She had instantly banished them, and now she saw with pleasure that the shades of her own choosing were still on the lamps. Everything had remained as she had arranged it; he had seen that her way was best. A wood fire was burning on the hearth—not the detestable gas logs which Hermione had left behind her. She found herself wondering for the first time what Hermione had found—what Margaret had left. Then she remembered that Valentine had not bought the house in the simple days of Margaret's reign; he had had a small apartment far uptown and at first Margaret had had no servant.

A wish to know if Valentine had kept a paper cutter she had given him—lapis lazuli, the color of his eyes—made her get up and go to the desk. Yes, it was there, but something else was there, too: an unframed photograph propped against a paper weight—the photograph of a woman.

She bent cautiously to look at it, as one bends to examine the spot where the trembling of the grass suggests the presence of a venomous serpent. It was the picture of a slender woman with heavy dark hair and long slanting eyes, the cruelty of her high cheek bones softened by the sweet drooping curve of her mouth. A terrible and fascinating woman. Then as the light struck across the surface of the picture she saw it was a glossy print for reproduction. It might mean business—a feature for the syndicate—not love.

She was sitting far away from the desk when, a minute or two later, Valentine entered—Valentine a little thinner than before, but no less vital. He greeted her as if they had parted yesterday, or rather he did not greet her at all. He simply began to talk to her as he came into the room. He had a roll of blue prints in his hand.

"Now, my dear girl, these plans of yours—have you thought them over at all? . . . You practically made them? But don't you see what you've done—sacrificed everything to a patio. A patio—only good for hot weather, when you'll never be here anyhow. The whole comfort of the house arranged for the season you'll be away. They are without exception the most ridiculous plans— Oh! Yes, I sent down for a copy of them at once. I'm glad I did. If I hadn't—"

"But, Valentine," she interrupted—she knew by experience that you were forced to interrupt Valentine if you wished to speak at all—"it is my house, you know."

"And that's why I want it to be right for you," he answered. "But we'll get it right—never fear."

"It's exactly what I want as it is," she returned, and she heard with a mixture of disgust and fear that the old tone of false determination was creeping into her voice.

"It isn't at all what you want," he said. "You only imagine it is, Cora."

"Valentine, I've thought it all out with the greatest care."

"But it's absurd—you won't like it. Do listen to reason. Don't be obstinate."

Obstinate—the old accusation.

"That's what you always say when I insist on doing anything my own way."

"But your way is wrong. Now just listen to me, my dear girl—"

It was, to the identical phrases, the quarrel of their whole short turbulent married life. He had always made her feel that she was pig-headed and unreasonable not to yield at once to his superior knowledge of her own inmost wishes. The trouble was that the turmoil and the fighting slowly extinguished her own wishes—they weren't changed, they were killed—so that after a little while she was left gallantly defending a corpse; she ceased to care what happened; whereas Valentine's poignant interest grew with each word he uttered—and he uttered a great many—until he seemed to burn with an almost religious conviction that she must not do the thing in the way she wanted to do it.

It always ended the same way: "Now, my dear girl, don't be so obstinate." Was she obstinate? she wondered; and as she wondered Valentine rushed in like an army through a breach in the wall. He was doing it now.

"All I ask," he was saying, "is that you should look at the set of plans I had my man draw—he's a real architect—not a bungalow wizard like that fellow you employed. Now you might at least do that—it isn't much to ask that you should just look at them. Oh, well, you'll see they call for another piece of land, but honestly, Cora, I cannot let you settle on that switching yard, that you picked out—"

She could not refuse to look at his plans; in fact, she was not a little touched by the idea that he had taken such an infinity of trouble for her.

And at this instant Thorpe entered. Valentine shouted at him to get that other roll of plans from his room.

"Yes, sir," said Thorpe, "directly; but the message has come that the steamer is docking and I've sent for a taxi, sir."

Valentine collected himself. "Oh, yes, the steamer," he said, and then he glanced at Cora. "I don't think I'll go to the steamer, Thorpe."

Cora's heart rose; she knew that look, that tone; he did not want to go. She looked at Thorpe; not a muscle of his face had changed, and yet she knew he was in opposition.

"Yes, sir," he said. "Would you have any objection if I went to the dock? I doubt if the princess will understand the American customs without assistance, sir."

There was a little pause.

"The princess?" said Cora.

Valentine waved toward the photograph on the desk. "She's coming—Hungarian princess. Great stuff, if she's as per invoice. I'm sending her to China for the syndicate. Hun to Hun, you know. Good idea, isn't it? Thorpe told me about her. He lived with her uncle when he was ambassador in London; the uncle, you know, not Thorpe—though why not?"

Valentine rose. The recital of the facts in the case of the princess had revived his interest in her.

"I'll just go and grasp her by the hand. We've got her transportation for the Coast this evening, and she may not relish starting at once, unless it's put just right. I'll show her it's the best thing for her to do. Her last cable suggested she wished to linger in New York, but she would enjoy it more on her way back. I'll explain that to her. It won't take a minute. You'll wait, won't you? Stay and dine with me. I'm alone. Or no; I see by Thorpe's face that I have someone to dinner."

"Indeed, you have, sir.'

"Who is it? I don't remember."

"Mrs. Johnson-Bing, sir."

"Oh, Margaret—good old Margaret—so it is." Thorpe and Cora, a little embarrassed for him, averted their eyes, but Valentine was not embarrassed at all. "You have no idea how good she was to me when

I was at the hospital. And I wasn't very grateful—out of my head, you know. I thought I ought to tell her— You'll wait, Cora; just give you time to look over my plans, and when I come back I'll tell you about the land I bought for you. Well, I have an option on it—"

She lost the end of his sentence, for Thorpe, who during the speech had been putting him into his overcoat and handing him his hat and gloves, finally succeeded in hurrying him out of the door, still talking. But Cora did not require the end of the sentence; no woman who has lived two years with a man does. She knew what he was going to say, but even more important, she knew what was in his mind—that her welfare was as important to him as it had ever been. The marriage ceremony, she had always known, did not unite people, but now she was discovering that a decree of divorce did not always separate them. She was as much married to Valentine as she had ever been—no more and no less. How astonishing!

She sank into a chair. Perhaps the really astonishing fact was that they should ever have parted. They parted because they quarreled, but now she saw that their quarreling was the expression of their love. Her relations with everyone in the world except Valentine were suave and untroubled. And she was sure there was no one else with whom Valentine enjoyed the struggle for mastery. The mere notion of attempting to master the docile Margaret was comic, and as for Hermione, she was like a dish of blanc mange—you liked it and ate it or else you let it alone. No, it was useless to evade the truth that she, Cora, of all women was to him unique.

Thorpe returned presently and brought the new plans. She nodded without looking at him and told him to leave them on the table. She had plenty of time. Valentine's few minutes were always an hour.

"If you don't care to wait, madam, I'm sure Mr. Bing would be very glad to have you take them home with you," said Thorpe.

Cora did not trouble to repress a smile. "I shall wait, Thorpe," she said, with the good humor that comes from perfect confidence.

Thorpe bent very slightly from the waist, and left the room.

At last she rose and began to unroll the plans. She became immediately absorbed in them; they were not only beautiful and ingenious but, better to her than any beauty, they showed how he had remembered her tastes, her needs. She had always loved growing plants, and he had arranged a glassed passageway with sun and heat to be a small conservatory for her; there was a place for her piano; a clever

ALICE DUER MILLER

arrangement for hanging her dresses. He had remembered, or rather he had never forgotten. The idea came to her that this was not a house for her alone, but for her and him together. How simply that would explain his passionate interest in the prospect of her building. She began to read the plans as if they were a love letter.

She was still bending over them when later—much later—the door opened and closed. She did not immediately look up. It was not her plan to betray that she had guessed what lay behind his actions. She waited with bent head for Valentine's accustomed opening, and then hearing nothing she looked up, to find the newcomer was Margaret.

In their last meeting the shadow of death had obliterated the pattern of convention, but now both women were aware of an awkward moment. Margaret smiled first.

"I suppose, as no one sees us, we may shake hands," she said. Cora looked at her predecessor. Even in the low becoming lights of Valentine's big room she was frankly middle-aged, large waisted and dowdy, and yet glowingly human. Cora held out her hand.

"Is it so late?" she said. "Valentine mentioned that you were coming to dinner. He said he hadn't thanked you for all you did for him when he was ill."

Mrs. Johnson-Bings smiled. "That isn't what he wants," she said. She undid her coat and began to remove stout black gloves. She was in a high dark dress—very different from what Cora would have worn if she had decided to come back and dine with Valentine.

"What does he want?" Cora asked. She was really curious to hear.

"He's heard I'm going into business—supplying food to invalids. He wants me to organize according to his ideas, and not according to mine." Margaret smiled. "But poor Valentine doesn't know anything about invalids; just wants the fun of having everything done his way."

The words for some reason sounded like a knell in Cora's ears. Was that all Valentine really cared about—getting his own way? There was a brief silence; far away in someother part of the house she was dimly aware of a clock striking and a telephone bell ringing. It must be dinnertime, she thought—Margaret's hour. No, they couldn't both stay to dinner. She found herself wondering which of them Val would put at the head of the table. He would sit there himself, of course, with one on each side of him. "I suppose you'll do it all just as he says," she remarked mechanically.

Margaret laughed; she had a pleasant laugh, almost a chuckle. "Indeed I shan't!" she answered. "But I may let him think I'm going to. It saves such a lot of trouble, as I suppose you found out too."

No, Cora had not found that out. She felt shocked and admiring—as a little boy feels who sees another one smoking. How was it that Hermione, the faithless, and Margaret, the maternal, dared to treat Valentine more carelessly than she did? Perhaps they did not understand him as well as she did, with her more subtle reactions.

Before she could answer, Thorpe was in the room. When she thought of that moment afterwards she appreciated the power of the man, for there was no trace of elation or excitement or even hurry about him. He addressed Margaret:

"Mr. Bing is very sorry, madam, he will not be able to get home to dinner tonight."

Cora's mind working with the quickness of lightning waited for a second part of the message—something that would detain her and let Margaret depart in peace. But Thorpe having delivered himself of this one sentence turned to the desk and began collecting various objects—a fountain pen, a package of letters.

"When will Mr. Bing be back?" Cora asked.

"Mr. Bing is obliged to start for China this evening, madam," said Thorpe, and his eye just wavered across hers. "I'm packing for him now as well as I can at such short notice." The reason, his tone suggested, was sufficient excuse for leaving the two ladies to see each other out. He left the room, his eyes still roving about in search of necessary objects.

In this bitter moment Cora felt vaguely envious of Margaret, who, unmoved by the intelligence, was beginning to replace her heavy gloves.

"To China," she observed placidly. "Now I wonder What the reason for that is."

Cora snatched up the glossy photograph and thrust it between Margaret's shapeless black fingers. "That's the reason!" she said passionately. "He left me for just half an hour to meet her steamer—a princess—'great stuff if as per invoice.' Well, evidently she is as 'per invoice,' if he's going to China with her the first time they meet—he and his princess!"

Margaret took the photograph and studied it with irritating calm.

"I don't suppose there ever lived a human male who would not enjoy going to China with a princess," she said, and she almost smiled at the thought of their departure.

Tears were already running down Cora's cheeks. "What does it mean?" she said. "Are men incapable of permanent attachments?"

"Oh, no," replied Margaret. "Valentine's attachments are very permanent—only they're not exclusive. He will always want me when he's sick—and you when he wants to test his will power."

She stopped, for Thorpe had come into the room again. He had come for the photograph, which he now took gently out of Margaret's unresisting hand. She hardly noticed his action, so intently was her mind working upon the question of Valentine's health.

"Thorpe," she said, as if consulting a fellow expert, "do you think Mr. Bing is strong enough to make this journey?"

For the first time Thorpe allowed himself a smile—a faint fleeting lighting of the eyes.

"Oh, yes, madam," he said. "I think now Mr. Bing is quite himself—quite normal. And then, madam, I shall be with him."

The Red Carpet

The Torbys were giving a large dinner-party, and a scarlet carpet was rolled out from the glass and iron of their grilled door to the curb of the Fifth Avenue gutter—a carpet as red as a cardinal's robe, as the flags in the Bolshevist meeting which was being held simultaneously two miles away in Madison Square and giving the police a good deal of trouble.

It was customary to put on new clothes and treasured jewels for the Torby parties, for they gave very good parties; they were fashionable, and as they had been important, financially and socially, in New York for two generations, and as most other New Yorkers had only lived there a year or two, the Torbys were generally assumed to be as aboriginal as the rocks of Manhattan Island.

As a matter of fact, the first identified Torby, Ephraim by name, had strolled down to the great city from a Vermont farm just before the Civil War, and had made his fortune in questionable real-estate deals during the following years of unrest. But when the present Torby, William, said, "My father used to say that when he held the property at the corner of Twenty-third Street—" it sounded as if the family had always been landed proprietors; and Trevillian Torby, William's son, just twenty-four and not deeply interested in ancestry, had actually come to believe, though he of course knew all the facts, that the Torbys were the oldest and best family in America, and he was very scornful of newcomers from other States or countries who drifted into the metropolis to make their fortunes.

Hewer, the Torby butler, stood in the hall, wearing the old-fashioned livery the Torbys affected. Hewer was not the kind of butler who opens the door; on the contrary, when the great double doors had been swung open by two footmen, Hewer was discovered standing back center, doing absolutely nothing, except, if a female guest should be so thoughtless as to direct her steps to the men's dressing-room, or a male to the women's, he set them right with a slight but autocratic gesture of the hand.

Hewer was rather a young man to be so very great. He was the son of one of the gamekeepers on the Duke of Wessex's place, and being ambitious and having a weak heart, he allowed it to be known through the proper channels, when the Torbys were staying with the Duke, that

ALICE DUER MILLER

he would like to go to America; and the Torbys, who had had a great deal of trouble with butlers, snapped him up at once.

At first Hewer had found social distinctions in America somewhat confusing. He had been brought up in the strictest sect of inherited aristocracy, but some of his friends who had been in the United States explained to him that there everything was plutocratic—that nothing mattered but money. Hewer thought this not such a bad idea; but when he reached New York, he found it wasn't true. Social distinctions were not entirely based on money—not nearly as much so as in London. He had a friend living second footman to the third or fourth richest family in America, and it appeared that they were asked nowhere. Of course his own Torbys were all right—absolutely all right; they not only had visiting royalties to stay with them, but what did not always follow, they stayed with those same royalties when they went abroad.

As the motor doors began to slam, Hewer placed one foot on the lower step of the Torbys' beautiful Italian stairway, banked on each side with white lilies in honor of the party, and prepared to announce the first guest who issued from the dressing-room. If he did not know the name (though he almost always did, for he was intelligent, interested in his job, and had been doing the telephoning for the Torby parties for several years), he just drooped his ear toward the guest's mouth for a dilatory second, and then having caught it, he moved straight away upstairs, like a hunting-dog that had picked up the scent.

Many of the guests—more than a dozen—had arrived before one came in who spoke to Hewer by name. This was a small, erect old lady, with eyes as bright as her diamonds in their old-fashioned settings, and a smile as fine as her long old hands.

"Ah, Hewer," she said with a brisk nod, "still here, are you? Do crowds like this always collect for the Torbys' parties?"

Hewer, standing on the lower step, seemed just twice as tall as the old lady as he answered: "Crowds, madam!" And then as she waved her hand toward the front door, he understood and added: "Oh, yes, madam, quite often a crowd collects. And how is Mr. Richard?"

"Oh, of course he's been wounded," said the old lady, as if that had been the least of her expectations, "but he's well again now, and on his way home." And then, noticing that other people were waiting,—bejeweled creatures whom she did not know,—she nodded again, to indicate that the conversation was over. Hewer mounted the stairs five steps ahead of her and announced, as if this time he were really saying something:

"Mrs. John Grey."

But all the time he was at work announcing other guests—"Admiral and Mrs. Simpsom. . . Lady Cecilia and Mr. Hume. . . Mr. Lossing. . . Miss Watkins"—his mind was grappling with the problem of what Mrs. John Grey was doing dining with the Torbys.

About a year before this, Hewer had left the Torbys and had been engaged by Mrs. Grey. He deeply respected Mrs. Grey, but her household had not been congenial to him. In the first place there was an elderly maid in spectacles who managed everything, and had even attempted to manage Hewer. Then, Mrs. Grey was a widow with an only son, often away, and when he was away, Mrs. Grey dined by the library fire on a chop and rice pudding, and she sometimes omitted the chop; and though when Mr. Richard was at home, he was very gay and good-tempered, on the whole Hewer felt the position to be depressing; and when the Torbys humbly asked him to come back at a higher wage, he had consented.

But he retained a strong admiration for Mrs. Grey. She was afraid of nothing, whereas he knew his present employers were afraid of many things—afraid of being laughed at, afraid of missing the turn of the social tide, afraid even of him, their butler, though they attempted to conceal this fear under a studied insolence of manner. It was because this insolence was not of the particular brand that Hewer admired that he had left them. He had often noticed, as he waited on table, that Mrs. Torby was afraid of having opinions; she always found out what other people thought about art and politics, and only when strongly backed by majority opinion would she express herself—with a good deal of arrogance. She never confessed ignorance of any subject under discussion—except possibly of a childhood friend.

Mrs. Grey, on the other hand, ripped out her opinions with the utmost confidence, and could say, "No, my dear, I never heard of it," when some new school of art or thought was under discussion, in a tone that made those who had been somewhat overpraising it wonder if they had not, after all, been making fools of themselves. Mr. Richard was the same way—never afraid of what people would think of him; perhaps it might have been better if he had been, judging from what Hewer himself had thought of some of Mr. Richard's more youthful escapades.

Now, the last thing Mrs. Grey had said to Hewer when he left her service was: "What, Mr. Hewer, back to those vulgar people?" The words had been a shock to Hewer, for the Torbys were so fashionable, so clearly sought-after, that he had not supposed anyone would apply such a term as *vulgar* to them. But he did know exactly what Mrs. Grey meant, and he had never forgotten the words, and so he wondered what Mrs. Grey was doing in the house of the people she had so contemptuously described. She was not like the Torbys, who seemed to go to their friends' houses chiefly for the sake of making an amusing story afterward of how dull and badly done their parties had been. Mrs. Grey did not go to the houses of those she considered her social inferiors, and as she considered almost everyone her social inferiors, and as most of them regarded her as a funny little old lady who didn't matter anyhow, she ate most of her meals quietly in her own house.

As so often happens, while Hewer was pondering the problem, the explanation of it was walking into the house—walking in with her head in the air, and a sapphire-blue satin cloak wrapped tightly about her. Hewer recognized her at once, but he did not know her name. She was the young lady who used to come and sit with Mrs. Grey and look pale and tearless during the terrible weeks when Mr. Richard was fighting in the Argonne—and would have liked to cry, Hewer had thought, if only Mrs. Grey had not been so dreadfully heroic, remarking like the Roman emperor, that after all, she had never been under the illusion that her son was immortal. She was the young lady whose photograph had dropped out of one of Mr. Richard's coats one day when he was brushing it. She was beautiful, and she came from far enough West to be aware of the existence of the letter *r*. She and Mrs. Grey used to have long amiable arguments as to whether or not well-bred people would recognize the letter *r*, except, of course, in such magnificent words as *Richard*. Hewer did not know this lady's name until she told it to him at the foot of the stairs—"Miss Evington." He repressed a start. It was the gossip belowstairs in the Torby household that Mr. Trevillian wanted to marry a Miss Evington, whom his family did not consider quite up to the Torbys' matrimonial standard. When Mrs. Torby had given Hewer the cards and the diagram of the table, and he had seen that Miss Evington's place was next to Mr. Trevillian, he had taken this as a sign that the thing was settled. He never knew how much he had liked Mr. Richard until he felt a wave of contempt for this beautiful young creature who preferred Trevillian and his millions.

Hewer announced "Miss Evington" with quite a sniff.

When he went downstairs, another guest had arrived and was taking his dinner-card from the tray a footman was offering him. It was Mr. Barnsell. Barnsell was a sleek, brown, middle-aged man whose only interest in life was comfort; and as his means were limited and his tastes luxurious, the attainment of supreme comfort had become both an art and sport to him.

"Ah, good evening, Hewer!" he said.

"Good evening, sir," said Hewer without the slightest change of expression. He hated and despised Barnsell, for the reason that he was one of those people who demand a far higher standard of comfort from other people's houses and servants than he did from his own. When he stayed at the Torbys,—as he did for long periods,—he gave a great deal of trouble, and had been known to send a suit of clothes downstairs three times because it had not been properly pressed, although Hewer knew very well that at home his clothes were very sketchily taken care of by the housemaid. Hewer's only revenge was to force upward the whole scale of Mr. Barnsell's tips. Hewer himself did not care much about money and was very well paid by the Torbys, but in the interests of pure justice, he received Mr. Barnsell's crinkled bill with an air of cold surprise that made him double it next time.

"Gad, Hewer," Mr. Barnsell was saying, "there's a pretty ugly situation outside there—a crowd around the door, and marching up Fifth Avenue. They nearly pulled my chauffeur off the box. If they'd laid a finger on me, I'd have let them have it, I can tell you."

"I hope they did not hurt the chauffeur, sir."

"Oh, no," said Barnsell positively; but Hewer knew from his tone that he had not waited to see.

Immediately after this, terrible things began to happen to the Torbys' nice party—things that had never happened to any of their parties before. The meeting in Madison Square having been broken up by methods which the participants described as being a little short of massacre, and which the police said were too velvet-gloved to be effective, had drifted away into smaller groups, all looking for trouble. Perhaps it was the color of the Torby's carpet, or the size or ugliness of a house built in the worst taste of the '80's, or the delicious smell of terrapin which came floating out of the kitchen windows; but for whatever reason, a crowd had collected about the door and was mocking at and jostling the guests in such a threatening manner that the night watchman rushed in to tell a footman to telephone at once to the police, and poor fat little Mrs. McFarlane arrived with her tiara quite on one side and a conviction that she had just escaped being strung up to a lamp-post in the best style of the French Revolution.

The McFarlanes, who took themselves seriously in every position, made a dramatic entrance into the drawing-room. Mr. McFarlane held up his hand for silence and then said:

"We are in grave danger."

He was a tall, solemn, hawk-nosed man, who had made a fortune after forty, and had been elected president of a great bank after fifty—an office which he accepted as if it were a sort of financial priesthood. Mrs. McFarlane, who went in for jeweled crowns and sweeping velvets, was suspected by her friends of a repressed wish to be queenly—nor indeed was her height and figure so different from that of the late Victoria.

"Hewer, send down and have the outer doors closed," said Mr. Torby. And Hewer, having announced the last guest, who was a good deal flustered from having had his high hat smashed over his nose—left the room to obey.

"They are bloodthirsty, simply bloodthirsty," continued Mr. McFarlane. "One villainous-looking fellow shouted at my wife: 'You don't look as if you needed another square meal for a year; give us a chance.'"

"Accurate observers, at least," said Mrs. Grey in a twinkling aside to Miss Evington. "Come and sit down, my dear, and let us talk while these people regain their poise."

"Do you think we are in any danger from the mob, Mrs. Grey?" asked the girl quietly.

"The mob inside, or the mob out?"

Miss Evington laughed. "Oh," she said. "Feeling like that about them, why did you come?"

"I came," answered Mrs. Grey, "because I knew these people are trying to dazzle you with all their hideous possessions; and I wanted," she added simply, "to give you some standard of comparison."

Miss Evington turned away to hide a smile, or perhaps it was a tear, at the old lady's self-confidence. She had an impulse to explain that if she refused the Torby millions, it would not be on account of Mrs. Grey's high breeding; and then she stopped to wonder whether, after all, it had not something to do with the situation—indirectly.

Mr. Barnsell approached them, shaking his head. "Well," he said, "now I hope Washington will see the consequence of coddling the lower classes." Mr. Barnsell's railroad investments had declined.

"This should be a great lesson to the Administration," said Mr. Lossing—a slim, elderly man, who seemed to have decreased in bulk through constant shrinking from outrages against his notion of good taste and good manners. "As my dear old father used to say—"

"It's the French Revolution over again," said Mrs. McFarlane, still panting a little. "It's the hatred of the common man for the aristocrat."

"The aristocrat, my dear!" murmured Mrs. Grey to her young friend. "Her father-in-law was my father's gardener, and she must know I know it."

At this moment a stone crashed through one of the long French windows of the drawing-room. Trevillian Torby rushed to Miss Evington's side. "Don't be alarmed," he said. "Don't be alarmed, Mrs. Grey."

"Thank you—I'm not," said Mrs. Grey, tossing her gray head slightly, as if to say it was a pretty state of affairs when Trevillian Torby could intervene in her fate. "If you won't think me rude, I must say the evening is turning out more amusing than I had expected."

Trevillian, fortunately, was not looking for malice from one so small and gray and feminine, and he went on hotly: "I wonder what this rabble thinks they could do with this country without us—without the leadership of people like ourselves."

"They'll soon find out, it seems," answered Mrs. Grey.

"The trouble with this country," continued Trevillian, "is the growing contempt for law and order. No one is brought up to respect the state— the Government. What would the poor do without the ruling class? Do you realize that the hospitals and charitable institutions of this country would have to close? And what would happen then, I should like to know?"

"They would be run by the state, of course," said Miss Evington, who knew her way about sociology.

"The state!" cried Trevillian. "Do you mean government ownership? Well, let me tell you that the state is about the most inefficient, the most corrupt—"

"I thought we ought to respect it," said Miss Evington.

Mrs. Grey laughed out loud. "Ah, Mr. Torby," she said, "women ought not to attempt argument, ought they?"

ALICE DUER MILLER

Trevillian felt soothed by this remark. "I own," he replied, "that I do not think a woman appears at her best in argument." And he never understood why it was that he seemed to have made a very good joke.

They now began to go in to dinner—the dining-room was safely situated across the back of the house. The table was magnificent. Gold vases of pink and white flowers alternated down its length with gold bowls of yellow and orange fruit. Tall wineglasses of crystal engraved in gold stood like little groves at each plate. The Torbys' engraved glass was famous.

"But I thought," Lady Cecilia was heard saying to her host, who was of course taking her in to dinner, "I thought there were no classes in the United States?"

Mr. Torby was shocked that Lady Cecilia, who had had so many opportunities, like the present, for observing, should make such a mistake.

"Oh," he said, "I should hardly say that. I yield to none in my belief in the principles of democracy—from the political point of view; but socially, my dear Lady Cecilia, every country in the world has a class—how shall I define it—"

He succeeded in defining it so that it included himself and excluded most of the rest of the world. Aristocracy nowadays, he thought, consisted in having had for two or three generations the advantages of a large fortune with all the cultivation and refinement and responsibility that it brings. A college president, who was present, was equally sure that it was all a question of education. Mr. McFarlane, the head of a large bank, thought it meant the group of men in any country who control the financial destinies—and therefore all the destinies—of a country. Mrs. Grey did not find it worth while to define anything, but sat thinking: "It's being ladies and gentlemen, if they only knew it."

Suddenly there was a tremendous sound of cracking and tearing—a crash as if the stout double outer doors had given way, a shouting, the noise of an ambulance gong, or of a police-wagon. Some people sprang up from the table, but Mr. Torby urged them to remain seated.

"Hewer," he said, "go downstairs and see what is happening."

Hewer immediately left the room, and did not return for a long time.

In the downstairs hall Hewer found the night watchman with a dislocated wrist, several policemen, a young man mopping his brow, whom he did not at first notice, and a great deal of broken glass.

The whole trouble, it appeared, had arisen over the red carpet—the Bolshevist meeting not being able to understand why, if they were not allowed to display red flags in Madison Square, Mr. Torby should be allowed to display a carpet of exactly the same hue in Fifth Avenue. In the interests of pure logic, the participants in the late meeting decided to point out this inconsistency to the municipal authorities, by cutting the Torby's carpet into small pieces and carrying them away. A number of returned sailors and soldiers, who felt perhaps that to fight for a poor cause was better than not fighting at all, had decided to defend the carpet. The complete harmony of everyone was proved by the fact that when driven away by the police-reserves, both parties were soon jointly engaged in upsetting all the ash-cans in a neighboring side-street.

Hewer sent the night-watchman to the housekeeper to get his wrist bandaged, got rid of the police by giving them some of Mr. Torby's second-best cigars and a great deal of irrelevant information which they said was necessary to the preservation of order, directed that the broken glass should be swept up, and then turned his attention to the young man.

"Why, Mr. Richard!" he exclaimed.

"Look here, Hewer," said Mr. Richard, "I know that Miss Evington is dining here—I saw her going in, as I happened to be passing." He glanced quickly at the butler to see if there was any criticism of an officer in the United States Army hanging about doorways to watch young ladies go in and out. "Is everyone in there frightened to death over this shindy?"

"Well, you know, sir," said Hewer temperately, "they have been very nervous about this Bolshevist movement for a long time; and they do seem anxious—all except Mrs. Grey, sir."

"What!" cried the Captain. "Is my mother dining here?" And Hewer could see that this was the last straw—that his mother should have gone over to the enemy. Hewer was sorry, but felt it his duty to go back to the dining-room. "They are anxious, sir, for fear the mob may have overpowered the police, and I ought to go back and tell them that everything is quiet."

"No, Hewer," said the Captain firmly. "Go back, but tell them just the opposite. Tell them that the police have been driven off, that the mob is in control, that a soviet committee has been formed, which will send a representative to question them and decide on the merits of each of their cases, and say that if a finger is laid on the people's delegate, the house will be blown up with T N T."

Hewer could not help smiling at the plan, but he shook his head. "I'd like to oblige you, sir," he said, "but I'd lose my job."

"Oh, the cream's off your job anyhow, Hewer," said Mr. Richard decisively. "You don't want to be a butler under the new order. I've just got a good job with a Western railroad. Come with me and run our dining-car service."

The Great War has far-reaching effects. It was the war that made Hewer yield to this insane suggestion—the sense of dissatisfaction with himself because a weak heart had kept him from fighting, and the sense of power in Grey which a year and a half of being obeyed had thrown into his tone.

"But you can't go upstairs like that, sir—they'd all know you."

"You do your part, and I'll do mine," said Richard.

When Hewer entered the dining-room again, the tension had increased. Some of the guests had arisen from the table and were looking for weapons. All had decided to behave nobly. The six footmen, as if paralyzed by the consciousness that they had identified themselves with the capitalistic class, were standing idly about the room, not attempting to go on with the serving of dinner. Mrs. McFarlane had almost fainted again, but finding that no one had time to bring her to, she was coming to by herself. Only Mrs. Grey was finishing her soup in a thorough but not inelegant manner.

Hewer bent to whisper in Mr. Torby's ear.

"Good God!" said Mr. Torby; and an electric thrill ran through the company, who did not know that the exclamation expressed anger rather than fear.

"Don't be alarmed," said Mr. Torby, addressing the table. "Keep perfectly calm. Hewer tells me the situation is this: the police have been temporarily driven off. These Bolshevist rascals are in control for a minute or two—nothing more, I am sure. I should advise our yielding for the moment to their demands."

"But what are their demands?" asked Mrs. McFarlane nervously, with a vague recollection of a program about women which her respectable morning paper had not been able to print in full, but which she had looked up later in the chauffeur's more liberal journal, while he was putting on the chains.

Divining her fears, Mrs. Torby gracefully hastened to allay them. "They demand nothing more than that we receive a delegate from their committee, and answer his questions."

"Receive him," said the Admiral with that terrible calm which seems to have replaced the old quarter-deck manner. "We'll receive him a good deal more warmly than he'll like."

Mr. Torby held up his hand. "No," he said. "Our safety, the safety of these ladies, is dependent upon the safe-conduct back of this delegate. The mob, probably through the culpable carelessness of the Administration—"

"Not a word against the Administration, sir," cried the Admiral, "—the Administration under whom this country has just won one of the most signal tri—"

"I'm afraid, sir," said Hewer most respectfully, "that the committee is not inclined to wait very much longer."

It was decided to admit the People's delegate at once. After all, however detestable his philosophy, he would be only one man against twenty-four guests, six footmen and Hewer. But when Hewer opened the dining-room door and announced in his very best manner, "The Representative of the Soviet Committee," everyone saw that confidence had been premature.

The delegate was an alarming figure. He was in his shirt-sleeves, without collar and round his waist was tied a long strip of the Torby's carpet; from this protruded the handle of an army revolver. The lower part of his face was hidden by a black silk handkerchief; and a soft hat, rather too large for him, was pulled down to his brows. It was a hat which Trevillian had passed on to Hewer some months before, but fortunately there is no way of identifying a soft felt hat. Below the brim a pair of piercing gray eyes ran over the company like the glint of steel.

The delegate was tall, and he stood in the doorway with folded arms. Mrs. McFarlane, declaring that at last the aristocracy knew how to die, burst into tears; and Trevillian Torby, bending over Miss Evington, declared in a passionate undertone that he would give his life for hers. But Miss Evington, with her eye fixed on the delegate, drew back almost rudely from Trevillian's protecting droop and said quite loudly: "Nonsense, Trevillian! I don't feel myself in any danger."

"I am here," said the delegate in a deep, rough voice, "as a representative of the first soviet committee—a form of government which, as you now doubtless understand, will soon take over this entire country—indeed, the world. How dare you, a little, idle, parasitic group, eat like this, drink like this—and," he added, snatching a bottle of champagne from the nerveless hand of a footman and quickly returning it, "and such a

ALICE DUER MILLER

rotten brand, too? By what right, I say, do you feast, while better people are starving? But we are not cruel or unreasonable, and anyone here who can show that he or his immediate family belong to the proletariat and has worked with his hands, will be spared."

A confused silence greeted this speech. The company did not really take in the meaning of his words, for the reason that any identification of themselves with the proletariat—what they would have called the lower classes—seemed to them simply fantastic. Though they were continually readjusting their social standing with each other, they no more doubted their general superiority to the rest of humanity than they doubted the fact of the skies being above the earth.

Mr. Barnsell, who had had more practice than most of them in adapting himself to his surroundings, spoke first. Getting up, with his hands in his pockets, he said coolly:

"Oh, come, my dear fellow! This is ridiculous. This is un-American—extremely un-American. There are no class-distinctions in this country. We all in a sense belong to the proletariat."

"Speak for yourself," said Mrs. Grey.

Mrs. Torby bent over to her next-door neighbor and whispered, "Exactly what do they mean by proletariat?" with the manner of one who, being about to be elected to a club, would like to know what the organization signified.

"You will have to offer proof of your assertions," said the delegate in a more threatening tone. "A leisure class is a criminal class, and its wealth will be confiscated for the common good. Are you or are you not members of a leisure class?"

At this the company, which had so far shown a good deal of courage, in face of one of the most terrifying agencies in the world,—an angry mob,—began to show evidence of panic. A threat to human life, even their own, seemed to them less horrible than this danger to the existing order of society. The right of property—not their own property, but the divine right of property in general—seemed worth defending at great cost. A babel of voices arose, out of which Mr. McFarlane's soared like a lark:

"I did, I did," he was saying. "I used to help my father pick the beets and the rose-bugs. My father was a gardener. This lady"—indicating Mrs. Grey—"knows that what I say is true. My father was her father's gardener."

"Is this true?" asked the delegate.

"Yes," answered Mrs. Grey, "and a very coarse, uneducated man too, as I remember him."

"Thank you—oh, thank you," said Mr. McFarlane warmly; and his wife, raising her tiara-ed head, added:

"Yes, and as a girl I used to take in plain—"

"Hush, Maria!" said her husband. "It is unnecessary. A wife always takes the rank of her husband in any society."

Mrs. McFarlane caught the idea at once, and leaning back with folded hands, she looked about patronizingly on those whose position under the new order was less solidly founded than her own.

The complete success of Mr. McFarlane pointed the way to others, whose training had made them quick to learn new methods of pleasing—when they wanted to please. In a few minutes astounding revelations had been made on all sides. Mr. Lossing, the haughty and exclusive Mr. Lossing, confessed, or rather he loudly and repeatedly asserted, that he had long been secretly married to his cook—than whom, he insisted, no one was a more persistent and skillful manual worker. Mr. Barnsell, who had always seemed to live remarkably well on the proceeds of a somewhat tenuous law-practice, pleaded for publicity for the fact that his father had kept a tailor's shop—and he offered to produce photographs in proof of his statement.

"Did you ever work in this shop?" asked the delegate.

"I'm afraid not," answered Mr. Barnsell reluctantly. "My mother,— you know how petty women are about class distinctions,—she wanted me to rise in the world—"

"*Rise!*" exclaimed the delegate haughtily. "You are untrue to your class, sir."

"Perhaps—a little," murmured Mr. Barnsell meekly.

"But we will pass you," said the delegate, "for the sake of your father."

By a somewhat unexpected application of Bolshevist principles, the delegate exempted members of the military and naval services, and visiting foreigners, from any examination. He showed a tendency also to pass over Mrs. Grey, although she kept asserting that none of her ancestors had ever done anything useful. "Unless," she added thoughtfully, "Lionel Grey, whom they sent to the Tower for a day or two in 1673 for killing his valet. He may have had to sweep out his room. And I have a son," she added more loudly, "who is just as bad."

"You mean your son does not work?" said the delegate, as if he felt the statement so unlikely that he was ready to contradict it.

"I shouldn't call him usefully employed at this moment," replied the old lady. "Would you like me to describe what he is doing?"

"Be silent, madam," said the delegate, and turned hastily away to the examination of the Torby family.

Asked rather roughly what he had to say for himself, Mr. Torby rose. "I have to say," he began, "that I agree with my friend Mr. Barnsell, that this whole movement is extremely un-American. This country is a democracy—our forefathers died to make it so; and for you to attempt to introduce all these dangerous ideas of class antagonism is opposed to all the ideals of the founders of this nation. There are no class distinctions in America. I may rise today, and you tomorrow—or you might have, if you had not cast in your lot with these lawless rascals who all will end in jail. Take the example of Mr. Barnsell here—proud to own his father's trade." (Mr. Barnsell tried to oblige with a proud look.) "And I too—my father was a farmer. He tilled the soil with his own hands. That, ladies and gentlemen, is America."

"Ah, that's easy to say," replied the delegate, strangely unimpressed by an oration that had drawn tears to Mr. Barnsell's eyes. "It's easy to say that your father was a farmer, but can you prove it? Only yesterday I saw an interview with you in our capitalistic press on the occasion of your being elected president of one of these aristocratic social clubs,—which the people will raze to the ground immediately,—and this interview stated on your own authority that yours was one of the oldest and idlest families in this country."

"The reporter misunderstood me," said Mr. Torby with the firmness of a man whose public life has made him long familiar with the phrase.

Trevillian Torby sprang to his feet. "Father," he said pleadingly, "let me go upstairs and bring down Grandfather."

"Goodness," exclaimed Mrs. Grey, "don't tell me that the original Ephraim is still alive!"

"My father-in-law is very old," murmured Mrs. Torby faintly. "He shuns society."

For the first time since the entrance of the People's delegate, the interest of the company turned from him and rested on the door through which Trevillian had departed. The idea that the great Ephraim—the founder of the colossal Torby fortune, the ancestor who had become almost a myth—was not only alive but living somewhere in the top of the palace which his money had built, was an overwhelming surprise to everyone. Everyone began calculating what his age must be, and having reached the conclusion that he was well over eighty, they were prepared to see Trevillian lead, wheel, or even carry him into the room; but the reality was very different.

Ephraim Torby strode in ahead of his grandson. He was tall, over six feet, and the long plum-colored dressing-gown he was wearing made him look taller. The whiskers, which he wore in accordance with the fashion of his youth, gave to his shaven upper lip an added expression of shrewd humor. A slight smile wrinkled the upper part of his face, and his bright black eyes twinkled. From the moment he entered the room, the situation was in his hands.

"Well," he said in a leisurely tone, addressing the delegate, "what's all this about?"

The delegate in a few words, made less fluent by the fact that the old man had put on a pair of gold-rimmed spectacles and was now studying the delegate in detail, explained the principles of the Bolshevist movement, and the relation of these principles to the present company.

"Foolishness!" said the old man. "For the land's sake, what are clever fellars like you doing wasting your time fighting these folks?" And he waved his hand toward the dinner-table. "Ain't you got sense enough to see that you're jest the same—jest the same? Both against justice and law and order—both discontented— Oh, yes, Bill, you are discontented, and Trevillian too. They don't get any fun out of life—not out of spending the money I had such a heap of fun making. And you'll find, young fellar," he added to the delegate, "that there's only two kinds of folks worth fussing over in this world—them that enjoys life, and them that would jest as lief jump off the bridge tomorrow. You're both discontented, and you're both narrer: you can't see anybody's interest but your own, and you're both as selfish as the dickens—want to run the world jest for the sake of your own folks. Why, you two ought to be able to get together. But the fellars who are going to beat you both—and you're going to be beaten—is the fellars with a cheap car and a couple of acres, or a three-room flat, who are having too good a time out of it to let you bust it up. And you'll never get past them—never in your lifetime, young fellar."

"We've got a good way already," said the delegate.

"Oh, maybe, maybe," answered the old man. "And I presume you're having a good time out of trying—and if you want any advice about organization, you might drop in to see me some afternoon, when Bill is out. You can't tell; I might even want to subscribe to your campaign-fund—"

"Father," said William Torby, displaying more feeling than at anytime during the evening, "that would be being untrue to your class."

"Why, Trevillian was just a-telling me, Bill, that you said there were no classes in America," answered his father.

In the slight pause that followed, Mrs. Grey rose, and approaching Ephraim, she said in her most gracious manner—and that was very gracious:

"Do come over and sit down, Mr. Torby. I should like so much to talk to you."

But the People's delegate interfered. "No, madam," he said fiercely. "As you have shown no connection whatsoever with the proletariat, I must trouble you to come with me."

Mrs. Grey nodded at the terrified company. "Goodnight," she said. "Such a pleasant evening! Do ask me again sometime, dear Mrs. Torby." And then she added to the delegate: "I insist on Miss Evington's accompanying me. She's quite as bad in her own way as I am in mine."

"No," shouted Trevillian.

"Yes, we'll take her along," said the delegate; and the three left the room hastily, taking the precaution to lock the door behind them.

When safely in the taxicab, which Hewer had waiting for them, Miss Evington said: "Oh, Dick, can you ever forgive me for having been a little bit dazzled by those people?"

"Well, Richard," said his mother, "I should think this would mean a jail-sentence for you when it comes out. But I shall always think it was well worth while, well worth while."

"They'll never tell if we don't," said Richard confidently.

"Perhaps not," said Mrs. Grey, settling back comfortably in her corner. "I want to say this—not that I don't know that you are holding Evalina's hand behind my back, and I should know it, even if I were as blind as a bat, which I'm thankful to say I am not—I want to say that I think I believe in democracy, after all. The only really interesting and agreeable man there this evening, except yourself, my dear Richard, was that delightful old farmer. Evidently the thing that makes American society so dull is not the people they let in nowadays, as I had always imagined, but the people they keep out. Yes, Richard, you have converted me to democracy."

But Richard and Evalina were not paying as much attention to this philosophy as it undoubtedly deserved.

The Widow's Might

Fifth: To my executors hereinafter named, or to such of them as shall qualify, and the survivors of them, I give and bequeath the sum of one million dollars ($1,000,000) in trust to hold, invest and reinvest the same and to collect the income, issues and profits thereof and pay over the whole of said income, issues and profits, accruing from the date of my death, in semiannual payments, less proper charges and expenses, to my wife, Doris Helen Southgate, as long as she shall remain my widow; and upon the death or remarriage of my said wife, I direct that the principal of said trust shall be paid over to my sister, Antonia Southgate, or in the event of her death—

It was this fifth clause that Vincent Williams, the dead man's lawyer, found himself considering as he drove uptown with a copy of the will in his pocket. Was or was not a man justified in cutting his wife off in case of her remarriage? After all, why should a fellow work hard all his life to support his successor and perhaps his successor's children? The absolute possession of a large fortune may be a definite danger to a young woman of twenty-five. Yes, there was much to be said in favor of such a provision; and yet, when he had said it all, Williams found himself feeling as he had felt when he drew the will—that it was an unwarranted insult, an ungracious gesture of possession from the grave. He himself couldn't imagine making such a will; but then he had not married a girl thirty-five years his junior. Southgate may have had a vision of some pale, sleek-headed professional dancer, or dark-skinned South European with a criminal record—

Williams was shocked to find he was thinking that the widow would have a right even to such companions as these, if these were what she wanted. He had no clew as to what she did want, for he had never seen her, although he had been Southgate's lawyer for many years. Southgate, since his marriage five years before, had spent most of his time at Pasadena, although he always kept the house on Riverside open.

It was toward this house that Williams was now driving. There was a touch of the mausoleum about it—just the kind of house that a man who had made his fortune in coffins ought to have owned. It was built of cold, smooth graystone, and the door was wider at the bottom than at the top, in the manner of an Egyptian tomb. You went down a few steps into the hall, and Williams always half expected to hear a trapdoor clang behind him and find that, Rhadames in the last act of Aïda, he was walled up for good.

Nichols, Southgate's old manservant, opened the door for him and conducted him to the drawing-room, which ran across the front of the house on the second story, with three windows, somewhat contracted by stone decorations, which looked on the river.

It was an ugly, pretentious room, done in the period of modern satinwood, striped silks and small oil paintings in immense gold frames. Over the mantelpiece hung a portrait of Southgate by Bonnat—a fine, blatant picture, against a red background, of a man in a frock coat with a square beard.

The house was well constructed and the carpets were deep, so that complete silence reigned. Williams walked to the middle window and looked out. It was the end of February and a wild wind was blowing across the Hudson, but even a ruffled dark gray river was more agreeable to look at than the drawing-room. He stood staring out at an empty freighter making her way slowly upstream to her anchorage, until a rustling of new crape garments made him turn, as Miss Southgate entered.

She was tall—her brother had been tall too; nearly six feet; her face was white as alabaster, and her hair, though she was nearly sixty, was still jet black. Her mourning made her seem more majestic than ever, though Williams would have said she could not possibly have been more majestic than she had been the last time he saw her.

His first impression was that she was alone, but a second later he saw that she was followed by a tiny creature, who looked as much out of scale beside Antonia as if the Creator had been experimenting in different sizes of human beings and had somehow got the two sets mixed up—a little blond-headed doll with eyes the color of Delft china. Miss Southgate held out a solid hand, white as a camellia. "I don't think you know my sister-in-law," she said in her deep voice. "A very old friend of Alexander's, my dear—Mr. Williams."

Williams smiled encouragingly in answer, assuming that anything so small must be timid; but little Mrs. Southgate betrayed no symptom of alarm. She bent her slender throat and sat down on the sofa beside Antonia, with her hands, palms up, in her lap. She did it with a certain crispness, like a good child doing what it has been taught as exactly the right thing to do. She sat perfectly still; whereas Antonia kept up a slow, magnificent undulation of shoulders and hips, as Williams took the will out of his pocket.

"You are familiar with the terms of the will?" he asked, scrupulously including both ladies in the question.

"Yes," said Antonia, "my brother discussed the will with me in great detail before he made it, and I told Doris What you had said to me yesterday after the funeral. I think she understands. You do understand, my dear, don't you, that my brother left you the income of his estate during your life?"

Mrs. Southgate nodded, without the least change of expression.

"During her life or until her remarriage," said Williams, giving the word full weight.

"I shall not remarry," said Mrs. Southgate in a quick, sweet, whispering voice—the sort of voice which made everyone lean forward, although it was perfectly audible.

Antonia looked down at her sister-in-law and smiled, and Williams recognized with surprise that she was obviously attached to the little creature. He was surprised, because he knew that Miss Southgate had disapproved of the marriage; and even if the marriage had been less open to hostile criticism than it was, no one would expect a sister, who had for many years been at the head of her brother's house and a partner in his business, to welcome the intrusion of a young blond-headed wife. It really spoke well for both women, he thought, that they had managed to get on.

He began to go over the will, paragraph by paragraph. In the sixteenth clause it was stated that the jewels now in possession of Mrs. Southgate, in especial a string of pearls and pigeon's-blood rubies, were not to be regarded as gifts, but as part of the estate. He glanced at the widow.

"I suppose that was your understanding," he said.

"I never thought about it," she answered. "If Alexander says so, of course he knew what he meant."

At this moment the door softly opened and Nichols appeared with a visiting card on a salver, which he presented to Antonia. Miss Southgate began feeling for her lorgnette.

"We can see no one," she said reprovingly to Nichols; then as she found her glasses and read the card, she added, "I never heard of such a person. Is it for me?"

"No, madam," said Nichols; "the gentleman asked for Mrs. Southgate."

"Explain to him that we can see no one," said Antonia; and then, as Nichols left the room, she decided as an afterthought to give the card to her sister-in-law—merely for information, however, for the door had already shut behind Nichols.

As the little widow read the card she looked up with large, startled eyes, which from having been light blue suddenly turned without any warning at all to a deep, shiny black, and she colored until not only her face and neck but even her tiny wrists were pink. It was really, Williams thought, very interesting to watch; all the more because Antonia, who was talking about a legacy to an old servant, was utterly unaware of what was going on at her elbow. Mrs. Southgate had made no muscular movement at all, except to turn her palms over, so that her two hands were now domed above the visiting card. She sat quite still, gazing into vacancy and obviously not hearing a single word that was said.

But half an hour later, when Williams stood up to go, she came back to life, and said to him without the least preamble, "You did not tell me what would happen if I did remarry."

Antonia turned the full front of her majesty upon her sister-in-law, and said, "You would lose the name of Southgate."

"I am glad you asked that question," said Williams. "You ought to understand exactly what your situation is. In the event of your remarriage, you would have an income from another small fund—amounting to about forty-five hundred dollars a year, I should think."

She nodded thoughtfully; and Antonia, laying her hand on her shoulder, said gently: "Now I have still a few family matters to discuss with Mr. Williams; but you need not wait, if you want to finish your letters, although we shall be very glad to have you with us if you wish to stay."

It was clear to Williams that she did not wish to stay. She held out her hand to him—thin and narrow, but as strong as steel—gave him a smile and left the room. She always had a little difficulty, like a child, with the handle of a door.

Williams and Miss Southgate smiled at each other, and he expressed a common thought as he said, "If I met Mrs. Southgate unexpectedly in the woods, I shouldn't need any photographs to make me believe in fairies."

"She's a dear little thing," said Antonia as she seated herself again, rather heavily. "Very intelligent in some ways, but in business matters—

almost a case of arrested development. My brother never even gave her the trouble of signing a check."

"He just paid her bills?"

"She had very few. She has never been extravagant. She seems to have no wishes at all. I often hope that she will learn to assert herself more as she grows older."

Williams doubted if Miss Southgate would enjoy the realization of this hope, but he only said, "An income of fifty thousand is apt to increase human assertiveness."

"I sincerely hope so," said Miss Southgate. "It's a great care, Mr. Williams, and no special pleasure to find yourself obliged to direct every action, almost every thought, of another person's life. What I wanted to say to you was that I think you had better consult me about all the business details. You see how little grasp she has of them. My brother never discussed anything of the kind with her. He was more like a father than a husband—thirty-five years' difference in age—"

Miss Southgate shook her head.

"And yet," said Williams, "the marriage turned out well, wouldn't you say?"

Antonia's fine arched black brows went up in doubt.

"It hadn't the disadvantages you ordinarily expect from such marriages," she answered. "She did not run about flirting with young men or spending my brother's money foolishly. On the other hand, she did not introduce any of that gayety and youth into his daily life, any of that humor and high spirits— She is a curious little person, good as gold, but not vital, not alive."

Williams went away wondering. Corpses don't blush like that, he thought. The wind had died down as the sun set; and now, with a red sky over the Palisades, the Riverside was not a bad place for a walk. He strolled southward, trying to remember, now that he had seen Doris Helen Southgate in the flesh, all that he had heard about her in the days when she was only a name—the folly of an otherwise shrewd client.

He thought he remembered that she was some relation to the clergyman of the Southgates' church—an orphan trying to support herself by one of those extremely ill-paid occupations which are considered ladylike. He thought she had come to the Southgate house to read to Antonia during a temporary affliction of the eyes. Before he had seen her he had thought of her as a serpent, insinuating herself into the household and then coiling herself so firmly that she could never be driven out; but now it seemed to him more as if a kitten had strayed into that great mausoleum and had been shut up there for life.

He remembered a frequent phrase of Southgate's, which he had never noticed much at the time: "Yes, I read it with great interest—at least my wife read it to me." He had been fond of being read aloud to, especially at night, when he couldn't sleep. Williams wondered whether Doris Helen had spent six years reading aloud—above the rustling of the avenue of palms at Pasadena, above the rattle of the private car as they went back and forth and across the continent. Mercy, it was no wonder she wasn't much alive. And Southgate had never given her the trouble of signing a check, hadn't be? Well, that was one way to put it. No, of course, he said to himself, he did not want to see the little widow break loose—to hear that she was gambling at Monte Carlo or being robbed of her jewels at some café on the Left Bank; but he would have been glad to see her acting on the emotion that had turned her eyes so black that afternoon.

Although he went to the house several times again in the course of the next few days, he did not see Mrs. Southgate. She was always engaged with the correspondence which had resulted from her husband's death.

"She writes a very nice letter, if I give her a general idea of what ought to be said," Antonia had explained to Williams.

One afternoon about a month after Southgate's death, as Williams was leaving his office in Nassau Street, a card was brought to him. He did not know the name, and he sent word that he was just going home. If the gentleman could give him some idea—

Word came back that the gentleman was an old friend of Mrs. Southgate. Then Williams knew that he was holding in his hand the mate of the card that Doris Helen had pressed down upon her lap so tenderly that afternoon. The name was Dominic Hale.

Even Antonia could not have complained of lack of vitality in the young man who presently walked into Williams' private office. There was something vigorous about the way he was built, the way he moved, the way his thick brown hair grew, like a close dark cap on his head. He spoke at once.

"I wanted to see you, Mr. Williams, as a friend of Mrs. Southgate's. You are a friend, aren't you?"

"Yes," said Williams, speaking as a man; and then added as a lawyer, "Though I must confess I have seen her only once in my life."

"My goodness!" said Hale, with a shake of his head, "I never knew of such a thing! I can't find that anyone has seen her more than once or twice in the course of the last five years. Wasn't she allowed friends?"

"Perhaps she did not want any."

Hale gave what in a tiger would have been a growl, but which in a man was merely a sound expressing complete disagreement.

"A girl of twenty-five—" he said; and added without pause, "Mr. Williams, I want to marry Mrs. Southgate."

The exclamation "Good!" which rose to Williams' lips was suppressed in favor of "I see." Then he went on, "And does she want to marry you?"

"She says not."

"But does not convince you of her sincerity?"

"Well, she said not in just the same tone seven years ago, when we became engaged."

"Oh, you and she were engaged before her marriage?"

"Yes, we called it that. We had no possible prospect of ever getting married. Then just before I went abroad to study—"

"And may I ask what it was you went abroad to study, Mr. Hale?"

The young man looked at him a moment in surprise before he answered, "Painting. I'm Dominic Hale."

Williams shook his head.

"Ought I to know?"

Hale laughed.

"You perfectly well might," he said. "Doris broke our engagement before I went. We did not part in a very friendly spirit."

"I see. She had already decided—"

"Oh, no! This was months before she went to the Southgates. She thought it was wrong for us to be tangled up with each other so hopelessly. It made me furious. She was so firm and clear about— She has a will of iron, that girl."

This last statement interested Williams almost more than anything Hale had said, for he suddenly appreciated the fact that he himself had had the same impression of the widow.

"Miss Southgate finds her almost too pliable and docile," he said.

"Then," answered Hale, "Miss Southgate has never tried to make her do something she did not want to. Oh, she's not petty—Doris! She'll drift quietly along with the stream, until something which makes a difference to her comes along, and then—"

He wagged his head, compressing his lips in thought.

"I don't see exactly how I can help you in the matter—if she thinks she does not want to marry you, and she has an iron will."

"I don't want help; I want advice," said Hale. "I think she cares about me, but how much? If she really loves me, losing the fortune makes no difference. But if she doesn't—if she's just fond of me as an old friend— can I urge her to give up a million for the fun of being poor with me?"

"Does it occur to you," asked Williams—"I don't want to say anything painful, but we must face facts—that she might love you a great deal and yet hesitate to give up the income from a million?"

"Of course it has occurred to me," answered Hale, "and if I thought it was true I'd kidnap her."

"Well, of course, you can't do that," said the lawyer; but his tone seemed to admit it wouldn't be a bad thing to do.

He was surprised after his visitor had left to find how sincerely he hoped that Hale would succeed in marrying the little widow. He owned that he himself would not give up a million for any romance in the world; but then he was a middle-aged man who had lived his life, not a pretty young woman who had spent five years of her youth almost as an upper servant.

She ought, he thought, to be unafraid of the adventure of poverty; though he was obliged to confess that there was an element of adventure, too, in spending a large income; an adventure which would appeal more strongly to most people. Only, he thought, there wouldn't be much joy in riches if one remained forever under the iron rule of Antonia.

Soon after this, that first day of spring arrived which always comes to deceive New Yorkers sometime in March; that day when the air is warm and the sky a pale even blue, and the north side of the street is dry and clear and the south side still runs in slush and rivulets. Then almost everyone does something foolish—from wearing thin clothes and letting the furnace go out to mistakes of a more devastating sort.

Williams, who was prudent by nature, did nothing worse than, in returning from arguing a case in Jersey City, to take the ferry instead of the tube. As he stood watching the boat for which he was waiting bumping its way into its slip, his attention was attracted by two people seated on the upper deck, with their elbows hooked over the rail and their bent heads close together, evidently at that delightful stage of intimacy when it is possible to talk—or rather whisper—simultaneously without either one losing a single word of what the other is saying.

They showed no disposition to get off, no realization even that the boat had reached the shore, though the process of winding up the dock and letting down the drawbridges and opening the gates is not a quiet one. They were simply going to and fro on the river, for when the deck hand came to collect their fare it was obviously a repeated performance.

Williams had recognized Hale first, but the next second he had seen that the diminutive figure in black could be no other than Doris Helen. He did not disturb them, but from the window of the upper cabin he watched them—rather wistfully. Now and then they seemed to be saying something of the most serious importance, and, looking at each other in the middle of a sentence, they would forget to complete it. At other times they were evidently extremely frivolous, speaking with a manner common to those a little drunk and those deeply in love, a manner as if only they themselves could appreciate how deliciously ridiculous they were.

Williams was not much surprised the very next day to be called on the telephone by Miss Southgate, who wished to see him at once. She said she would come to his office, where they could talk without interruption.

She came. Her handsome alabaster mask was never allowed to express emotion, but she undulated her vast shoulders more than usual. A young man by the name of Hale—a painter—was coming everyday to the house, and that morning Doris had admitted that he wanted to marry her.

"And my brother hardly a month in his grave!" said Miss Southgate, with all the concentrated bitterness of Hamlet's first soliloquy.

She was so deeply outraged by the idea that Williams did not dare point out to her that she would profit by the marriage. There was something noble about her utter indifference to this aspect of it, but there was something bitter and egotistical in her anger against her sister-in-law for daring to suggest the control of her own destiny. Williams remembered having seen Antonia show the same ruthless, pitiless bitterness toward a servant who had left her voluntarily. She regarded it as an insult from an inferior. Yet in her emotion there was also the wish to protect her brother's memory.

"It will make my brother ridiculous—an old man's widow," she said. "It was bad enough when he married her, but he and I together managed to keep the marriage on a dignified plane. No one could have found anything to laugh at during his life; and now he is dead, after all his kindness and generosity to her, she shall not insult his memory."

"But has she any idea of doing it?" asked Williams. "There is a pretty heavy weight on the other side of the scale."

Miss Southgate clenched her hands.

"I don't know," she said, as if that were extraordinary enough. "I can't read her mind. She says not, and yet she sees him everyday."

Williams shook his head.

"She won't do it," he said, and fortunately Miss Southgate did not catch the note of regret in his voice.

He promised to come and dine alone with the two women that evening. He found the little widow more alive than before, more prone to smile and talk, but no less docile in her attitude toward Antonia. There was nothing of the rebel about her, no hint that she was preparing to defy the lightning. And Williams admitted, as he saw the violence of Antonia's determination that the marriage should not take place, that a great deal of courage would be required. As he walked away from the house that evening he said to himself that if he were Hale he would kidnap her and take his chances of happiness.

A day or so later, a jubilant though black-bordered note from Miss Southgate announced that the decision had been made.

"Doris has promised me that she will not marry this man, or any other, without my consent. She is to see him this afternoon at four. I should like you to be with me then, in case he makes a scene at his final dismissal."

Well, Williams said to himself, he was a lawyer; he had seen a good deal of life; he had always known that that was the way the thing would end. But how pitiful and how stupid! He thought of the ferryboat plying unnoticed from one bank of the Hudson to the other. Did Doris Helen suppose she would duplicate that afternoon for a million dollars?

He went punctually at four, and was ushered into the back drawing-room. The terrible room across the front of the house was already occupied by the parting lovers, where presumably the portrait of Alexander Southgate was dominating their farewells.

Antonia received him with a manner of calm triumph, unshadowed by the least doubt that her sister-in-law would keep her word. But after about an hour a silence fell upon her, and Williams became aware that she was listening with increasing eagerness for the sound of the opening of the front drawing-room door. At last she rose to her feet.

"This is unbearable," she said.

"An hour isn't so very long," he returned, "for two people who love each other to take an eternal good-by."

"It's over two hours," said Antonia. "And she had nothing to say to him but no."

A suspicion suddenly came to Williams that perhaps the other room was empty, that perhaps Hale had been driven to the alternative of carrying her off. He sprang to his feet.

"Just wait here," he said to Antonia.

The hallway between the two rooms was in shadow. As he stepped into it, the door of the front room opened and Doris and Hale came out of it together. They did not see Williams, for they both turned at once toward the staircase, Hale in order to descend it and Doris leaning on the balustrade, raising her shoulders and almost taking her feet off the ground. Their manner was not that of people who have parted forever.

"There isn't another woman in the world would make such a sacrifice for a fellow like me," Hale said. Williams could not see the smile she gave him, but it must have been potent. He took her in his arms, wrenched himself away, walked down about three steps, turned and walked up them again, kissed her a second time—a good satisfactory hug, and then exclaiming, "I can't bear to go," bounded down the stairs and was gone. The front door banged behind him, and Doris Helen lifted her hands from the balustrade. She hardly noticed Williams as he opened the door.

Antonia was still standing.

"Well, Doris," she said as the younger woman entered, and the tone of her voice was deep and bell-like.

Doris sat down on the edge of the sofa—she always sat on the edge of her chair so that her feet could touch the ground. Her hands, folded as usual in her lap, were perfectly quiet, yet something in the way her eyes darted from point to point made Williams feel that she was nervous.

"Well," he said briskly, "what did you decide?"

She looked at him wonderingly.

"I promised Antonia I would not marry without her consent. I shall keep my word, of course."

Her sister-in-law held out a hand to her, and with the other covered her eyes.

"Thank God!" she said.

Williams looked at the widow. Obviously she was deceiving either Hale or Antonia. That was no rejected lover who had just left the house.

He speculated how the drama was going to unfold. There was no special purpose in deceiving Antonia. If there was to be a marriage, she would necessarily know it.

Perhaps Doris Helen was one of those people who couldn't say disagreeable things, but could write them.

Miss Southgate removed her hand from her eyes.

"And now," she said, "that nightmare is over, let us go back to Pasadena and begin our work editing my brother's memoirs."

Williams was aware of a certain bitter satisfaction in the thought that such a life was about all the little creature deserved, but the little creature was calmly shaking her head.

"No," she was saying gently; "no, I'm not going back to Pasadena, Antonia. I'm going to Spain."

Her sister-in-law stared at her.

"To Spain? But I don't want to go to Spain, Doris, and you can hardly go alone."

"I'm not going alone," answered Doris. "Mr. Hale is going with me."

Thirty years of training at the bar barely saved Williams from laughing aloud; the solution was so simple and so complete. The recollection flashed through his mind of the daughter of a friend of his, who when discovered in the act of smoking a cigar explained that she had promised her mother never to smoke a cigarette. He took himself in hand. The thing was serious and must be stopped. Evidently the word "sacrifice" had applied not to the loss of an income of fifty thousand dollars but to the resignation of the less tangible asset—reputation. Miss Southgate was already rolling out a magnificent invective. Doris Helen did not attempt to interrupt her. She sat still, with her eyes raised with interested surprise to Antonia's angry face. Only once she spoke.

She said quietly, "No, not as my lover, Antonia—as my secretary."

"And what difference does it make—what you call it?"

"Antonia!" Mrs. Southgate's tone protested. "It makes a great deal of difference what it is."

Her sister-in-law felt the reproach.

"I mean, no one will believe it, no one will care—the scandal will be the same."

Doris made gesture with her thin hands as if one couldn't go changing all one's plans for every shred of gossip that drifted across the horizon.

"One only cares what one's friends say," she explained, "and I haven't any friends—except you, Antonia."

"Are you utterly indifferent to the name of an honorable man who was your husband?"

"While my husband lived I tried to do my duty to him," said Doris firmly. "I gave my whole life to it, and my reward is that he tries to reach out of the grave and prevent my having the normal freedom that any woman of my age ought to have."

Williams had only to look into her set little face to see that it was hopeless to argue with her, but he had hopes of Hale. He had formed a favorable opinion of the young man and simply did not believe he was a party to any such plan.

"I should like to have a talk with Hale," he said.

"He's gone out of town," answered Doris. "He won't be back until a day or two before we sail."

Antonia gave a sound between a bleat and a whinny.

"You're sailing on the same steamer?"

"Of course—with my secretary."

She left the room.

In the course of the next few minutes Williams was surprised to discover the words included in the vocabulary of so majestic a woman as Antonia. There was nothing she did not call her sister-in-law, although she ended each sentence with an assertion that she wouldn't really do it.

"I wouldn't count on that," said Williams. "Most people are restrained by the opinion of their social group; but, as Mrs. Southgate says, she doesn't seem to have any group."

"Do you forget there is such a thing as a moral sense?" asked Antonia.

"If you had listened attentively," he replied, "you would have gathered as I did that there is nothing contrary to morals in this plan of your sister-in-law's—a lack of convention, yes."

"We will not allow it," said Antonia.

It was Williams' duty to point out that persuasion was the only method open to them. His sympathies were with the lovers, but he felt it his duty to mention to Miss Southgate his conviction that the best way to stop the whole thing was to send for Dominic Hale.

"This is not Hale's plan," he said. "I am sure he would not stand for it. If you send for him and have a talk you will find that he believes they are going to be married before they sail."

But Miss Southgate was too angry to listen to him. She tossed the suggestion aside with the utmost contempt.

"How can you be so innocent?" she exclaimed. "The whole plan is his. Doris would never have the imagination to think of such a thing. She has simply fallen into the hands of a designing man. She has no will of her own. You are utterly mistaken."

Well, perhaps he was; but he wanted to find Hale and have a talk with him; but as he could find no trace of the young man, he was obliged to content himself with an interview with Doris. He wanted to point out to her that she was ruining Hale irretrievably. It was the sort of thing a man could never live down. It would be said that he preferred to live on the dead husband's money rather than to make the widow his wife. He put it as badly as he could, but Doris was unshaken. She nodded her head.

"Yes, I know," she said. "No one will understand. He sacrifices his reputation too—not anymore than I do, Mr. Williams, though perhaps not any less. We must learn to live without the world, but we can—we shall have each other."

Williams thumped his hand on his knee.

"I can't believe it of him," he said. "Such a disgusting rôle! So unmanly!"

Doris smiled at him sadly.

"Does it seem unmanly to you?" she said meditatively. "It seems to me it wouldn't be manly to say no to a woman who loves him and has been as unhappy as I have been."

Yes, Williams could see that point of view too. Hale might say to himself that a girl who had lived those years of self-abnegation had a right to his love and Southgate's money, if she wanted them both; that it wasn't his part to take a noble stand for which she must pay. There was a certain nobility in not caring what the world said of him.

And yet—

He tried one last argument.

"Well, then for yourself; can't you see that it's contemptible to cling so to a fortune? What's poverty, after all? You're young. Marry the young man."

She stared at him.

"But, Mr. Williams," she said, "that's exactly what I promised Antonia I wouldn't do."

"Break your promise."

She looked really shocked.

"What a funny thing for you to say—a lawyer!" She shook her head. "I never broke my word in all my life. Besides, Antonia says that Alexander particularly disliked the idea of my remarriage."

Williams thought this was too trifling.

"You can hardly suppose," he said stiffly, "that you will be fulfilling the wishes of your husband by going to Spain with a man to whom you are not married."

She raised her shoulders as if beset by inconsistencies.

"What can I do?"

"You can give up the whole thing."

"Give up Dominic? No! I gave him up once because I thought it was better for him. I don't think I'd do it again, even for that—certainly not for anything else. I love him, Mr. Williams, and I'm of rather a persistent sort of nature."

Williams reported his failure to Antonia. He began to feel sorry for Antonia. Her age, her previous power and, above all, her mere bulk made it seem somehow humiliating that she could make no impression on this calm, steely chit of a girl. He was struck, too, by the depth and sincerity of her emotion.

"Don't care so much, my dear Miss Southgate," he said. "You've done your best to protect your brother's memory. Wash your hands of it all and go back to California. Forget there ever was such a person."

And then he saw what perhaps he had been stupid not to see before, that under all Miss Southgate's anger and family pride was a more creditable feeling—a love of Doris Helen, an almost maternal desire to protect her. As soon as Williams understood this—and he did not understand for some weeks—he advised compromise.

"Offer her half the income and let her marry the fellow."

Antonia's eyes flashed.

"Let myself be blackmailed?" she said. "You admit they are trying to blackmail me?"

"I admit they are in the stronger position," said Williams, as if in the experience of a lawyer it was pretty much the same thing.

"I shall not yield—for her own sake," answered Antonia.

In spite of the bitter issue between them the two women continued to live in the same house, and to discuss with interest and sometimes with affection all those endless daily details which two people who live in the same house must discuss. It was the preparations for the trip that finally drove Antonia to the wall: Doris' passport, her letter of credit from Southgate's bank, and the trunks all marked with the name of Southgate—"in red, with a bright-red band," Antonia explained to Williams, "so that no one can fail to notice them."

The final item was a dozen black-bordered pocket handkerchiefs. Williams, coming in late one afternoon, at the time when the shops are making their last delivery, found Antonia sobbing on the sofa and the little widow erect and pale, with the small, flat, square box open between them.

He looked questioningly at Doris, and she answered, pointing to the handkerchiefs, "It seems as if she did not want me to wear mourning. But I can hardly go into colors when Alexander has been dead such a short time."

Antonia sobbed out without raising her head, "Can she go careering about Europe in widow's mourning with that dreadful young man in bright colours?"

"Dominic's clothes are not bright," said Doris gently.

"They're not black like yours," returned Antonia.

The widow looked up at Williams.

"I don't think it's necessary for Dominic to wear black for my husband," she said, as one open to reason. "One puts one's footman in black, but not one's secretary."

At that terrible word "secretary" Antonia gave way.

"I can't let her do it!" she wailed. "In crape and he in colors—at hotels! Oh, Doris, it's horrible—what you're doing, but I must save you from utter ruin! I will make proper legal arrangements to give you half the income from the estate, and you can marry this—this person."

She covered her large statuesque face with her large white hands. Doris patted the heaving shoulder, but she did not leap at the offer. For an instant Williams thought she was going to bargain. She was, but not for money.

"Antonia, it's very kind of you," she said; "but I don't see how I could take your money—money which at least legally would have become yours—to do something that you hated."

"You can't expect me to approve of your marriage."

"If you don't, I won't do it," said Doris. "I'll just go—the way I said."

And on this she obstinately took her stand. Nor would she be content with Antonia's cry that she disapproved less of marriage than of this other horrible immoral plan.

"There was nothing immoral in my plan," answered Doris proudly, "and I cannot let you say so."

She insisted on being approved, and at length Antonia approved of her—or said she did. And so the papers were drawn up and signed, and the arrangements for the wedding went forward, and at last Hale returned.

Williams had been waiting eagerly for this. He was more curious than he had ever been in his life. His whole estimate of his own judgment of men was at stake. Did Hale know, or didn't he? Five minutes alone with the young artist would tell him, but those five minutes were hard to get; Doris Helen was always there. Even when Williams made an appointment with Hale at his office, the young widow was with him.

They were married early one morning, and their vessel was to sail at noon. Then at last, while Doris was changing her clothes, Hale was left alone in the front drawing-room with Antonia and the lawyer. Antonia, who still clung to her belief that her sister-in-law was an innocent instrument in the hands of a wicked man, would not speak to Hale, but sat erect, with her eyes fixed on her brother's portrait. It was Hale who opened the conversation.

"Miss Southgate," he said, with his engaging energy, "I can understand you don't like me much for taking Doris away, but I do hope you'll let me tell you how nobly I think you have behaved."

Antonia stared at him as if in her emptied safe she had discovered a bread-and-butter letter from the burglar. Then without an articulated word she rose and swept out of the room. Hale sighed.

"I do wish she didn't hate me so," he said. "Doris tells me she says she approves of our marriage, but she doesn't behave as if she did."

"At least," said Williams, "she made it possible."

Hale took him up quickly.

"Not a bit of it. It was settled quite irrespective of her—that day when you saw me kiss Doris in the hall. It was all arranged then; only, of course, we thought we were going to be hard up. I shall never forget that, Mr. Williams—that Doris was willing to give up that enormous income for me."

"Was she?" said Williams. And as Hale nodded to himself he went on, "Why did you go away like that for a month?"

"Doris wanted me to," he answered. "She thought it was only fair to Miss Southgate. I felt perfectly safe. I had her promise, and she thought she might bring Miss Southgate round to approving of the marriage. I never thought she'd succeed; but, you see, she did. She's a very remarkable woman, is Doris."

"She is, indeed," said Williams cordially.

Presently she came downstairs—the very remarkable woman—hand in hand with Antonia, and she and Hale drove away to the steamer.

Williams found himself holding Antonia's large, heavy, white hand.

"I think you've been wonderful, Miss Southgate," he said.

She wiped her eyes.

"I did not want to make it impossible for her to come back," she said, "when she finds that man out."

The lawyer did not answer, for it was his opinion that if there was to be any finding out it would be done by Hale.

Whose Petard Was It?

Aunt Georgy Hadley was rather unpopular with her own generation because she did not think the younger one so terrible. "I can't see," she insisted, "that they are so different from what we were." For an unmarried lady of forty to admit that she had ever had anything in common with the young people of the present day shocked her contemporaries.

Aunt Georgy was a pale, plain, brilliant-eyed woman, who liked to talk, to listen to other people talk, and to read. She simply hated to do anything else. As a girl she had always said that the dream of her life was to be bedridden; and so when, after she had ceased to be young, she had broken her hip so badly as to make walking difficult many people regarded it as a judgment from heaven. Georgy herself said it was a triumph of mind over matter; she was now freed from all active obligations, while it became the duty of her friends and relations to come and sit beside her sofa and tell her the news, of which, since she lived in a small town, there was always a great deal.

Her two sisters, married and mothers both, differed with her most violently about the younger generation. Her sister Fanny, who had produced three robust, handsome members of the gang under discussion, asked passionately, "Did we carry flasks to parties?"

"How silly it would have been if we had, when it was always there waiting for us," answered Georgy.

Her sister Evelyn, who had produced one perfect flower—little Evie—demanded, "Did we motor thirty miles at midnight to dance in disreputable road houses?"

"No," said Georgina, "because in our day we did not have motors; but we did pretty well with the environment at our disposal. I remember that Evelyn was once becalmed on the Sound all night in a catboat with a young man, and Fanny was caught just stepping off to a masked ball in the Garden, only—"

"I was not," said Fanny, as one who slams the door in the face of an unwelcome guest.

"Imagine Georgy's mind being just a sink for all those old scandals!" said Evelyn pleasantly, but without taking up the question of the truth or falsity of the facts stated.

Although Georgy was the youngest of the three Hadley sisters she, being unmarried, had inherited the red-brick house in Maple Street.

It had a small grass plot in front—at least, it would have been a grass plot if the roots of the two maple trees which stood in it had not long ago come through the soil. There was, however, a nice old-fashioned garden at the back of the house; and the sitting room looked out on this. Here Aunt Georgy's sofa stood, beside the fire in winter and beside the window in summer. The room was rather crowded with books and light blue satin furniture, and steel engravings of Raphael Madonnas and the Death of Saint Jerome; and over the mantelpiece hung a portrait by Sully of Aunt Georgy's grandmother, looking, everyone said, exactly as little Evie looked today.

It was to the circle round the blue satin sofa that people came, bearing news—from nieces and nephews fresh from some new atrocity, to the mayor of the town, worried over the gift of a too costly museum. Jefferson was the sort of town that bred news. In the first place, it was old—Washington had stopped there on his way to or from Philadelphia once—so it had magnificent old-fashioned ideals and traditions to be violated, as they constantly were. In the second place, it was near New York; most of the population commuted daily, thus keeping in close touch with all the more dangerous features of metropolitan life. And last, everyone had known everyone else since the cradle, and most of them were related to one another.

There was never any dearth of news, and everyone came to recount, not to consult. Aunt Georgy did not like to be consulted. One presented life to her as a narrative, not as a problem. There was no use in asking her for advice, because she simply would not give it.

"No," she would say, holding up a thin, rather bony hand, "I can't advise you. I lose all the wonderful surge and excitement of your story if I know I shall have to do something useful about it at the end. It's like reading a book for review—quite destroys my pleasure, my sense of drama."

That was exactly what she conveyed to those who talked to her—a sense of the drama, not of her life but of their own. The smallest incident—the sort that most of one's friends don't even hear when it is told to them—became so significant, so amusing when recounted to Aunt Georgy that you went on and on—and told her things.

Even her sisters, shocked as they constantly were by something they described as "Georgy's disloyalty to the way we were all brought up," told her everything. Step by step, the progress, or the decadence, by which the customs of one generation change into the customs of the next one was fought out by the three ladies, *née* Hadley, at the side of that blue satin sofa.

It began with cigarettes for girls and the new dances for both sexes. At that remote epoch none of the nieces and nephews were old enough either to smoke or dance; so, although the line of the battle had been the same—Fanny and Evelyn anti and Georgy pro—the battle itself had not been so bitter and personal as it afterward became.

The first time that Fanny's life was permanently blighted was when Norma, her eldest child, was called out and publicly rebuked in dancing school for shimmying. She wept—Fanny of course, not Norma, who didn't mind at all—and said that she could never hold up her head again. But she must have lifted it, for it was bowed every few months for many years subsequently. Aunt Georgy at once sent for her niece and insisted on having a private performance of the offensive dance, over which she laughed heartily. It looked to her, she said, so much like the old horse trying to shake off a horsefly.

The next time that the social fabric in Jefferson tottered and Fanny's head was again bowed was at the discovery that the younger set was not wearing corsets. Fanny tiptoed over and shut the sitting-room door before she breathed this bad news into her sister's ear.

"None of them," she said.

"But you wouldn't want the boys to, would you?" answered Georgy.

Fanny explained that she meant the girls didn't.

"Mercy!" exclaimed her sister. "We were all scolded because we did. Elderly gentlemen used to write embarrassing articles about how we were sacrificing the health of the next generation to our vanity, and how the Venus de Milo was the ideal feminine figure; and now these girls are just as much scolded—"

"The worst of it is," said Fanny, rolling her eyes and not listening, "that they take them off and leave them in the dressing room. They say that at the Brownes' the other evening there was a pile that high."

Still, in spite of her disapproval, Fanny's head was not so permanently bowed this time, because every mother in Jefferson was in the same situation. But craps struck Fanny a shrewder blow, because her child, Norma, was a conspicuous offender here, whereas little Evie, her sister's child, didn't care for craps. She said it wasn't amusing.

In order to decide the point Aunt Georgy asked Norma to teach her the game, and they were thus engaged when Mr. Gordon, the hollow-cheeked young clergyman, came to pay his first parochial visit. He said he wasn't at all shocked, and turned to Evie, who was sitting demurely behind the tea table eager to give him a cup of Aunt Georgy's excellent tea.

There was something a little mid-Victorian about Evie, and the only blot on Aunt Georgy's perfect liberalism was that in her heart she preferred her to the more modern nieces. Evie parted her thick light-brown hair in the middle and had a little pointed chin, like a picture in an old annual or a flattered likeness of Queen Victoria as a girl. She was small and decidedly pretty, though not a beauty like her large, rollicking, black-haired cousin Norma.

Norma's love affairs—if they were love affairs, and whether they were or not was a topic often discussed about the blue satin sofa—were carried on with the utmost candor. Suddenly one day it would become evident that Norma was dancing, golfing, motoring with a new young man. Everybody would report to Aunt Gregory the number of hours a day that he and Norma spent together, and Aunt Gregory would say to Norma, "Are you in love with him, Norma?" and Norma would answer "Yes" or "No" or "I'm trying to find out."

"There's no mystery about this generation," Fanny would say.

"Why should there be?" Norma would say, and would stamp out again, and would be heard hailing the young man of the minute, "We're considered minus on romance, Bill"; and ten of them would get into a car intended for four and drive away, looking like a basketful of puppies.

But about little Evie's love affairs there was some mystery. Aunt Georgy did not know that Evie had ever spoken to the mayor—a middle-aged banker of great wealth—and yet one day when he came to tell Miss Hadley about the museum he told her instead about how Evie had refused to marry him, and how unhappy he was. The nice young clergyman, too, who preached so interestingly and pleased the parish in every detail, was thinking of getting himself transferred to a city in California because the sight of an attentive but unattainable Evie in the front pew every Sunday almost broke his heart.

Aunt Georgy exonerated Evie from blame as far as the mayor was concerned, but she wasn't so sure about the Reverend Mr. Gordon.

"Evie," she said, "did you try to enmesh that nice-looking man of God?"

Evie shook her head.

"I don't get anywhere if I try, Aunt Georgy," she answered. "It has to come of itself or not at all. If Norma sees a man she fancies she swims out after him like a Newfoundland dog. But I have to sit on the shore until the tide washes something up at my feet. I don't always like what it washes up either."

The simile amused Aunt Georgy, but the more she reflected the more she doubted its accuracy. Those tides that washed things up—Evie had some mysterious control of them, whether she knew it or not. Evie's method and Norma's differed enormously in technic, but wasn't the elemental aggression about the same?

Life in Jefferson was never more interesting to Aunt Georgy than when psychoanalysis swept over them. Of course, they had all known about it, and read Freud, or articles about Freud; but the whole subject was revived and made personal by the arrival of Lisburn. Lisburn was not a doctor of medicine but of philosophy. He was an assistant professor of psychology in a New York college. He had written his dissertation on The Unconscious as Portrayed in Poetic Images. With an astonishing erudition he brought all poetry from Homer to Edna St. Vincent Millay into line with the new psychology. Besides this, he was an exceedingly handsome young man—tall, dark, decided, and a trifle offhand and contemptuous in his manner. What girl could ask more? Norma did not ask a bit more. The moment she saw him she—in Evie's language—swam out after him. She met him at dinner one evening, and the next day her conversation was all about dreams and fixations and inhibitions. Mothers began to assemble rapidly about the blue satin sofa. Craps had been vulgar, the shimmy immoral, but this was the worst of all.

"Georgy," said Fanny solemnly, "they go and sit on that young man's piazza, and they talk about things—things which you and I did not know existed, and if we did know they existed we did not know words for them; and if we did know words for them we did not take the slightest interest in them."

"Then there can't be any harm in them," said Georgy, "because I'm sure when we were girls we took an interest in everything there was any harm in. But it sounds to me just like a new way of holding hands—like palmistry in our day. You remember when you took up palmistry, Evelyn. It made me so jealous to see you holding my young men's hands!"

"It's not at all the same thing," answered Evelyn. "There was nothing in palmistry that wasn't perfectly nice."

"Oh, yes, there was," said Georgy. "There was that line, you know, round the base of the two middle fingers. We all felt a little shocked if we had it and a little disappointed if we hadn't."

But her sisters were too much worried to be amused. Their children, they said, were talking about things that could not be named. Fanny did name them, however, and was grimly glad to see that even Georgy, the liberal, reeled under the blow.

She recovered enough to say, "Well, after all, is it so different? We called people Puritans instead of saying that they had inhibitions. We didn't say a boy had a fixation on the mother, but we called him mother's little carpet knight. And as for dreams, Fanny, when a young man told me he had a dream about me I did not need a doctor of philosophy to tell me what that meant."

Even Fanny was obliged to confess that her younger son Robert had been cured of his incipient stammer after a few interviews with Lisburn. And the young Carters, who, after three months of marriage, were confiding to everyone their longing for divorce, had been reconciled. There was a dream in this—about a large white gardenia—and there was an incident connected with it—a girl in a florist's shop—

About this time the mayor, still worrying over the upkeep of the museum, wanted some sort of entertainment given in order to raise money. It was suggested that a lecture on psychoanalysis by Lisburn would be popular. Norma was delegated to go and ask him—make him, was the way the committee put it. Needless to say, she returned triumphant.

Aunt Georgy was among the first to arrive at the town hall on the evening the lecture took place. She had become curious about the young man and wanted a front seat. She limped up the aisle, leaning on her grandfather's heavy ivory-headed cane, with little Evie beside her. Norma was busy taking—one might almost say snatching—tickets at the door. It is a peculiar feature of modern life that so much time is spent first in getting lecturers to consent to lecture and then in drumming up an audience to hear them. But this time the audience was not difficult to get. They came in crowds.

The mayor opened the meeting. He was not a ready speaker, and the sight of Evie, sitting so attentive in the front row, embarrassed him hideously. He said a few panting words about the needs of the museum and turned the meeting over to the Reverend Mr. Gordon, who was going to introduce the speaker—who was going, in fact, to do a little bit more than that.

He advanced to the edge of the platform, looked down at Evie and smiled—after all, he wasn't in the pulpit—folded his hands as if lawn frills ought to have been dripping from them, and began:

"It is my great pleasure and privilege to introduce the speaker of the evening, although I myself am not at all in sympathy with the subject about which—which—about which he—"

Aunt Georgy had a second of agony. Could he avoid using the verb "to speak"? It seemed impossible; but she underrated his mental agility.

"—about which he is to make his interesting and instructive address." Mr. Gordon pulled down his waistcoat with a slight gesture of triumph. "The church," he continued, "has never been in very cordial sympathy with what I may be permitted, perhaps, to call these lay miracle workers."

Here he threw a smile over his shoulder to Lisburn—a smile intended to be friendly and reassuring; but as it had in it something acid and scornful, it only served to make his words more hostile. "The church endures," he went on, "and watches in each generation the rise and fall of a new science, a new philosophy, a new panacea, a new popular fad like this one."

Having done what he could to discredit the lecture, he gave the lecturer himself a flattering sentence: "A professor in one of our great universities, a new resident in this community, and my very good friend, Mr. Kenneth Lisburn."

The Reverend Mr. Gordon had been standing between Aunt Georgy and the speaker, so that she did not really get a good look at him until he stood up.

Then she said "Mercy!" in a hissing whisper in Evie's ear.

"Mercy what?" asked little Evie, rather coldly.

"So good-looking!" murmured Aunt Georgy.

Evie moved her shoulders about.

"Roughhewn," she whispered back.

Perhaps his features were a trifle rugged; but Aunt Georgy admired his hair—black as a crow under the bright though sometimes intermittent light of the Jefferson Light and Power Company. His eyes—black also—gleamed from deep sockets—"Like a rat's in a cave," Evie said. Lecturing was evidently nothing of an adventure to him. It did not embarrass him as it had embarrassed the mayor; it did not stimulate him to an eloquence too suave and fluent as it did Mr. Gordon. It created not the least change in his personality. He stood on the platform as he swung in his chair in his college room, ready to say what he had to say as simply and as clearly as he could.

He wasn't so sure, he began, that his subject was popular. He found most people enjoyed the exploration of other people's unconscious, not of their own. In fact you could generally tell whether you were right in a diagnosis or not by the passion with which the victim contradicted you and the rapidity with which he invented explanations other than the true one. He was not, however, going to talk about psychoanalysis in general—rather too large a subject—with its relations to art and medicine. He was going to talk about the simple, commonplace actions of everyday life as clews to the unconscious—first, the so-called trivial ones. Nothing is really trivial. The tunes we whistle, the songs we sing, nine times out of ten have a wish-thought behind them. An amusing case of this had come to him the other day. A man had consulted him because he was being driven mad by a tune that ran in his head night and day. It was the Funeral March of a Marionette. Well, when it turned out that he was unhappily married and that his wife's name was Dolly it wasn't very hard to see whose funeral it was that he was mentally staging.

Aunt Georgy was perfectly delighted. She saw that psychoanalysis was going to make life in Jefferson infinitely more entertaining. The sphere of gossip was so remarkably extended. In old times one could only talk about what had been done, said or written; but now what was dreamed, what was desired, and, best of all, what was entirely omitted could be made as interesting as a crime. She wriggled down into her chair with pleasure as he went on to take up the question of the types that people fell in love with. Of course, we have all noticed how people tend to fall in love again and again with the same type. The spoiled weak son is forever looking for a mother type to take care of him; the girl brought up under the domination of the father idea is attracted by nothing but protective older types of men.

Lisburn went on to describe such cases in greater detail so accurately that all through the audience married couples were nodding to one another and themselves. He described also a variant of this: How some people always abused the type that attracted them most; the virile man who is forever making fun of feminine weaknesses, the womanly woman always taking on about man's wickedness; they're afraid of the black magic they attack; they are trying to exorcise the spell—

As soon as the lecture was over, and while eager members of the audience were crowding to the platform to discuss with the speaker the cases of mysterious friends who had dreamed this and forgotten that, Aunt Georgy beckoned to Norma.

"Do," she said, "go and disentangle that interesting young man from his votaries, or whatever they are, and bring him down to be introduced to me."

"It was interesting, wasn't it?" said Norma, with an effort at detachment.

"I can never be sufficiently grateful," answered Aunt Georgy. "It is so satisfactory the way he lays the strictly virtuous open to attack—the sort of people we've wanted to catch in a scandal and never been able to."

Norma nodded.

"Oh, yes," she said, "Ken thinks people like that have a very foul unconscious."

Aunt Georgy gave a slight snort and asked Norma if she remembered the Bab Ballad about:

> *For only scoundrels dare to do*
> *What we consider just and true;*
> *And only good men do in fact,*
> *What we should think a dirty act.*

But Norma did not enjoy a humorous approach to a subject which she had only recently made her own. She withdrew; frowning slightly, and saying that she would try to get a word with him.

"Oh, don't let's wait," said Evie after a few minutes, during which the crowd on the platform increased.

And so Aunt Georgy was led home by the mayor and her small niece without getting a word with the speaker. But she was a determined woman; and though Lisburn was a busy man, between lecturing at his college in the daytime and conferences with mentally maladjusted in Jefferson in the evening and giving a good many spare hours to Norma, a free afternoon was finally found and Norma brought him to tea. Little Evie, who happened to be spending a week or two with her aunt, immediately announced her intention of being out.

"I don't like that man," she said.

Aunt Georgy, always eager for information, inquired why she didn't.

Evie thought a long time, and then said, "Because he invades one's private life."

"Does Norma feel that way?"

Little Evie laughed. "Norma hasn't got a private life," she answered.

At five o'clock, when Aunt Georgy was settled on her blue sofa, with her cane beside her and her tea set in front, Evie stole quietly out of the back door into the garden as Norma and the seer entered at the front.

"Well, here he is, Aunt Georgy," Norma shouted from the threshold, as if she had done a good deal for an elderly relation.

He came in and shook hands, unruffled by Norma's introduction.

"Where's Evie?" Norma went on in a tone rather like a sheriff's officer.

"She was so sorry—she had an engagement," said Aunt Georgy, quite as if it were true.

Norma gave a short shout.

"Oh, Ken knows she doesn't like him," she said; "and as a matter of fact, he isn't very keen about her."

Lisburn looked at Miss Hadley, not exactly embarrassed, but as if to say that when you told a thing to Norma you told it to the whole world. Aunt Georgy was interested in his not denying the accusation. She had never before happened to meet a man who actually did not like Evie.

"You don't admire my little niece?" she said, in her tone of seeking information merely.

"No," shouted Norma from the hearthrug. "He thinks she's too colorless, too much tied up with inhibitions to be interesting."

"Of course, I see your niece's great charm," he answered; "but, as I said the other night, we all have our own type—the type that particularly appeals—and I am attracted to a more active, aggressive type."

"That's why he likes me," said Norma, with her mouth not empty of chocolate cake—"because I lead a great, free, ramping life. Isn't that true, Ken?"

"I'm sure it's true you lead a great, free, ramping life, Norma," said her aunt.

"Yes, and that's why I'm so healthy," answered Norma, and she danced a little on her flat-heeled shoes. They were large shoes, but then, she was a large woman.

Aunt Georgy was surprised to find herself a partisan. It annoyed her to hear her favorite niece dismissed as attractive to other men but not to this reader of human hearts.

She said almost pettishly, "Evie is healthy, too—one of the healthiest people I ever knew."

"I bet she has dreams," said Norma.

"I doubt it."

"Everybody dreams, Aunt Georgy," said Norma, really astonished at her aunt's ignorance of the facts of life. "If you don't remember your dreams, that only shows that they are so awful that you don't allow them to come up into your conscious at all."

Aunt Georgy was opening her mouth to contradict, but found that Lisburn was speaking.

"That's the theory, Miss Hadley," he said, less positively than Norma; "that everyone dreams, and that our dreams represent our unfulfilled and unacknowledged desires. A type like—like Miss—"

"Like Evie," said Norma, a foe to last names.

"That type," Lisburn went on—"so restrained, so inhibited, so what is called well-bred, is particularly likely to have dreams and almost certain to be unwilling to admit having them."

He stopped as a slight sound at the door that led to the garden made them all turn. Little Evie was standing there—had evidently been standing there for sometime. She had on a sky-blue dress, a large childish hat and her arms were full of cherry blossoms. She looked more than usually like a fashion plate of the '40's.

Norma immediately shouted at her, "You do dream, don't you, Evie? Be honest for once in your life."

Aunt Georgy, who was herself an honest person, was aware of an utterly unsuppressed wish that, whatever the facts were, Evie would say that she had never had a dream in her life. Instead the girl, with her blue eyes fixed on Lisburn, was nodding slowly.

"I've begun to dream lately," she said in a low tone.

Norma was delighted.

"I knew it," she said. "I'd have bet on it. It's extraordinary how one gets to know these things. Tell us what your dream is about, Evie."

"Mercy!" exclaimed Aunt Georgy. "Isn't a person allowed more than one dream nowadays?"

Evie sank down on the sofa at her aunt's feet.

"Mine's always the same," she murmured.

"Ah," said Lisburn, "a recurrent dream." He looked at her with interest. "Does it trouble you?"

Evie made a cooing sound like a dove, in doubt. Norma began to tease her to tell. Aunt Georgy thought she was tiresome, nagging and bothering like that. She told her to let Evie alone. Norma shrugged her shoulders.

"It's so characteristic of that introverted type," she said, "not to be willing to be frank enough to be cured."

"Can one be cured?" asked Evie, and she raised her eyes to Lisburn.

He was a busy man, and he had stood up to go.

"I might—if it troubles you—be able to help you."

"Even," said Evie, "though you are not interested in my type?"

"Oh," cried Norma, "isn't that like you, Evie! You overheard the whole thing, and instead of having it out then and there, as I should have, you wait and give him a poisoned dig in the ribs when he's trying to be nice to you."

Evie repeated in exactly the same tone: "Even though you are not interested in my type?"

"I'm always interested in a case," he answered.

They exchanged unfriendly looks. Then he came to the sofa to say good-by to Aunt Georgy. She was rummaging for a pencil among the litter of papers and books beside her. She wanted to write down the name of his book, but he insisted very civilly on sending it to her.

When he and Norma had gone Aunt Georgy turned to Evie.

"I'm glad," she said, "that you did not tell them what your dream was about. They would have been sure to make something horrid out of it."

"I couldn't tell them."

"You mean it is horrid?"

"I hadn't made it up yet," answered Evie. "Dear Aunt Georgy, I never, never dream. I'm always asleep before I get the covers well tucked in at the nape of my neck, and I never wake up until someone comes in and opens the shutters. Norma was so determined that I should have a dream—perhaps she won't be so pleased. Mine is going to be a hard one to interpret. Interested in cases, is he? Well, mine is going to be an interesting one. Wait till we get his book."

The book was left at the door after dinner, and Aunt Georgy plunged at once into it. She habitually read as a famished animal eats, tearing the heart out of a book, utterly oblivious of the world until she had finished. At last she looked up.

"Really, Evie," she exclaimed, "I'm afraid you can't get a dream out of this. I'm not old-fashioned, but I must say—" She did not say what it was she must say.

Evie took the book calmly.

"Of course, I shall be perfectly innocent as to what my dream means, Aunt Georgy," she said. "Let's see. X, a young employe in a shoe factory, dreamed— My goodness, what an unpleasant man X must have been! Now this isn't bad— Or, no, that would involve mother. I don't want to drag poor mother into it. Something wonderful might be done with a tune—Old Black Joe, if only his name were Joe, which it isn't. . . And I shall begin to do a strange and apparently meaningless thing—to have a compulsion. I mean—like buttering my bread on both sides—"

"Don't you think it's a little dangerous?" said Aunt Georgy. "They interpret everything so oddly."

"Yes, it's dangerous; but everything is. If you do nothing, that's the worst of all." And Evie sank into the book.

A few days later, when Lisburn reached home in the late afternoon, he found a note waiting for him at his house. It was written in Evie's neat, fine hand, and said:

Dear Mr. Lisburn:

Do you remember offering to help me in case the dream— of which I think I spoke to you—began to give me trouble? I must say I hesitate to take up your time, as the whole thing seems so trivial (Lisburn gave a little shake of his head, an indication that such experiences were far from trivial) but it would be a relief to me to talk it over with you, and I shall stop at your house for a few minutes this evening on the chance that you may have a spare minute.

He laid the letter on the table and eyed it sideways as he lit his pipe. Then he went to the telephone and called up Norma. He said he was sorry, but that he wouldn't be able to come that evening for bridge. Norma, as she herself had observed, did not suffer from inhibitions. Her emotions found easy expression, and her emotion on this occasion was disappointment mingled with anger. She expressed it freely over the telephone. Lisburn hung up the receiver sharply. Self-expression was all very well, he thought; but there was such a thing as having no self-control. It was necessary for him to have a calm and receptive mind in order to be of any assistance to this child who was coming to consult him. He must make a mental picture of her personality and recall her gestures, her vocabulary.

Soon after eight he heard her step on the piazza and went to the door himself. She entered with that timid, conscious, apologetic manner which had become so familiar to him in his patients. It seemed as if she would have liked to make fun of herself for coming if only she had been less frightened at finding herself there. The hand she gave him shook. He drew forward a deep comfortable chair for her.

"Now tell me everything you can think of," he said; "your own way; I won't interrupt."

She drew an uncertain breath.

"Well, I didn't think anything about it—you know how casually I spoke the other day—but now I find it is beginning to affect my conduct. I find I cannot bring myself to get into an automobile. I have never driven a car myself, but I have always enjoyed driving with other people; but now— This dream of mine is about a car."

She described the dream at great length, though it was strangely lacking in incident. It was merely that she was driving a small car of her own—a very pretty white car with a good deal of blue about it. She was driving along a wide street, and suddenly the car began to skid, slowly at first and then faster and faster; and though her agony became extreme and she turned the steering wheel more and more, she could do nothing—the car made straight for the bushes, where some terrific but unseen and unknown object was lurking.

He made her go over the details of it two or three times. The shade of blue was about the same shade as the dress she was wearing, but he elicited very little more. She could not, she said, get any clew as to what was hidden in the bushes, except that it was something she was horribly afraid of.

"And yet," he said, "you go toward it?"

"Yes; but entirely against my will, Mr. Lisburn."

"You're sure you go against your will?"

Her voice was almost hysterical as she protested, "Yes—yes, indeed!"

"And yet you go?"

"No, Mr. Lisburn, the car goes."

"Don't you think you and the car are the same?"

She gave him a long wondering stare, and presently insisted that she must go. She promised, however, that she would do everything in her power to find out what was hidden in those sinister bushes. She was to keep a pencil and paper beside her bed and write down everything she could remember as soon as she waked up in the morning.

She hurried home to tell Aunt Georgy all that had occurred and was disappointed to find her aunt established at the bridge table with Norma and two of Norma's friends. It seemed that Mr. Lisburn had been expected as a fourth and they had been obliged to come to Aunt Georgy at the last minute to make up the table. Norma was still angry.

"They can't have it both ways—these psychoanalysts," Norma was saying. "It's always a Freudian forgetting—a wish-thought—when you forget an engagement with them, and something quite professional and unavoidable when they break an engagement with you."

"What Norma means, Evie," said Aunt Georgy, without raising her eyes from the interesting hand which had just been dealt her, "is that she suspects Mr. Lisburn of having had something more amusing to do."

Evie shook her head as if you couldn't be sure with men like that.

"Perhaps he had," she said.

Then Aunt Georgy knew the interview had gone well.

Three days later, not having heard anything more from her, he came to the house late in the afternoon. He was in his own car, and he suggested that perhaps he could help her to overcome her repugnance to motoring. At first she refused with every appearance of terror; but soon she admitted that with him she would feel perfectly safe, and so she yielded and got in.

She spoke little, and he could hear that she drew her breath in a tremulous and disturbing manner. At last, in a lonely road, her terror seemed to overmaster her, and she opened the door and would have sprung out while the car was going thirty-five miles an hour if Lisburn had not held her in.

As soon as he had brought the car to a standstill he took his arm away, while little Evie cowered in the seat beside him.

"You see," she said at last, "how it is with me? If you had not been there I should have jumped out and been killed. It's stronger than I am."

"I see," he answered gently. "Well, if it happens again I won't force you to stay in the car. You shall get out and walk home."

She thanked him warmly for his concession, but it did not happen again.

After this they had conferences every evening, as her stay at Jefferson was coming to an end, and she still did not seem to be able to see what was the emotional center of her dream.

The fact that Lisburn was trying to help little Evie soon began to be known, and the knowledge affected different people differently. Norma said that she should think Evie would be ashamed to take up so much of Mr. Lisburn's time, considering how contemptuous she had been about the whole science of psychoanalysis. The Reverend Mr. Gordon said that he had never been in any doubt that the human spirit needed the confessional, but that only a man in holy orders was fit to receive confession. The mayor was a little more violent. He said that it appeared to him that this fellow was practicing medicine without a license, and that if the law could not reach him it ought to be able to. He hoped it wasn't doing little Miss Evie any harm. Aunt Georgy tried to reassure him, and said Evie seemed in the best of health and spirits, at which the mayor, looking gloomier than ever, said he was much relieved. Aunt Georgy had just been telling this to Evie as she was about to start for her last conference. She was going away the next day.

"Have you decided what it is that is hidden in the bushes?" her aunt asked her.

Evie nodded.

"Yes," she said; "it's a black panther—a beautiful, lithe, vigorous, graceful, dangerous wild animal."

"Mercy!" exclaimed Aunt Georgy. "He'll think it's himself."

"Do you think he's a vain man, Aunt Georgy?"

"Everyone's as vain as that."

"Well, that isn't my fault," said Evie, and went on her way.

Aunt Georgy shook her head. Life was often like that, she thought—a woman despised a man for believing something that she had exercised all her ingenuity to make him believe.

Lisburn was on his feet when Evie entered, and as soon as he had seen her settled in the deep chair he began to pace up and down; like a panther, she thought, but did not say so; that would have been crude.

"Well," he said, fixing his black eyes on her, "you've found out what it is, haven't you?"

She nodded.

"You are clever," she answered. "I don't know what you'll make of it— it sounds so silly." She looked up at him, rubbing the back of one hand against the palm of the other. "It's—it's a panther; just a beautiful black panther; a splendid, lithe, graceful, dangerous wild animal." Even little Evie was susceptible at times to embarrassment, and at this moment she could not endure the piercing stare of those black eyes. She dropped her eyes modestly and murmured, "Oh, Mr. Lisburn, do you think you can help me?"

"I'm sure I can," he answered; "at least, I can if I may be perfectly candid."

Evie said that was all she asked—candor.

"In that case—" said he. He walked to the door and leaned against it as if the revelations he was about to make were such that she might try to escape before she heard him out. "In that case," he repeated, in that smooth, almost honeyed tone in which the psychoanalyst clothes even the most shocking statements, "let me say that you are the most phenomenal little liar, little Evie, that I have ever met—yes, among all the many I have known I gladly hand you the palm."

"Mr. Lisburn!" said Evie, but she was so much surprised and interested that she did not do justice to her protest.

"What makes me angry," he went on in his civil tone, "is that you should imagine you could get away with it. However much of an ass you may consider me, you ought to have known that there was enough in the science of psychoanalysis to show from the very beginning that you were a fraud."

"Not from the beginning!" said Evie.

"From the first evening. You haven't one single symptom of a person with a neurosis—not one. If you knew a little bit more—pooh, if you knew anything at all about the subject—"

"I read your book," she answered, as if this put the blame on him.

"Not very intelligently, then, or you would have done a better fraud."

"You were willing to waste a lot of time on a fraud."

"It hasn't been wasted. And that brings me to my second point. I will now tell you what perhaps you don't know, and that is why you did it."

"I know perfectly well, thank you," replied Evie. "I did it because you were so poisonous about me that afternoon at Aunt Georgy's. I thought I'd like to show you—"

"That is a rationalization," he interrupted, waving it away with one hand. "You did it because you are strongly attracted to me."

"Attracted to you!" said Evie in a most offensive tone.

"I am the panther in the bushes."

Evie laughed contemptuously.

"I knew you'd think you were the panther," she said; "I simply knew it."

"Of course you did," he answered. "That's the very reason you dreamed it."

"But I didn't dream it," she returned triumphantly. "I thought you had grasped that. I didn't dream it. I never dream."

He was not triumphed over.

"Well," he said, "you made it up; that's the same thing—a daydream, a romance."

"I made it up particularly in order to deceive you," Evie explained.

"That's what you think," he answered; "but it isn't true. You made it up in order to let me know you were attracted to me, for I repeat that you are attracted to me."

Little Evie sprang up from the deep chair in which she had sat at ease during so many evening conferences.

"You may repeat it until you are black in the face," she said; "but I'm not, I'm not, I'm not!"

"Don't you see that the emotion with which you repudiate the idea proves that it's the truth?"

An inspiration came to her.

"Then why," she demanded—"the other afternoon when you explained so much why you didn't like me—why doesn't that prove that you are attracted to me?"

"Little Evie," he said, "it does. That's the truth. You are almost everything of which I disapprove in woman. I love you."

He approached and took her in his arms.

"I hate you," said Evie, in a tone too conversational to be impressive.

He behaved as if she had not spoken. She drew away from him, though not wholly out of the circle of his arms.

"I don't think you can have understood me," she remarked coldly. "I said I hated you."

"I feel more sure of you than if you had said you loved me."

"Then I'll say I love you."

"Yes, dear, I know you do."

She sighed.

"You're not a very consistent man, are you?" she said.

She spoke in a tone of remote philosophy, but she leaned her forehead against his chest.

When the story came out, as of course it was bound to do—for both Evie and Lisburn seemed to think they had been rather clever about the whole thing, and they told everybody—Fanny was deeply shocked. In fact, she owned that if she had been Evie's mother she would never have held up her head again.

"To think," she said, "of Evie, who has always seemed so dignified and well-bred and not of this generation at all—to think that she invented the whole thing in order to attract Mr. Lisburn's attention!"

"Fanny," said Aunt Georgy, "do you remember the first day you met your present husband? You twisted your ankle just so that he might have to carry you upstairs to your room. Well, my dear, you recovered entirely as soon as he had gone, and walked all over everywhere. A strange young man carried you in his arms, Fanny. If you ask me, I call the new technique more delicate and modest than the old."

The New Stoics

M r. Brougham stood waiting in the wings. Never before had he made a speech; never had he been upon a stage, except to sit safely with a delegation, in a row, behind the ice-water pitcher. He had a small dry patch in his throat which constant swallowing failed to improve, and the tips of his fingers kept getting cold and very distant. He was about to make a Liberty Loan speech, and he was suffering more than he had expected; but, as he kept murmuring to himself, *"Dulce et decorum est."*

At twenty-eight he had volunteered among the first in the Spanish War, and it had been no fault of his that he had never got any nearer the front than Chattanooga. At forty-eight he could still speak for his country—at least he hoped he could. How absurd to be nervous! This was no time to be thinking of one's own feelings. He took out his handkerchief and wiped the palms of his hands. "Well, Mr. Brougham," said the loud bold voice of the local chairman, "shall we go on?" What was one victim more or less to him in his insatiable campaign for speakers?

"By all means," answered Brougham in a tone which even in his own ears sounded like that of a total stranger.

His only conscious thought was grateful remembrance that his wife was kept at the canteen that evening, and couldn't be in the audience, which he found himself regarding as a hostile body waiting to devour him. He sat trying to relax the muscles of his face during the chairman's short address; and then the fatal sentence began: ". . . the great pleasure. . . introduce. . . so well known. . . Mr. Walter Brougham, who will say a few rousing words to you on this great subject."

What a silly adjective "rousing" was, Brougham thought as he came forward. He had no intention whatever of being rousing. He wondered if he had the intention of being anything except absolutely silent. He lifted the lid and looked into his mind as into an unexplored box. Was there anything in it? Why, yes; rather to his surprise he found there was.

"My friends," he began, "this is no time for oratory." Hearty, and to Brougham totally unexpected, applause greeted this sentiment. "This is a time for cool, steady, clear-eyed vision." That was a mistake; of course vision was clear-eyed. "This is a time to ask ourselves this

ALICE DUER MILLER

question: How is it that we hesitate to give our money, and yet stand ready—everyone of us—to give our lives and—harder still—our sons' lives?"

"Hear, hear!" cried a voice from the audience, fresh, young and familiar. Brougham looked down; yes, there they were—his own two boys, David, not eighteen, and Lawrence, hardly fifteen. Their blond, well-brushed heads towered above the rest of the row and were easily recognizable. He could see the expressions of their faces—cool, serene, friendly approval. They're too damned philosophical, he said to himself; and as he went on speaking, with all that was mortal in him concentrated on his words, in some entirely different part of his being a veil was suddenly lifted and he saw something that he had been trying not to see for months—namely, that he was dissatisfied with his elder son's attitude toward the war—it was cool; cool like his approval of the speech. Not that Mr. Brougham wanted his son to volunteer at his age—quite the contrary; he sincerely believed it was every man's duty to wait until he had reached the age designated by his country; but he did want the boy to want to volunteer. He wanted to be able to say at the club as other fathers were saying: "What gets into these young fellows? I've had to forbid my boy—" Perhaps if his self-vision had been perfect he would have admitted that he had sometimes said it.

And then it occurred to him that this was the moment to stir their hearts—to make one of those speeches which might not touch the audience but which would inflame the patriotism of youth. Forgetting his recent pledge he plunged into oratory—the inherited oratory of the Fourth of July, he snatched up any adjectives as long as they came in threes, called patriotism by name, and spoke of the flag as Old Glory. Hurried on by his own warmth he reached his climax too soon, ended his speech before the audience expected and began asking for subscriptions before anyone was ready.

There was an awkward silence. Then a young voice spoke up: "One one-hundred-dollar bond." Yes, it was David. Mr. Brougham's heart leaped with hope; had the boy been moved? Was this the first fruit of repentance? He looked down, hoping to meet the upward glance of a devotee, but David was whispering something to his younger brother which made the latter giggle foolishly.

The ball once set rolling went fast. Subscriptions poured in; it was a successful evening—almost as successful as the evening made famous by a great screen artist. Mr. Brougham was warmly congratulated by the local chairman.

"We shall call on you again, Brougham," he said gayly.

Mr. Brougham nodded, but his thought was: Is nothing enough for these fellows?

His two boys were waiting for him at the stage door. "You're good, sir, you're good!" they cried, patting him on the back.

"I never thought he'd let them have it so mild," said Lawrence.

Mr. Brougham did not mind being laughed at—at least he always said he didn't—but he couldn't bear to have patriotism in any form held up to ridicule. He thought to himself:

"They don't know what it costs a man of my age to go on a stage and make a speech. I don't enjoy making myself conspicuous."

"We'll stop and get your mother at the canteen," he said sternly.

"Oh, yes, this is mother's night for saving the country, isn't it?" said Lawrence.

"Did you know," said David to his brother, across his father's head, for they were both taller than he, "did you know that a gob tipped mother the other evening? So pleased with his coffee that he flicked her a dime for herself."

"Oh, you sailor-boys!" said Lawrence in a high falsetto.

This was really more than Mr. Brougham could bear in his exalted state. "I don't like that, boys," he said.

"No, father," answered David; "but you know we never tipped mother; in fact, it's always been quite the other way."

"I mean I don't like your tone of ridicule, of—of—of—" He couldn't think of the word he wanted, and felt conscious that David had it on the tip of his tongue but was too tactful to interrupt. "You boys don't seem to appreciate the sacrifice, the physical strain for a woman of your mother's age—standing all evening handing out sandwiches—not accustomed to hard work either."

Both boys looked gravely ahead of them, and Mr. Brougham had a sickening conviction they were both trying to think of something to say that would calm him.

The canteen was just closing, and the two boys made themselves useful in putting things away. "Just as if it were a school picnic," their father thought.

As soon as they were on their way home Mrs. Brougham asked about the speech. Had it gone well?

"Oh, father was great, mother," David answered. "He took it from them in wads, and presented Lawrence and me to his country with every bond."

"A lady behind us was awfully affected," said Lawrence. "She kept whispering that she understood the speaker had two lovely boys of his own."

"I could hardly keep Lawrence from telling her that she had not been misinformed."

Mr. Brougham sighed. This was not the tone of young men suddenly roused to a new vision of patriotism. He said aloud: "I was glad you felt financially able to take a bond yourself, David."

"Oh, yes," answered his son. "I sold my boat yesterday."

Mr. Brougham was not so Spartan a parent that he did not feel a pang to think of the boy without his favorite pastime on this perhaps his last summer.

"Quite right," he said. "This is no year for pleasure boats."

"You get a good price for boats this year," said David.

There it was again—that note Mr. Brougham didn't like. Even if David's motives had been financial and not patriotic he might have allowed Lawrence to see an example of self-sacrifice. Instead Lawrence was getting just like his brother.

Brougham was not a man who habitually eased his burdens by casting them on his wife, but that night when they went upstairs he took her into his confidence.

"Are you satisfied with David's attitude toward the war?" he began.

She was a silent, deep woman whose actions always astonished those who had no intuitive knowledge of the great general trends of her nature. She and David usually understood each other fairly well.

Now she shook her head. "No," she said.

"Good Lord!" said poor Mr. Brougham. "I don't want the boy shot in a trench. I think it's his duty to wait a year or two; but I can't see that he has any enthusiasm, any eagerness, hardly any interest. He seized the paper last evening, and I supposed that he wanted to read about the offensive. Not at all! After a glance at the headlines he turned to the baseball news. Do you understand him?"

"No," said his mother.

"At his age I should have been in this war, with or without my parents' consent. Mind you, I don't want him in it—not for a year or two. But why doesn't he want to get in? He's not a coward."

"No," said his mother, and then she added: "I've thought a great deal about it, and I think it's because he's so young—so immature."

"Immature!" cried Mr. Brougham. "Why, he's always using words I don't know the meaning of!"

"Perhaps he doesn't either," said his wife. "That's immature, isn't it? But I meant the immaturity of not seeing responsibilities—not taking them up, at least. You see, my dear, he's very young—only a year out of school. It's natural enough."

"It's not natural at all," answered Mr. Brougham. "Just out of school—school is the very place to learn patriotism—drilling and all that—and I'm sure Granby is one of the most patriotic men I ever knew. He inspires most of his boys. No, I don't understand. I shall speak to David about his attitude."

"Oh, don't! You'll have him enlisting tomorrow."

"No; for I shall explain to him that he must wait."

She smiled. "You're going to stir him up to want to do something which you won't allow him to do. Is that sensible, dear?"

It wasn't sensible, but—more important—it was inevitable. Mr. Brougham, feeling as he did, could not be silent. He had always been proud of his boys, had always assumed they were stuff to be proud of. They had done decently in their lessons, well in their athletics. What could a father ask more? Now for the first time he found himself questioning his right to be proud, and the doubt was like poison in his system. He must speak to his son.

The difficulty of "speaking to" people is that we either take too portentous a tone, and thus ruffle the minds we mean to impress, or else that we speak so casually as to make no impression at all. Mr. Brougham's leanings were all to the former manner, and recognizing this weakness he made one more effort at the indirect attack. Hearing that his nephew, a lieutenant of infantry, was about to sail, he sent for him to come and dine. In his greeting of the young man he tried to express his respect for the uniform, even when decorated by nothing more than a gold bar.

"I envy you, my boy," he said. "I remember how I felt when I first put on those clothes in 1898—not that we can compare that war with this, but the emotion is the same—the emotion is always the same. We all envy you in this house."

David looked rather impish. "Envy him!" he said. "And him such a bad sailor!"

At this Brougham's brows contracted, but the lieutenant smiled.

"Yes," he said; "won't I wish I had stayed at home!"

This sentiment would have shocked Mr. Brougham except that he believed he recognized in it the decent Anglo-Saxon cloak of a profound feeling—very different from David's cold inaction.

As soon as dinner was over he left the boys alone and took a chair on the piazza, from which he could watch the expressions of their faces. They fell at once into a conversation of the deepest interest; so interesting that they began to move their hands about in unaccustomed gestures. Once David lifted his and brought it down with a sidewise swoop.

"That's it!" a voice rang out. "It's great!"

Mr. Brougham felt justified in moving a little nearer. He then found that the subject of discussion was jazz-band records for the phonograph.

The next morning, looking out of his window early, he saw David in his bathing suit trying, with a seriousness that might have drilled a company, to teach a new handspring to Lawrence. And this made it impossible for Mr. Brougham to be silent any longer.

When David came back to the house, dressed, but with his hair still dark and wet from his swim, his father stopped him.

"Sit down a minute," he said. "I want to speak to you. I want you to explain your attitude toward this war."

This opening sentence, which he had thought of while the handsprings were going on, would have been excellent if he could have given his son time to answer it, but he couldn't; his emotions swept him on, and at the end of five minutes he was still talking:

"The Civil War was fought by boys your age or younger. I don't say it was best, but it's the fact. And here you are—you've had every advantage—of education, of luxury, of protection. Don't you care for the traditions of your country? You're not a child anymore. You're old enough to understand that a hideous catastrophe has come upon the world, and before long you must take your part in remedying it. What's your attitude to the war?"

"I think we're going to win it, sir, in the end."

"Other people are going to win it?"

"Would you approve of my enlisting at once? I understood—"

"No, I would not approve of it, as I've told you," answered his father, feeling that somehow he was being unjustly cornered. "But because a man's too young to make a soldier, that doesn't mean he shouldn't have any patriotism in his make-up—should be absolutely indifferent, with his head full of handsprings and jazz bands."

"I'm not indifferent," said David; "and as for jazz bands, even the men at the Front like them."

"But you're not at the Front—if you get my point."

"I don't believe I do," said David.

Civil as David's tone was there was of course a trace of hostility in the words themselves, and in his distress Mr. Brougham decided to go and consult Granby, the head of the school where David had been for five years and where Lawrence still was.

Brougham only went to Granby in desperate straits, for he was a little afraid of his son's schoolmaster. Granby was a tall bald man of fifty, with an expression at once stern and humble—stern with the habit of innumerable decisions, humble with the consciousness that half of them had been wrong. Brougham admired him, but could not be his friend, owing to the fact that he always became in Granby's presence an essential parent and nothing else. Mrs. Brougham, with the protection of her long silences, managed better to retain her individuality in his presence.

"I've come to consult you about David," he began.

Granby visibly shrank. "Don't tell me he's gone too!"

"No—he hasn't; that's it."

Brougham managed to tell his story very satisfactorily, for Granby had the power, rarer than is supposed, of extracting an idea from spoken words.

"He has no enthusiasm—no emotion. I can't understand him. At his age, I venture to say, I would— Well, I've come to you. You've had thirty years' experience of boys."

"Yes," said Granby with his reserved, pedagogic manner. "I've been at it thirty years." He stared at the floor and then, looking up, added: "But I've only had four years of boys as they are now."

This was a new idea to Brougham.

"You mean boys are different?"

"Of course, they're different!" said Granby. "Even we are different, and they— Boys I was giving demerits to and scolding about Latin prose last winter are fighting the war for us today. Roberts—I used to make Roberts' life a burden to him about the dative of reference—he was killed last month rescuing his machine gun; and here I am doing the same safe task— Well, I never felt like that about my work before. Different? Of course they're different! They are not boys anymore. They are men; and we are old men."

There was, naturally enough, a pause, for this was by no means a conception of life which Mr. Brougham could accept offhand; and in the silence the door opened and David himself strode in—and stopped with every appearance of disappointment on seeing his father.

"I beg your pardon," he said. "I'm afraid I'm interrupting you. I'll come back."

"What did you want?" said Mr. Granby.

David paused, looking less like a man and more like a boy in his indecision. Then his jaw set as he took his determination.

"I wanted you to tell my father something, but as long as he's here I'd better tell him myself. I took the examinations last month for an aviation camp, and I've just heard that I'm accepted."

Relief and horror struggling in Mr. Brougham like opposing waves resulted in calm.

"But, my son," he said, "why have you concealed it? You did not think I'd oppose you?"

David moved restlessly.

"Oh, no," he answered. "It wasn't that." He looked at Mr. Granby and smiled. "Father's awfully tyrannical about this war," he said. "He wants everyone to feel just as he does."

"But don't you feel as I do?" asked his father. "Why, you've just proved that you do!"

"Not a bit!" said David, and he spoke with a force neither of the men had ever heard from him before. "I don't feel a bit as you do, sir, and what's more, I don't want to!" He stopped. "But we needn't go into that," he added, and seemed about to leave the room.

Granby looked at Brougham. "It must be right here if we could get at it," he said. "Tell us, David, what is it in your father's attitude that you don't sympathize with?"

"And my mother's too."

"And mine?" asked Granby.

David hesitated an instant.

"You don't seem to care so much about having us all feel the way you do if what we do is right. But my father and mother don't care what I do unless I get excited about it."

"A healthy emotion is not excitement," said Mr. Brougham. "But you have been cold, absolutely cold to the horror of the world's bleeding to death, to all this unnatural disaster that has come upon us."

"It doesn't seem exactly unnatural to me," answered the boy slowly. "At least I've got used to it. You see, sir, ever since I knew anything—ever since I was Lawrence's age—war has been about the most natural thing going. I suppose it's very different for all of you. Coming at the end of a perfectly peaceful life, it must seem like a sort of dirty accident; but even so, it's awfully queer to me the way you and mother have to lash yourselves up to doing anything—"

"Lash ourselves up?" exclaimed Mr. Brougham.

"Yes, with the idea of patriotism and self-sacrifice, when it's so perfectly clear what we all have to do. Why, father, I feel just as if I were a policeman, or, no, a fireman—I feel as if I were a fireman and you expected me to get off something about patriotism and self-sacrifice everytime I went to put out a fire. A fireman goes, all right—it's his job; but I dare say he often wishes he could stay in bed. No one says his heart is cold, and no more it is, to my mind. It must be fun to go off in a burst of patriotic enthusiasm. I know, for I've often felt like that about football. But this is different. This isn't a sport—it's a long disagreeable job. And I must say, father, it makes me pretty tired to have you think me a slacker because I don't get, and don't want to get, excited about it."

"You misunderstand me," said his father. "I don't think any man a slacker who waits to think it over before he makes the supreme sacrifice and offers"—Mr. Brougham's voice took a deeper note—"his life."

David turned sharply to Granby.

"There," he said, "that's what I hate! I hate that attitude toward death—as if it were something you couldn't speak of in the drawing-room. Death isn't so bad," he added, as if saying what he could for an absent friend.

With this Mr. Brougham couldn't even pretend to agree; death seemed to him very bad indeed—about the worst possible, though not to be evaded by brave men on that account.

"Ah," he said to Granby, "that's the beauty of youth—it doesn't think about death at all."

"Nonsense," said David. "I beg your pardon, sir, but isn't it nonsense? Of course, we think of it—a lot more than you do. The chances are about one in twenty that I'll be killed. When you were my age you were planning your career, and college, and you thought you'd

ALICE DUER MILLER

be married sometime, and you were getting your name put up at clubs you couldn't get into for years. But fellows of my age aren't making any plans—it would be pretty foolish if we did. We haven't got any future, as you had it. I don't know if you call that thinking about death. I do—thinking about it as a fact, not a horror. We've been up against it for the last four years, and we've got used to it. That's what none of you older people seem to be able to get into your heads. We don't particularly mind the idea of dying. And now I think I'll run home and tell my mother."

Neither of the men spoke for a few minutes after he had gone. Mr. Brougham was shocked. He had just caught himself back from telling David that he ought to be afraid of dying—which of course was not at all what he meant. He himself had always feared death—most of the men he knew feared it—only hadn't allowed that fear to influence their actions. He had always regarded this fear as a great universal limitation. He felt as if a great gulf had suddenly opened between him and his son. More than that, he felt that to live free from the terror was too great an emancipation for one so young.

"If they're not afraid of death, what are they afraid of?" he found himself thinking.

He himself in his youth had never thought about dying—except sometimes in church in connection with music and crowns and glassy seas. Then once, when he was only a little younger than David, he had been very ill in the school infirmary; another boy had died, and then, he remembered, he did for the first time consider the possibility of his, Walter Brougham's, coming to an end, stopping, going out perhaps like a candle. It had been an uncomfortable experience, and when his mother had come to take care of him he had distinctly clung to her—as if she could have done any good. Had these boys gone through that and come out on the other side? He found it alarmed him to think that David wasn't afraid.

Good heavens, what would they do—this new generation, young and healthy and unafraid of death, not because they had never thought about it but because they had been familiar with it since they went into long trousers?

Mr. Granby broke the silence. He said: "To order ourselves lowly and reverently to all our betters?"

Brougham was puzzled by these words, and he felt that it was no time for puzzling him.

"Did you think David was impertinent to me, Mr. Granby?" he asked. "Is that what you meant?"

"No, that isn't what I meant, Mr. Brougham."

Brougham didn't inquire any further. He shook his head and went home. He found his wife and David sitting hand in hand on the piazza looking out to sea, with the same blank grave look on both their faces. Yet they were thinking very different thoughts.

Mrs. Brougham was thinking that she had been strangely stupid not to know that this was just exactly the way David would do it; but she added to herself she had allowed her vision to be clouded by her husband.

David was carefully reviewing the small stock of his technical knowledge of aëroplanes.

Worse Than Married

Miss Wilbur sat up and wrung the water out of her hair. Most of us have looked about a dinner-table and wondered which of the party would make the pleasantest companion on a desert island; Juliana had done it often enough, but now the comic touch was lacking. Far out, hung on some unknown reef, the prow of the vessel stuck up black and tall, almost as if she were still pursuing a triumphant course landward, though a list to starboard betrayed her desperate condition, and a second glance showed that the waves were breaking over her stern. The heavy swell was all that was left of the storm. The sun had just risen in a cloudless sky, above a dark-blue sea. It was perhaps that bright horizontal ray which had waked Miss Wilbur. It had not disturbed her rescuer, who, more provident, had hidden his face in his arm.

It seems hardly possible for a young lady to be dragged from her berth in the dead of night, hauled to the deck, and literally dumped into a small boat, to be tossed out of the boat and dragged to shore— all by a man whose face and name were equally unknown. But the more she looked at the back of that damp head, and the line of those shoulders, the less familiar did they appear. This was hardly surprising, for since she and her maid had taken the steamer at Trinidad, she had made so little effort at *rapprochement* with her fellow passengers that she could hardly call any of them to mind—a great German from a banking house in Caracas; a sunburnt native botanist bound for the Smithsonian; a little Englishman from the Argentine; these were the only three figures she could remember. Who was this man? A sailor? A commercial traveler? Of what standing and what nationality?

She coughed presently: "I wish you'd wake up," she said, "and let me thank you for saving my life."

The first result of this remark was that the man grunted and buried his nose deeper in the sand. Then he rolled over, stood up, and comprehensively hitching up what remained of his trousers, he looked carefully round the horizon, then at the wall of palm-trees behind them, and last of all at Miss Wilbur, without the smallest change of expression.

"Did I save you?" he asked.

"Yes, don't you remember? You caught me up in the dark—"

"I had a notion it was Mrs. Morale's son." Again his eyes sought the horizon, and he turned to move away, but she arrested him with a question.

"Do you think we shall be rescued?" she said.

He stopped, eyed her, and again turned away. His silence annoyed her. "Why don't you answer my question?"

"Because I thought it just about worthy of someone who wakes up a tired man to thank him for saving her life. Do I think we'll be rescued? That depends on whether we are in the track of vessels; and I know neither the track of vessels nor where we are. It depends on whether any of the other boats lived through the night. But I'll tell you one thing. It looks to me as if they needn't trouble to come at all, if they don't come soon. I'm going to hunt up breakfast."

He disappeared into the forest of palms, leaving her alone. She would have liked to call him back and ask him what he thought of the probabilities of snakes on the island. Tact, however, that civilized substitute for terror, restrained her. She thought him very peculiar. "I wonder if he's a little crazy," she thought. "I wonder if something hit him on the head."

He was gone a long time, and when he returned carried a bunch of bananas and three cocoanuts. He stopped short on seeing her. "Do you mean to say," he cried, "that you haven't been drying your clothes? What do you suppose I stayed away so long for? But no matter. Have your breakfast first."

She refrained from expressing, at once, a profound distaste for cocoanuts, but when he cut one and handed it to her, the smell overcame her resolutions. "Oh!" she said, drawing back, "I can't bear them."

"You will order something else on the menu?"

The tone was not agreeable, and Miss Wilbur eyed the speaker. No wonder she was at a loss, for hitherto her measure of men had been the people they knew, the clothes they wore, and, more especially, their friendliness to herself. In the present case, none of these were much help, and she decided to resort to the simpler means of the direct question. Besides, it had always been Juliana's custom to converse during her meals and, peculiar though this one appeared, she saw no reason for making it an exception.

"Doesn't it seem strange," she began, "that I don't even know your name?"

"Nathaniel or Spens?"

"Oh! Spens, of course," she answered, quite as if they had met in a ballroom. "And don't you think," she went on, "that it would be nice if we knew a little more about each other than just our names?"

"A little more?" he exclaimed. "My idea was we were getting near the too much point."

"But I meant our past selves, our everyday selves—our *real* selves."

"So did I. I hope we sha'n't get any realler. This is real enough to suit me." He continued under his breath to ring the changes on this idea to his own intense satisfaction.

Miss Wilbur gave up and began again. "I think it would be interesting to tell each other a little of our lives—who we are, and where we came from. For instance I'm willing to begin—I'm a New Yorker. My mother died when I was sixteen, and I have been at the head of my father's house ever since—he has retired from business. We are quite free, and we travel a great deal. I came down here on a yacht. You may ask why I left it—well, a little difficulty arose—a situation. The owner, one of my best and oldest friends—" She paused. As she talked, questions had floated through her mind. Does he take in the sort of person I am at home? Does he realize how his toil is lightened by the contrast of my presence in the benighted spot? Does he know what a privilege it is to be cast away with me? He was saying to himself: "If only I can get home before the first, I'll increase that quarterly dividend."

She took up her narrative. "The owner, as I say, was one of my best and oldest friends; and yet, you know—"

"And yet you quarreled like one o'clock."

"Oh, no," said Miss Wilbur. "We did not quarrel. It would have been better if we had."

"Just sulked, you mean?"

This was more than she could bear. "He wanted to marry me," she said firmly.

"Not really!" he exclaimed, and then, studying her more carefully, he added: "But of course—very naturally. I am sure to some types of men you would be excessively desirable."

This was the nearest approach to a compliment that she had had since the ship struck, and she gulped at it eagerly.

"Desirable is not quite the word," she answered. "But perhaps I should rather have you think of me as desirable than not at all," and she smiled fascinatingly.

"Great Cæsar's ghost!" he exclaimed. "Did I say I was thinking of you? But there, I mean—I mean—" But it was unnecessary to complete the sentence, for Miss Wilbur rose, with what dignity a tattered dressing gown allowed, and moved away. He followed her and explained with the utmost civility where there was another beach, how she should spread out her clothes to the sun, and added gravely, holding up one finger: "And remember to keep in the shade yourself."

"Oh, the sun never affects me," said Juliana.

This answer plainly tried him, but with some self-control he merely repeated his injunction in exactly the same words.

Miss Wilbur's costume was not elaborate. It comprised, all told, a night-gown, a pink quilted dressing-gown, a pair of men's sneakers, and a bit of Cartier jewelry about her throat. She wished that dressing-gown had been more becoming. Just before she sailed she had sent her maid out to buy something warm, and the pink atrocity had been the result. She had thought it did not matter then, but, now that she might have to spend the rest of her life in it, she wished she had taken the trouble to choose it herself.

Even if she had been completely alone on this Caribbean island, she was too much a child of civilization to remove all her clothes at once. The process took time. As she sat under the trees and waited, she considered her position.

Feelings of dislike for, and dependence upon, her rescuer grew together in her mind. She did not say, even to herself, that she was afraid of him, very much in the same way in which she had once been afraid of her schoolmistress—afraid of his criticism and his contempt, but she expressed the same idea by saying "he was not very nice to her." That he "was rather rude"! She thought how differently any of the men she had left on the yacht at Trinidad would have behaved. Alfred, for instance. It would have been rather fun to have been cast away with Alfred. He would have been tender and solicitous. Poor Alfred! She began to think it had been an absurd scruple that had made her leave the party. It had seemed as if she could not cruise another day on the yacht of a man she had refused so decidedly to marry. After such a scene, too! Miss Wilbur frowned and shook her head at the recollection. As a matter of fact, she liked scenes.

She had so far used the freedom of her life in eliminating from her consciousness those who did not contribute to her self-esteem. Sometimes she created admiration where it had not existed. Sometimes,

　　　　ALICE DUER MILLER

when this seemed impossible, she simply withdrew. The latter method was obviously out of the question on this little dot of an island.

But the other? One of the unquestioned facts in Miss Wilbur's life was her own extreme charm; and this thought brought another to her mind. The picture of the traditional male—the beast of prey! In spite of the American girl's strange mixture of inexperience and sophistication, she is not entirely without the instinct of self-preservation. She remembered his long Yankee jaw with relief.

When she returned she found he had erected four poles with cross beams and was attempting to thatch it with banana-leaves, to the accompaniment of a low sibilant whistle.

"What's that?" she asked. He completed the phrase diminuendo before answering.

"This," he said, "is where you are going to sleep, and, if it doesn't fall in on you in the night, I'll build another for myself tomorrow. Look out where you step. I'm drying two vestas on that rock. If they light, we'll have a fire, and perhaps some day something to eat. Suppose you go and find some wood?"

She hesitated. "Do you think there are snakes on this island?" she hazarded; and oh, with what enthusiasm such a suggestion of femininity would have been received on the yacht!

"Think not," said her companion; "but I'd look out for scorpions and centipedes and things like that, you know."

The suggestion did not increase her enthusiasm for her task. She hung about a few minutes longer and then collected a few twigs along the beach, raising them carefully between her thumb and forefinger. They did not make an imposing pile, as she felt when her rescuer came to inspect it, looking first at it and then at her, with his hands in his pockets.

"I hope you won't overdo?" he said.

Juliana colored. "Did you expect me to carry great logs?" she asked. "Women can't do that sort of thing."

He moved away without answering, and presently had collected enough wood for many fires.

"I'd like to see you lay a fire," he said.

She threw some of the small sticks together, then the larger ones, as she had seen the housemaid do at home. Then, embarrassed at his silent observation, she drew back.

"Of course I can't do it, if you watch me," she exclaimed.

"You can't do it anyhow, because you don't know the principle. The first thing a fire needs is air. It's done like this." He tore down and re-erected her structure.

If Miss Wilbur had followed her impulse, she would have kicked it down as he finished, but she managed a fine aloofness instead. He did not appear to notice her chin in the air.

"Yes," he observed as he rose from his knees, "it's a handy thing to know—how to lay a fire, and as you say, one is naturally grateful to the fellow who teaches one. I'm going to look for food. Keep a lookout for ships."

He had hardly gone when he came bounding back again, waving two small fish by the tails. "Got 'em," he shouted. "Dug out some ponds this morning, but never thought it would work, but here they are. Now we'll light the fire."

His excitement was contagious. She sprang up, held the skirt of her dressing-gown to shield the match, blew the flame, almost blew it out. Finally, with the help of both matches the fire was lit.

"I'm so hungry," she said. "Do you think they'll taste good?"

He did not answer. She could not but be impressed by the deftness with which he split and boned the fish, and the invention he displayed in evolving cooking utensils out of shells and sticks.

"You know," he said suddenly, "this fire must never go out. This will be your job. Sort of vestal-virgin idea."

The charge made her nervous. The responsibility was serious. During one of his absences she began to think the flame was dying down. She put in a stick. It blazed too quickly. A crash followed and one of the fish disappeared into the fire.

After a time she managed to drag it out, black and sandy. She dreaded his return. How could she make clear to him that it had not been her fault? She decided on a comic manner. Holding it up by the tail, she smiled at him. "Doesn't that look delicious?" she asked gayly.

His brow darkened. "All right, if you like them that way," he returned.

"Don't you think the other is large enough for two?"

His answer was to remove the other from the fire and to eat it himself.

Miss Wilbur watched him to the end, and then she could contain herself no longer. She had been extremely hungry.

"Upon my word," she said, "I've known a good many selfish men, but

I never before saw one who would not have taken the bread out of his mouth to give to a hungry woman."

Her rescuer looked at her unshaken. "You don't think that was just?" he inquired.

"I am not talking of justice, but of chivalry," replied Miss Wilbur passionately. "Of consideration for the weak. You are physically stronger than I—"

"And I intend to remain so."

"At my expense?"

"If you fell ill, I should be sorry. If I fell ill, you would die." He turned away sharply, but half-way up to the beach thought better of it and returned.

"See here," he said, "I'm an irritable man, and a tired man. This whole thing isn't going to be easy for either of us. And what do we find, the first crack out of the box? That you are not only incompetent, but that you want to be social and pleasant over it. Great Scott! what folly! Well, if it's any satisfaction to you, I know I'm not behaving well either. But you don't seem aware of even that much, or of anything, indeed"—he smiled faintly—"except your own good looks."

He left her to meditate.

Battle, murder, and sudden death are not as great a shock to some people as their own failure to please. Miss Wilbur, being incapable of looking within for the cause of this phenomenon, looked at her companion. Evidently he *was* a peculiar, nervous sort of a creature, and, after all, had he been so successful? He hardly came up to the desert-island standard set by the father of the Swiss Family Robinson. She reviewed him with a critical eye. He was a nice-looking young man of the clean-shaven type. He lacked the great air, she told herself, which was not surprising, since eighteen months before there had been nothing whatever to distinguish him from any of the other shrewd young men produced in such numbers by the State of Connecticut. But chance had waved her wand, and it had fallen to his lot to head a congenial band of patriots who, controlling a group of trolleys, had parted with them at a barefaced price to the New York, New Haven and Hartford Railway. Since this *coup* he had rather rested on his laurels, spending most of his time with a classmate in New York, where he had acquired a tailor and had succeeded in getting himself elected to the directorate of The General Fruit Company—an organization which, as every Italian vender knows, deals in such miscellaneous commodities as bananas, hides, coffee, rubber, sugar, copper-mines, and narrow-gauge railroads along the Caribbean shores, with an argosy for transportation to Spokane, New Orleans, Baltimore, Boston, Bristol, or Bordeaux.

For some reason his mastery of the desert island was not complete. His race's traditional handiness seemed to be slightly in abeyance; perhaps because luck was against him, perhaps on account of a too pervasive feminine presence. But for whatever reason, things did not improve. Nothing came ashore from the wreck—not even when, after a small gale, it turned over and disappeared. The banana shelter leaked in the rain, and as Miss Wilbur sat steaming in the sunshine which immediately succeeded she felt inclined to attribute all her discomforts to Spens. He seemed to have no faculty whatever for evolving things out of nothing, which, she had always understood, was the great occupation of desert-island life. Their food continued to be bananas and cocoanuts, varied by an occasional fish; and, instead of being apologetic for such meagre fare, he seemed to think she ought to be grateful.

Now Miss Wilbur could have been grateful, if he had not roused her antagonism by his continual adverse criticism of herself. She wished to show him that she could be critical too; and so she sniffed at his fish, and took no interest in his roofing arrangements, and treated him, in short, exactly as the providing male should not be treated. Man cannot stoop to ask for praise, but he can eternally sulk if he does not get it. The domestic atmosphere of the island was anything but cordial.

After all, she used to say to herself, why should she labor under any profound sense of obligation? Even when he appeared to be considering her comfort she saw an ulterior motive. He came, for instance, one day, civilly enough, and pointed out a little row of white stones marking off a portion of the island.

"The beach beyond this line is ceded to you," he observed gravely. "No fooling. I'm in earnest. Of course I understand that you like to be alone sometimes. Here you'll never be disturbed. When I annoy you past bearing, you can come here." For a moment she was touched by his kindness, the next he had added: "And would you mind allowing me a similar privilege on the other side of the island?"

His tone was a trifle more nipping than he had intended, but no suavity could have concealed his meaning. His plan had been designed not to please her, but to protect himself. No one before had ever plotted to relieve himself of Miss Wilbur's company. Subterfuges had always had an opposite intention. She had been clamored for and quarreled over. She withdrew immediately to the indicated asylum.

"I'm not accustomed to such people," she said to herself. "He makes me feel different—horrid. I can't be myself." It was not the first time she had talked to herself, and she wondered if her mind were beginning to give way under the strain of the situation. "I'd like to box his ears until they rang. Until they rang!" she repeated, and felt like a criminal. Who would have supposed she had such instincts!

For the tenth time that day she caught together the sleeve of the detested dressing-gown. How shocked Alfred and her father would be to think a man lived who could treat her so! but the thought of their horror soothed her less as it became more and more unlikely that they would ever know anything about it.

She stayed behind her stones until he called her to luncheon. They ate in silence. Toward the end she said gently:

"Would you mind not whistling quite so loud?"

"Certainly not, if the sound annoys you."

"Oh, it isn't the sound so much, only"—and she smiled angelically—"it always seems to me a little flat."

She had a great success. Spens colored.

"Well," he said, "I don't pretend to be a musician, but it has always been agreed that I had an excellent ear."

"In Green Springs, Connecticut?"

He did not answer, but moved gloomily away. Two or three times she heard him start an air and cut it short. A smile flickered across her face. So sweet to her was it to be the aggressor that she did not return behind the white stones, but remained, like a cat at a rat-hole, waiting beside the fire to which Spens would have to return eventually.

She had resolved that it must be kindly yet firmly made clear to him that he was not behaving like a gentleman, and if, as seemed possible, he did not understand all that the word implied, she felt quite competent to explain it to him.

Perhaps the idea that his conduct was not quite up even to his own standards had already occurred to him, for when he returned he carried a peace-offering.

He stood before her, holding something toward her. "I notice," he said, "that you go about in the sun bare-headed. You oughtn't to do that, and so I have made you this," and she saw the green mass in his hands was leaves carefully fashioned into the shape of a hat.

It may perhaps be forgiven to Miss Wilbur that her heart sank. Nevertheless, she took the offering, expressing her gratitude with a little too much volubility. "I must put it on at once," she said. Green had never become her, but she placed it firmly on her head.

Spens studied it critically. "It fits you exactly," he observed with pleasure. "You see I could only guess at the size. Isn't it fortunate that I guessed so exactly right!"

She saw that he was immensely gratified and, trying to enter into the spirit of the thing she said:

"What a pity I can't see the effect!"

"You can." He drew his watch from his pocket, and opened the back of the case. "It doesn't keep time any longer," he said, "but it can still serve as a looking-glass," and he held it up.

Now anyone who has ever looked at himself in the back of a watch-case knows that it does not make a becoming mirror; it enlarges the tip of the nose, and decreases the size of the eyes. Juliana had not so far had any vision of herself. Now, for the first time, in this unfavorable reflection, she took in her flattened hair, her tattered dressing-gown, and, above all, the flapping, intoxicated head-gear which she had just received. She snatched it from her head with a gesture quicker than thought.

"I believe you enjoy making me ridiculous," she said passionately.

"Nothing could be more ridiculous than to say that," he answered. "I wanted to save your health, but if you prefer sunstroke to an unbecoming hat—not that I thought it unbecoming—"

"It was hideous."

"I can only say that I don't think so."

Miss Wilbur slowly crushed the offending object and dropped it into the fire. Ridiculous or not, there would never be any question about that again.

"Of course," she observed after a pause, "I don't expect you to understand how I feel about this—how I feel about anything—how any lady feels about anything."

"Is it particularly ladylike not to wish to wear an unbecoming hat?"

This of course was war, and Miss Wilbur took it up with spirit. "Unhappily, it is ladylike," she answered, "to have been so sheltered from hardships that when rudeness and stupidity are added—"

"Come, come," said Spens, "we each feel we have too good a case to spoil by losing our tempers. Sit down, and let us discuss it calmly. You first. I promise not to interrupt. You object to my being rude and stupid. So far so good, but develop your idea."

The tone steadied Juliana. "I don't complain of the hardships," she began. "I don't speak of the lack of shelter and food. These are not your fault, although," she could not resist adding, "some people might have managed a little better, I fancy. What I complain of is your total lack of appreciation of what this situation means to me. I haven't knocked about the world like a man. I've never been away from home without my maid. I've never before been without everything that love and money could get me, and instead of pitying me for this you do everything in your power to make it harder. Instead of being considerate you are not even civil. No one could think you civil—no one that I know, at least. You do everything you can to make me feel that my presence, instead of being a help and a pleasure, is an unmitigated bother."

There was a pause. "Well," said Spens, "since we are being so candid, have you been a help? Have you even done your own share? Certainly not. I don't speak of the things you can't help—your burning of the fish—"

"The fish! I don't see how you have the effrontery to mention the fish."

"Nor of your upsetting our first supply of rain-water. Constitutional clumsiness is something no one can help, I suppose. But it does irritate me that you seem to find it all so confoundedly fascinating in you. You seemed to think it was cunning to burn the fish, and playful to upset the water. In other words, though I don't mind carrying a dead weight, I'm hanged if I'll regard it as a beauteous burden."

Miss Wilbur rose to her feet. "The trouble with you is," she said, "that you haven't the faintest idea how a gentleman behaves."

"Well, I'm learning all right how a lady behaves," he retorted.

After this it was impossible to give any consistent account of their conversation. They both spoke at once, phrases such as these emerging from the confusion: "—you talk about ladies and gentlemen." "Thank Heaven, I know something of men and women"; "—civilized life and the people I know"; "—never been tested before." "Do you think you have survived the test so well?"

The last sentence was Miss Wilbur's, and under cover of it she retreated to her own domains. Spens, left in possession of the field, presently withdrew to the other side of the island.

Here for two or three days he had had a secret from Juliana. He had invented, constructed, and was in process of perfecting himself in a game with shells and cocoanuts which bore a family resemblance to both quoits and hop-scotch. He turned to it now to soothe and distract him. It was a delightful game, and exactly suited his purpose, requiring as it did skill, concentration, and agility. He had just accomplished a particularly difficult feat which left him in the attitude of the Flying Mercury, when his eye fell upon a smutch of smoke upon the horizon, beneath which the funnel of a vessel was already apparent.

Spen's methods of showing joy were all his own. He threw the tattered remnants of his cap in the air, and when it came down he jumped on it again and again.

His next impulse was to run and call Juliana, but he did not follow it. Instead he piled wood on the fire until it was a veritable column of flame, and then with folded arms he took his stand on the beach.

Within a few minutes he became convinced that the vessel, a steamer of moderate size, had sighted his signal. They were going to be rescued. Very soon he and Juliana would be sailing back to civilization. He would be fitted out by the ship's officers, and Juliana would be very self-conscious about appearing in the stewardess's clothes. They would figure in the papers—a rising young capitalist, and a society girl. Her father would be on the pier. There would be explanations. He himself would be a child in their hands. A vision of engraved cards, a faint smell of orange-blossoms, floated through his mind. His resolve was taken. He sprang up, ran through the palms, and penetrated without knocking to where Miss Wilbur was sitting, with her back against a tree. She glanced up at him with the utmost detestation.

"I thought that here, at least—" she began, but he paid no attention.

"Juliana," he exclaimed in his excitement, "there is a vessel on the other side of the island. She'll be here in twenty minutes, and you are going home in her. Now, don't make any mistake. *You* are going home. I stay here. No, don't say anything. I've thought it over, and this is the only way. We can't both go home. Think of landing, think of the papers, think of introducing me to that distinguished bunch—the people you know. No, no, you've been here all alone, and you're an extraordinarily clever, capable girl, and have managed to make yourself wonderfully comfortable, considering. No, don't protest. I am not taking any risk. Here's a vessel at the end of ten days. Another may be here tomorrow. Anyhow, be sure it's what I prefer. A cocoanut and liberty. Good-by. Better be getting down to the beach to wave."

Miss Wilbur hesitated. "At least," she said, "let me know when you do get home."

"I'll telephone from Green Springs. Now run along," and taking her by the shoulders, he turned her toward the path.

She had, however, scarcely reached the beach, and seen the vessel now looming large and near, when she heard a hoarse whisper: "I've forgotten my tobacco." A face and arm gleamed out from the bush. He snatched the pouch, and this time was finally gone.

The keel of the ship's boat grated on the sand, and a flustered young officer sprang out. Juliana was inclined to make a moment of it, but it was getting dark, and the captain, what with carrying the mails and being well out of his course, was cross enough as it was.

"One of you men go up there and stamp out that fire," he said. "No use in bringing anyone else in here."

An expression of terror crossed Miss Wilbur's face, and a cry burst from her: "Oh, he'll be so angry." The officer caught only the terror, and, setting it down to natural hysteria, pushed off without more ado.

Night fell, and the stars came out with the startling rapidity of the tropics. There was no wind, but puffs of salt air lifted the fronds of the palms.

Suddenly over the water was borne the sharp jangle of an engine-room bell, and the beat of a vessel's propellers.

THE END

A Note About the Author

Alice Duer Miller (1874–1942) was an American novelist, poet, screenwriter, and women's rights activist. Born into wealth in New York City, she was raised in a family of politicians, businessmen, and academics. At Barnard College, she studied Astronomy and Mathematics while writing novels, essays, and poems. She married Henry Wise Miller in 1899, moving with him in their young son to Costa Rica where they struggled and failed to open a rubber plantation. Back in New York, Miller earned a reputation as a gifted poet whose satirical poems advocating for women's suffrage were collected in *Are Women People?* (1915). Over the next two decades, Miller published several collections of stories and poems, some of which would serve as source material for motion picture adaptations. *The White Cliffs* (1940), her final published work, is a verse novel that uses the story of a young women widowed during the Great War to pose important questions about the morality of conflict and patriotism in the leadup to the United States' entrance into World War II.

A Note from the Publisher

Spanning many genres, from non-fiction essays to literature classics to children's books and lyric poetry, Mint Edition books showcase the master works of our time in a modern new package. The text is freshly typeset, is clean and easy to read, and features a new note about the author in each volume. Many books also include exclusive new introductory material. Every book boasts a striking new cover, which makes it as appropriate for collecting as it is for gift giving. Mint Edition books are only printed when a reader orders them, so natural resources are not wasted. We're proud that our books are never manufactured in excess and exist only in the exact quantity they need to be read and enjoyed.

bookfinity™

Discover more of your favorite classics with Bookfinity™.

- Track your reading with custom book lists.
- Get great book recommendations for your personalized Reader Type.
- Add reviews for your favorite books.
- AND MUCH MORE!

Visit **bookfinity.com** and take the fun Reader Type quiz to get started.

Enjoy our classic and modern companion pairings!